D0499446

For the Love of a Goblin Warrior

Shona Husk

sourcebooks
casablanca

Published by Sourcebooks Casablanca, an imprint of Sourcebooks, Inc.
P.O. Box 4410, Naperville, Illinois 60567-4410
(630) 961-3900
Fax: (630) 961-2168
www.sourcebooks.com

Printed and bound in Canada.
WC 10 9 8 7 6 5 4 3 2 1

Chapter 1

WHAT WAS IT ABOUT THE FULL MOON THAT TURNED the emergency room into an overfull level of Hell? This was madness.

Already Nadine was dreaming of the end of her shift and going for a run. Running was her escape. In that hour, she was free, and all she had to do was breathe. For half a second, she let herself drift away from the chaos.

A nurse tapped her on the arm. "Nadine, you're wanted in triage."

Nadine frowned. She didn't work the front counter. "Why?"

"Dunno, I was just told to find you." The nurse was already moving away, leaving Nadine with no choice but to see why she'd been requested.

When she saw the cop, her stomach tightened. Police never brought good news. What had her father done now? He'd barely been out of prison for two weeks. She crossed her fingers by her side and sent up a prayer.

She gave the cop a tight smile and forced herself to be professional. She wasn't five, and she had nothing that could be taken away. "How can I help you?"

"I've got a man with a head injury who doesn't seem to speak English." The officer gave her a quick glance. "Can you help?"

Nadine looked past the cop to his partner, standing next to a sitting man who looked like he'd crawled out of a third-world jail. Blood ran down the side of his face and stuck in his shaggy hair. He was covered in dust or ash, almost as if he'd been pulled from a collapsed building. His loose-fitting tunic was worn with age, as were his pants and boots. But the cut was somehow wrong, as if he were wearing castoffs from another age. His gaze was firmly fixed on the floor, shoulders slumped as if defeated by whatever struggle he was facing.

"He's having some kind of episode. Freaked out when we brought him in."

"What did he do?" She had no intention of being attacked by a psychiatric patient, yet he didn't seem dangerous...just lost, locked in his own world. She'd seen that look before on a returned soldier who wasn't coping.

"He was being a nuisance." The cop paused, then leaned a little closer.

"And?" Nadine prompted.

"Waving a sword," the officer said quietly.

Right. A sword, of course. She glanced at the man, but he hadn't moved. "How'd he get hurt?"

"No idea. He speaks gibberish. Look, I don't want to take him down to the station. He needs medical attention. Can you get him a psych consult and help with his injuries?"

"Are you going to charge him?"

"He's been no trouble since we picked him up. He's unarmed. Will you at least check out his head and make sure it isn't serious, and see if you can make sense of what he's saying?"

If she said no, the scruffy man would spend the night in lockup with real criminals and be back on the street by morning no better off.

"I'll have a look at the wound, but unless he speaks French"—Nadine doubted he spoke her father's Sudanese language of Nuer, so she didn't mention it—"he'll have to wait until we can get a proper translator in." *A serious head injury could explain his lack of proper speech.*

"Thank you."

Yeah, off the cop's hands and into hers. If the man needed admitting, they'd have to make room for him and that would take some rearranging. "Will you wait while I examine him?"

"Sure."

Nadine grabbed a pair of gloves, went through the security door and into the waiting room. She cast her gaze over the people waiting to be seen. Some looked fine. Some were ill but having to wait their turn. Bleeders got seen fairly quickly—even if it was their own fault.

Prospective patients watched her. Even with the police officer at her side, she didn't feel safe. Despite the warning posters that violence toward staff wouldn't be tolerated, people did strange things when they were desperate. This was why she didn't like working at the triage counter. All she had to do was assess the man and decide if he needed to be moved to the ward—her ward.

The second cop pulled the scruffy man up from his hunched-over position. The man's gray eyes focused on her. Shadows she didn't understand gave him a haunted look, as if he'd seen too much. She couldn't leave him in the care of the police; he was already traumatized.

The man spoke, but his words were unintelligible. Fast and fluent. Definitely not gibberish. It had the rhythm of language. Just not one she'd ever heard.

Nadine bent down so she was at eye level, but far

enough back to be out of range if he lashed out with his feet. His hands were cuffed behind his back—even though the cops claimed he wasn't a threat. Still, she had to try something even if she didn't get a response.

"*Monsieur, parlez vous francais?*" She smiled encouragingly while she held his gaze and studied his eyes. The pupils were even and they weren't dilated.

The man's eyes darted between Nadine and the cops. His forehead furrowed, as if he were trying to make sense of her words.

His voice was quiet but strong as he spoke again. This time in a different language.

"*Pardon?*" Nadine moved closer as she listened.

He inclined his head at a crying baby and repeated the same words more slowly, as if she were simple.

She glanced at the baby and then at the man. He was talking about the crying child. *Infans*. It was only a small jump to English *infant*. But what was he saying? And in what language?

Nadine pointed to the shaggy man's bleeding head. "You're bleeding."

That he seemed to understand, but he shook his head, spoke, and looked at the baby, adding extra sentences filled with force. Yet his words were formal and he stumbled over some, as if it wasn't his first language. It was no one's language anymore. The realization rocked her back on her heels, and yet she was willing to bet all of tonight's pay he was speaking Latin.

She straightened up and looked at the cops. One raised his eyebrows as if expecting a miracle. She was fresh out of them, and all she had was a puzzle. The cops weren't going to like her answer—how were they supposed to get a translator for a dead language? Who was this man? "I think he's speaking Latin." As she said it aloud, it didn't seem possible. Maybe she was wrong and he was speaking an obscure dialect of…of what? Not Italian. Breton? She glanced at the dust-covered man again.

"Who the hell speaks Latin?"

"No one." Nadine frowned. He must have studied it at school and somehow the knock on his head bought it forth. "It's a dead language." And the man speaking it looked like he should be dead but had refused to quit. Yet he must have been someone once to be educated in Latin.

His gaze lingered on her, gray and endless. There was something about him…a half hidden nightmare glided through the back of her mind. The child nearby began wailing in a higher pitch. The noise cut through Nadine's thoughts. The man shook as if he couldn't bear the sound. Tears pooled in his eyes, and he hung his head as if to hide them, repeating the same line about the baby over and over.

She wasn't going to get anywhere with the man while the baby was crying.

"The baby." She turned to the cop who had come up to the counter. "Take the woman and baby up to triage and get them seen faster. The crying is making him worse…and it's a baby. She shouldn't be waiting."

She hated seeing children in distress. It brought back too many memories of her own childhood and the other foster children who'd been in and out of the homes she had lived in. Some of them made her odd habits seem normal, and that was saying a lot.

Nadine touched the man's shoulder to get his attention. He lifted his head as if expecting reproach. She smiled and softened her voice from the orders she'd given the cop.

"Look, the baby is getting help." She pointed at the mother and child, now getting fast-tracked through emergency. "Can I take a look at your head?" She pointed to his head, not sure how much he was understanding. But he didn't seem disorientated or confused. He just didn't understand the language.

He stared at her for a moment, then watched the woman with the baby as she was taken behind the doors. He blinked, but his tears had already tracked a line through the gray dust coating his face. Once the woman and child were gone, he nodded.

She brushed aside his hair to get a better look at the wound—and him. It was impossible to tell his age. While his skin was covered in dust, his hair was full of the gray powder and it clumped together in uneven chunks. Even his beard was full of it. Is that why his eyes had been watering? Was it concrete powder? She looked closer at his skin but saw no evidence of chemical burns where his tears had mixed with the dust.

"Where did you find him?" Nadine asked the cop.

"Adelaide Terrace."

She nodded. There were lots of luxury apartments being built down at the east end of Perth. "Construction site?"

"No. On the street."

"What's he covered in?"

"No idea."

Great.

The head injury didn't look too bad. His skull seemed undamaged, but she couldn't ask if he'd lost consciousness. For all she knew, his brain was bleeding and swelling. He should get a scan or be admitted for observation at a minimum. She covered his eyes with her hand, then removed it and watched to make sure his pupils reacted evenly to the light. They did. He didn't appear drug affected, and he didn't smell of alcohol. He smelled of nothing. Which was odd. Everyone had a smell, and given his appearance and well-worn clothes, he should have at least smelled unwashed. She sniffed again to be sure, but there wasn't even the scent of skin. Odd.

If he spoke no English, or remembered none, it was no wonder he was having an episode when the cops dragged him in. He had no idea what they were saying or where they were taking him. Yet he'd had enough compassion to ask that the baby be seen first. That said more about the man than anything else.

"Uncuff him and I'll bring him through to the ward for a proper examination." The cop gave a visible sigh and freed the man. For a heartbeat, the two cops and Nadine all waited to see what he'd do. He looked at her, smiled, and said something that had the tone of gratitude. He might not speak the language, but he understood some of what was going on.

He rubbed his wrists and she noted the fresh grazes and cuts, but they didn't bother her as much as the gray coating and possible damage to his eyes, or his lack of regular language. He was obviously educated. So what had happened to him to bring him here in such a state?

She noticed a gold broach holding the cloak over his shoulders. It was a beautiful piece, two wolves chasing each other in an endless circle. If he'd been living on the streets, that would've been stolen. And he'd been picked up carrying a sword. Nothing about this man was adding up.

She shook her head. "Who are you?"

Chapter 2

THE WOMAN IN FRONT OF MERYN SMILED. HER TEETH were white against the dark honey color of her skin and around her neck was a gold necklace. A crucifix. A man was forever dying at her throat. He flinched at the symbol of Roman punishment, and her friendly smile faltered. She spoke, a question in the other language. Not that it mattered. He didn't understand her any more than he understood the blue-clad soldiers. Her tone was one of concern not aggression…and yet she'd ordered the soldiers to take care of the baby, and they had obeyed. Despite the cruelty of her necklace, she appeared to be free, not a slave.

The woman's soft hands touched his and flexed his fingers, checking the cuts made when he'd fled the tower after being torn from the Shadowlands. The things his hands had done. So much blood. So much battle. The memories flickered past, half formed, but he couldn't quite grab hold of them.

It was only when he thought of the emptiness of the Shadowlands—the realm of the goblins—that his mind was still. The endless nothing. Gray land meeting gray sky. No sun to cast light and warmth, no stars to light the way, just nothing as far as he could see.

Except the rock spire.

It had joined sky and land, a testament to the power of the goblin king. The one goblin who had the power to cross to the human realm at will. That power had made him the envy of all other goblins. When they weren't fighting each other for scraps of gold, they were looking for the most powerful king, hoping to steal his treasure and magic. But Meryn knew no one had ever found the goblin king and lived to tell. He'd failed to find him at all. The spire had been empty. The king gone and Meryn had been trapped. Human in a world of nightmares.

Cursed. That's what the man claiming to be his cousin Dai had said as he pulled Meryn out of the Shadowlands. Meryn had been human once; he knew that. He'd always been different from the other goblins of the Shadowlands without knowing why.

But what kind of man had he been?

One who needed to be locked in a tower away from everyone else?

What crime had he committed as a human to warrant such a curse and punishment?

Memories of battle and blood tore at his mind. Things he didn't want to remember.

The woman with the beautiful smile touched his hand and spoke to him again, first in the same language the blue-clad soldiers used and then in softer, more lyrical words. He frowned, not understanding what she was saying yet wishing he could make sense of her words.

The Fixed Realm had changed in his absence. The people spoke a different language and were clothed differently. He glanced at the two identically dressed men. Only Romans stripped away individual identity. His thoughts tumbled and for a moment he was caught in the past. He needed to focus on the present.

He took a breath and grabbed on to the first piece of

logic that drifted past. The men had taken his sword, bound him, and brought him here to a place full of wounded. They might have brought him here as a prisoner, but it was so he could get his injury treated. That was a good thing. Meryn pushed down on the fear that made him want to run and tried to act like he knew what was going on. He had to act like everyone else and not draw attention, the way he'd done once before. Always watching, always alert. But he knew it hadn't helped him last time he'd been human. Somehow he'd failed and people had died.

The play of light on the woman's gold necklace held his gaze for a moment too long, as if he wasn't that far from turning goblin again. The chain and cross hung just out of reach. The need for gold didn't consume him the way it once had in the Shadowlands; instead, it offered salvation. Gold didn't hurt and cry and scream. As a goblin, he'd been numb to the memories of his life as a man. He wanted the silence of being goblin.

The crucifix swung in his vision as the bronze-skinned woman probed the wound on his head. Her hands were gentle on his tender skin. He wanted a piece of her calm and kindness. Every breath hurt his ribs and rasped over skin that the memories had stripped raw. The air was salt being rubbed into wounds that had never had a chance to heal.

In the Shadowlands there had been stillness. He'd known a measure of mindless peace. He didn't understand the Fixed Realm anymore. It had changed beyond his understanding. While the curse that had bound him to the Shadowlands and eased his pain had broken and made him human again, he wanted to go back. He wanted to be goblin again. He understood the rules of the Shadowlands. He knew how goblins behaved. If he returned, maybe he could forget. He blinked as his vision blurred and his eyes burned.

Gods, he was weak for wanting to go back.

He hadn't always been like this. He'd been a better man once. He knew that, the same way he knew that that man was gone. That man had died the night his wife and children were murdered. The body had kept going because it didn't know how to stop, even after his heart was broken. Now he was a skin full of unwanted memories with no reason to go on.

The gold around the woman's neck gleamed with a lure that promised everything and would deliver nothing. He'd fallen for its trap before, and he knew that for a goblin there was never enough gold to satisfy, but he would try. Could he lose himself in the mindless lust and become a heartless goblin again?

It would be so easy to give in.

The cross was only finger-lengths away. He could take the gold. Take enough gold to bury all feeling. He'd find a place to hoard it, and build a castle and fight all who'd tried to steal it from him. That was what goblins did. Yet the goal that had once sustained him now lacked true desire; it was empty, as if he was trying to force himself to want when he wasn't sure what he wanted. It would have to do. Gold would smother the other thoughts. Gold could always fix things for a goblin. But for a goblin there was nothing to fix but the need for more gold.

His gaze darted to the soldiers, but they weren't watching him. Could he steal from her? He shouldn't, but he needed the screaming of a thousand memories in his head to stop and gold had solved his problems for so long. The necklace swung closer and he gave in to the glittering temptation. If he took the gold, he'd become goblin and find peace. With a flick of his fingers, the gold came away in his hand. The woman didn't notice. Her gold burned his palm. He waited for the swell of desire, the pleasure of holding the precious metal, the rising need for more, but it didn't come.

Instead, there was silence as the screaming stopped and for a moment he glimpsed a clarity of mind he'd thought lost. Then it was wiped away as a slippery sense of disquiet took hold of his gut. Taking gold had never caused him discomfort before. He tried to push aside the unease and regain the calm, but it slid through his fingers. Goblins didn't have feelings. They had urges. He couldn't allow himself to feel. If he did, he would drown in despair.

He imagined gold, piles of it, the cold metal in his hands, and a hunger that couldn't be sated. But his skin didn't change to gray, and his joints didn't thicken. He remained stubbornly human.

How was that possible? He wanted gold. He was stealing gold. He should be goblin. He'd given in before and found peace, but this time he was denied and he knew the truth. The man who'd pulled him from the Shadowlands was right: Meryn had been cursed and was now free. He was human and couldn't go back. The realization brought no joy, only more of the heartache he couldn't fully explain.

The woman stood and beckoned him forward, her voice calm, her lips still curved. She hadn't noticed his theft. He fisted his hand so the points pressed into his palm. The guilt didn't fade. He should give the neck-lace back before it was too late, before she realized and labeled him a thief, but when she glanced at him, he couldn't. The look in her eyes would change from concern to hate. Her kindness would be gone, replaced by the fear he was more used to seeing. He sat frozen, unsure what to do next. The woman spoke again.

When he didn't move, one of the men in blue grabbed his arm and forced him to stand, then talked to the woman. She nodded as they spoke, her gaze flicking to him. And Meryn knew they were talking about him as if he were a simpleton.

He couldn't do anything right. He slipped the cross into the folds of his tunic and tried to listen as if he could force comprehension, but the words washed over him and didn't stick. Their language was too different and unfamiliar; they didn't understand him either. He sighed and bit back the frustration, then followed her because that seemed to be expected.

The soldiers didn't accompany the woman. What was going on? Where was she taking him? Should he make a run for it? He glanced over his shoulder; the men were still there, lingering by the door. Meryn forced himself to follow the woman. For the moment he would do as asked—at least until he had a better understanding of the world.

She picked up a piece of parchment and a stylus off the counter. They stood at the side near the door where the mother and children had gone. Was he about to be taken through the door? He didn't want to go there if that was where the crying child was. He couldn't listen to the screaming without hearing the echo of his own children. He swallowed the brittle points of anguish that lodged in his throat. Taking gold hadn't dulled the edges. How much would he have to steal to surrender his humanity again? Would he ever be able to breathe without hurting?

"Nadine." She pointed at her chest just below were the golden crucifix had hung, her neck now bare.

Her gold weighed heavy in his pocket. He shouldn't have stolen it, yet how could he give it back? She would know what he'd done and she would stop being nice to him. She was the first person to care in too long, and as a human, he needed that. The guilt swelled in his stomach, but he ignored it and focused on what she was saying. Her name.

Nadine. That wasn't a name he was familiar with. It wasn't Roman or Decangli. Where had her family originated?

She raised her dark eyebrows, waiting for him to respond.

He tapped his chest. "Meryn."

His name sounded strange on his lips. It had been a long time since he'd spoken it aloud, longer since he'd said anyone else's. Goblins didn't have names; even as a goblin he'd known that by having one he was different.

"Nadine." He pointed at her and copied the inflection in her voice. He'd learned Latin, the language of the invaders, by listening and repeating. He could do the same again. Maybe it would keep his mind occupied and away from the thoughts he didn't want to examine.

She nodded. As she wrote, she spoke, but all he understood was his name on her lips. He remembered the last woman to call his name had been his wife—not in love but in terror. She'd needed him as the Romans invaded their home and slaughtered their people. Instead, she had summoned a strange creature. A goblin. His wife hadn't recognized him in the body of a goblin. It was better that way. She'd have been horrified to see what he'd become.

He'd failed to help her when she needed him most.

Nadine glanced at him and then back at the page as if wondering what to write. He stared at the squiggles, but they made no sense—he could read a map, not words. She was educated and in a position of authority. Admitting his theft would result in his death. For a heartbeat he let himself consider dying. It should be easy to surrender to fate and know he would live again as another man in another life...but would he? What kind of afterlife waited for a man like him? He wouldn't be allowed into the Hall of the Gods to feast; he would be forced to wait outside and then be reborn into a life where he would have to make reparation for crimes he didn't remember.

He'd been cursed for a reason and then he'd given in to that curse.

Dying had never been an option; he'd always fought for life. Since becoming goblin again seemed out of reach, that left living. He released a slow breath. It had been so long since he'd been human in the Fixed Realm he didn't know how.

Nadine spoke to the woman on the other side of the counter. They both looked at him, and he recognized the look of disdain in the eyes of the other woman, as if she were judging him unworthy and beyond help.

Did he need help? He glanced at Nadine. She was talking to him and pointing at his head. He touched his forehead and his fingers came away red and sticky. Red blood, human blood. Not the black that lined goblin veins. He was all right. The wound wasn't fatal.

Nadine opened the door the woman and baby had gone through and indicated for him to follow. He hesitated, not sure what was on the other side. But she smiled again, and he trailed after her because she seemed to care and on the outside of the building there were people who'd try to attack him, and he no longer had weapons. With a shake of his head, Meryn took a step forward. The woman with the brilliant smile led him to a small room. Men in white coats followed. They talked among themselves. Then the men examined him the way Nadine had, checked his head, his eyes, and his pulse. A man addressed him, but his words made no sense.

When Meryn didn't respond, the man issued one order then left. Nadine sighed and studied him, a faint frown creasing her brow. He knew that look. She was tired, and he was a problem. If their roles were reversed, he'd have passed the problem on to someone else and gotten on with his job. He'd been someone of importance. His fingers touched the metal around his neck, a symbol of rank, the weight of responsibility. He'd failed more than his wife. He was a useless man in a world he didn't understand.

A young man in the same loose clothes as Nadine joined them. She spoke to the man, then turned to Meryn and addressed him as if he could understand. Her gaze remained steadily on him and he straightened his shoulders. He didn't feel so broken or lost in her eyes. She pointed to the man.

He glanced between the two of them. Nadine was handing him on to someone else. He understood that. But could he trust this newcomer? The man obviously listened to Nadine, because he nodded and smiled at Meryn. But it lacked the sincerity that Nadine's smile had; the man thought him an idiot.

Nadine raised her eyebrows and repeated whatever she was saying. He might not have understood the words, but by the way they moved their bodies and the tone of their words, he could at least grasp part of what was going on. And while he may not trust the man, he had to trust Nadine. There was nothing deceitful in her expression, and she'd shown him only kindness.

Meryn nodded and followed the man through lengths of white corridor. The man didn't speak or look at him, as if he wasn't worth the time and effort. The rudeness rubbed. It wasn't his fault he was here and unable to speak the language. But since he couldn't even voice his displeasure at being treated like an inconvenient slave, Meryn focused on his surroundings, looking for clues and details about the world.

Everything smelled odd. Not like the nothing of the Shadowlands. This place had a smell, a sharpness that tried to mask the scent of illness and death. He knew those scents too well, yet no one seemed to be dying here—at least not of battle wounds. Maybe it was plague or wasting illnesses.

He muttered a prayer to the gods that he wouldn't fall prey to whatever illness they had that needed such a large building, then stopped when the man gave him a quizzical glance. When the man looked away, he finished silently.

Why couldn't Nadine have come?

Tension crawled up his back and lodged around his skull, making the wound pulse. Warmth trickled down the side of his face. He wiped it away with the edge of his sleeve. Brilliant red stained the fabric. His stomach turned; he'd seen too much blood spilled without good reason. The man went into a small room and turned some handles. Rain began falling from a spout. Meryn stared, but the man was unconcerned; he put his hand under the water as if to check, then he pointed to Meryn and spoke a few words.

When Meryn didn't respond, the man pretended to wash his hands, then pointed to the water again. This time Meryn got it. He was supposed to get into the water.

Meryn unclasped the broach from his cloak. For a moment he stared at it as he remembered being given it. A gift from a king. That king had died, and his son, Roan, had taken the role even though he'd been too young and untried. Meryn held the wolves in his hand, unwilling to hand it over. The man tapped the wooden bench, so Meryn folded his cloak, placed it on the bench, and put the clasp on top. He stripped off his tunic and pouch. The gold inside clinked; Nadine's cross and his Roman coins. Then he pulled of his boots and trousers. The man was watching, but it was with bored indifference.

With one eye on his belongings, Meryn stepped into the water, expecting the bracing chill of rain. But the water was warm, hot on his skin, sluicing away the gray dust and leaving him clean. He tipped his face to the little rain and opened his mouth. It tasted clean. He scrubbed his face and beard, and ran his fingers through his shoulder-length hair, avoiding aggravating the gash on his head. The water drummed on his head and down his back. The cuts on his hands and head stung, but he didn't care. He hadn't been clean in so long.

The man spoke and held out a bottle of something. Meryn held out his hand and the man squirted a blob into his palm. He looked at it; he wanted to sniff it but the man was watching and waiting. So Meryn rubbed his hands together and went to wash it away, then it foamed in his hands. Soap.

Soap like nothing he'd ever seen. A liquid. He washed, everything and everywhere, scrubbing the remains of the Shadowlands from his skin, if not his mind. He would never be free of his memories. He closed his eyes and forced them back; he couldn't deal with them—any of them, and if he let them slip through, the screaming would start again.

He jerked his head up and tried to shake off the agony that filled his heart. He failed, but at least it wasn't crushing him with every breath. The man offered Meryn what looked like a small blanket and Meryn took the hint.

The blanket was thick and soft and soaked up the water. He rubbed himself down and dried his hair as best he could; his fingers brushed his torque. A sign of rank—or it had been. Again wolves, they faced each other around his neck. Pack animals. He'd helped lead the tribe. He and the king would meet and talk late at night, plotting a way to be free. They'd failed. He'd failed. The Romans had won.

His fingers closed around the metal as if to pull it off, but he couldn't. It had belonged to the man he had been, someone he'd been proud to be. Now he was a no one, dependent on some stranger to hand him clothes and show him how the world worked.

Meryn put on the pale blue pants and tunic that were offered. While his clothes were familiar, they were filthy, and he didn't want to be wearing the Shadowlands. He picked up the clasp and placed it in his pouch. Gray dust stuck to his damp fingers, but he didn't have a choice, so he put it on. The pouch contained everything he owned. Then he picked up his boots. He wasn't leaving his only pair of shoes either.

Satisfied, the man talked at him, not to him the way Nadine had, and then started walking away. Meryn glanced at his old clothes one last time, then walked away, hoping he could leave the Shadowlands behind so easily.

Chapter 3

NADINE HUNG MERYN'S CHART AT THE END OF A BED, ready for when he returned. He would be under observation until the specialist came down and did a neurological assessment. Then he'd either be admitted or turned out. A scan had already been ordered, since Meryn couldn't tell them what was wrong. Nadine just wanted him to be okay…and to know what had happened to him.

A man in hospital scrubs, a little taller than herself, followed the orderly into the ward. He was holding boots and around his neck was a band of metal. A torque. He looked at her and gave her a tentative smile. Nadine looked again and realized it was Meryn. Without all the dust he looked like a new man. Several other nurses paused to look at him, as if he commanded attention with just his presence.

Meryn acted like a man used to being obeyed. And while he couldn't communicate it, he knew it. He moved like a man who knew his place, and yet when she looked in his eyes she didn't see confidence, only uncertainty, as if he wasn't sure about anything. But he didn't glance around the ward the way many patients did, he still carried himself as if he feared nothing. He understood more than what he could say. She wanted to hear him speak again—in any language.

He placed his boots down and sat on the edge of the bed.

"How are you feeling?" Nadine did a quick couple of checks. He hadn't gotten worse. She checked the wound on his head. Now that she could see it clearly, it didn't seem that bad, but it could use a few stitches. But that would have to wait until the doctors had made a decision. All she could give him was a temporary bandage.

He glanced up at her and said a couple of words. Not Latin this time, but the language he'd first spoken. His voice was deep and melodic. She bit the inside of her lip to keep from smiling while wishing she could understand him, so she could ask him what had happened, why he'd had a sword, and what the torque around his neck meant. As usual, she had too many questions that would never be answered.

"Where are you from?" she asked, knowing he wouldn't be able to tell her but needing to fill the silence. "And what do you do for a living?"

Had he been living on the streets? His arms were strong, roped with muscle, and he had hard calluses on his hands. He had to have been working, and working hard, until very recently.

He spoke several complete sentences that made no sense, then again in what she was sure was Latin. The more she heard, the more convinced she was. And he was trying to tell her something that was important to him. She smiled and shook her head. For a moment they just looked at each other. His gray eyes unreadable, as if he didn't know how to make himself understood. She wished she had more time to spend with him, but they were too busy.

Nadine touched his hand and a shiver ran along his skin. It had been a long time since anyone had touched him. He'd been fighting goblins and killing for so long…long enough for the world to move beyond anything he might have imagined. The last person to lay a hand on him had been his wife. As if on cue, the screaming in his head grew louder, denying him any peace. He didn't deserve any after what he'd done.

The thousand misdeeds would haunt him forever.

Nadine placed a small cloth against his scalp. Whatever was on it stung the open wound. He pressed his teeth together and said nothing. Nothing he said meant anything anyway. When she was done, Nadine touched his shoulder for a moment, murmured something, and walked away.

For a while Meryn watched her work. She spoke to people, made notes about the ones in bed, and then hung those notes at the end of each bed. Most of the people looked worse than him. He shouldn't be here taking up space when he wasn't ill or gravely wounded. He rubbed his eyes to try to focus. He was tired, like he hadn't slept in days. How long had it been? There'd been no way to gauge the passing of time in the Shadowlands. Did goblins even sleep? He couldn't remember. He knew since becoming human again he'd only been able to snatch a few naps, but even then he'd been alert for the slightest sound. Maybe he should lie down, that's what everyone else was doing—those that weren't hidden behind curtains.

He swung his legs up onto the bed and rested his head on the pillow. He had nowhere else to be and being near the only person who treated him like a human seemed like a good idea. In his heart, he knew he was hiding. It was only a matter of time until Nadine realized what he'd done and what he'd been. Sooner rather than later, he was sure the man who'd pulled him from the Shadowlands would track him down and he'd be forced to face a past he could only remember in bits and pieces. He exhaled slowly and forced his muscles to relax.

Here was better than out there where the soldiers marched and people stared. And it was definitely better than the Shadowlands. But it wasn't home. He swallowed around the lump forming in his throat. He didn't have a home. It had been destroyed by the Romans. He closed his eyes and tried to forget, but some things couldn't be forgotten. The screaming filled his head again. He fought against the rising memories that wanted to suck him under. And he lost, defeated by simple exhaustion, a force no man could resist.

The blood spread around him, staining his gray skin crimson. Goblins didn't cry. He wanted to. He'd stood, unable to move, as the legionaries had cut his two daughters down. Their little bodies limp in his arms, cradled with the lifeless body of their mother. The baby in her belly never getting a chance to be born. His gnarled goblin hand rested on her stomach. He would give anything to take their places. But it didn't matter which god he called for assistance, none answered.

Because he'd supported his Decangli King over the druid, he'd been cursed—damned to the Shadowlands as goblin, forced to obey the summons of anyone who knew the proper words. He'd been summoned to watch the slaughter of the Decangli and been unable to lift his sword, bound by the magic of the curse. He was the leader of the army; he should've been there fighting with the men, but their plans had been spoiled. A traitor had betrayed them for Roman coin.

When he'd thought the night of blood and terror was over, he'd been summoned once more by the calls of his wife as she tried to defend their home and daughters from the Roman soldiers. She screamed at the sight of him, while the soldiers laughed. Once again he could do nothing but watch as everything he'd ever loved and lived for was taken away by a Roman blade.

The blood of his slain family cooled, and he called out for the tribe to avenge their deaths, to murder the Romans in their beds. But no one heard. They were all dead. Everyone was dead except those that had been cursed. Saved or damned, it didn't matter. He didn't care. He had no reason to go on. He howled his loss in the Fixed Realm; torn apart by grief, wounds opened that would never heal, the loss of his family leaving gaps that couldn't be filled. He was nothing more than a wounded monster.

Eventually he'd been pulled back to the Shadowlands, even though he'd resisted until his skin peeled and he'd expected to be torn apart. In the desolation, it had been easy to let the cold take him, seeking refuge from the pain in the curse. He'd failed his wife and his children. He'd failed his tribe. He'd failed his king. The grief he'd locked away when he'd surrendered to the curse sucked him under, ripping at his heart as the screams of his family echoed in his head.

"Meryn." A woman's voice shattered the nightmare.

He jerked awake at the sound of his name and sat up. His hands were coated with blood—red blood, human blood. His wife's blood. His heart hammered against his ribs. Where was he?

He glanced around the room, his hands curling into

fists. The woman next to him kept talking, her voice was soft, but she looked like she was ready to back away fast. Away from him. He looked at his hands. The blood was gone. He was human, not goblin. It had been a dream, nothing more. He opened his hands and made himself look at Nadine. Her gaze was wary, as if she wasn't sure he was safe to be around. That look was almost as bad the nightmare that had given his memories life.

"I'm all right." His voice was harsh, as if he'd been yelling. His heart slowed, but his breathing still came in heavy pants. "It was a dream." He closed his eyes.

Just a dream, a memory he'd suppressed. One he'd rather forget. But forgetting hadn't helped last time. The holes in his heart remained and no amount of gold had been able to fill the emptiness. Giving in to the curse had merely dulled the pain, saving it up for when his heart beat again. He took a slow breath and opened his eyes.

Nadine was looking at him…and so was everyone else. She spoke softly as if she was calming a child.

"I'm fine." He repeated, quieter this time. Then remembered she couldn't understand him.

She touched his arm and asked another question.

Like it made any difference what she asked.

He brushed aside her hand and her concern. He needed to leave now, before they called the soldiers back. He swung his legs off the bed. Nadine moved to stand in front of him, then she crossed her arms and shook her head.

"Let me pass. Put someone who's truly ill in the bed," he said in Decangli. This time he didn't bother repeating in Latin since she didn't speak it.

Nadine didn't move. She met his gaze without

flinching. Her full lips pressed tight together, her eyes hard as if she expected him to obey.

He clamped his teeth together and the muscle in his jaw twitched. He gave the orders; he didn't take orders, unless they had been coming from his wife. His heart gave a twinge, like a wound was opening, tearing wider with each breath. He couldn't function with the memories flooding his mind. He had to lock away the thoughts that hurt. He inhaled and with a wrench of will pushed everything down. Not forgotten but buried enough that he could think.

Nadine cocked her head and raised her dark eyebrows. No one had ever stared him down. He'd run the Decangli army. The only person who'd outranked him was the king. But he was no longer that man; that man had been killed with his wife and children. Meryn huffed out a breath and lay back on the bed. He crossed his arms and stared at the ceiling. He would not sleep again. He didn't want everyone staring when he had another nightmare. But he knew he'd have to sleep eventually, and when he did, everything he was trying to forget would rise back up.

From the corner of his eye he was aware of Nadine smiling, and he couldn't help the curving of his lips. He lay there staring at the ceiling, aware of her moving around the room even though he couldn't see her.

The noise in the room ebbed and flowed around him, but he didn't let it lull him to sleep. He stayed alert and listened, as if he could unravel the language if he did so hard enough. It would happen eventually if he paid attention. A man began shouting in anger not fear.

Meryn sat up slowly. His gaze landed on a wiry man

with wild eyes. The man began tearing at the bandages on his arm. His words were sharp and rising in pitch. Nadine walked closer, speaking calmly. Meryn's gaze darted between the two of them. He was like a drunk spoiling for a fight—only he was fighting with himself. Nadine reached for the man intent on ripping off his bandages. The man shoved her to the floor, and she landed on her butt. The man stepped closer, his arm bleeding, still shouting demands.

Meryn jumped off the bed. "Get back." He barked the order, expecting to be obeyed.

The man looked at him as if seeing him for the first time. In that moment of hesitation, Meryn put his hand out to Nadine. He kept his eye on the man as her fingers closed around his. As he pulled her up, he put himself between her and the man with dangerous eyes—he had the look of a boar about to charge.

Two men grabbed the crazy man from behind. He kicked and struggled, but they had him under control. Another man in uniform eyed Meryn as if deciding if he was a threat and Meryn realized he still held Nadine's hand. Her skin was cool and her palm smooth. He preferred it to the gloves she wore when she was checking his injury. He released her and stared back at the man, daring him to act. He'd done nothing wrong. He'd acted when no one else had.

Nadine spoke. Her words were clear but her voice had a tremor.

He turned to face her. "Are you hurt?"

She just shook her head and ushered him back to his bed, her gaze going back to the man who'd been tearing himself apart. She expected him to lie down as if nothing had happened. Was it like this all the time here? The noise and danger?

Then he realized he was part of it. No one could understand him, which meant no one knew what to expect from him. He didn't want to make her job harder, so he lay down, but this time he lay on his side so he could watch and make sure nothing else happened. But everything settled down. People went about their work. The patients lay still or moaned. Some were wheeled away, others walked. Wherever this place was, it was temporary, which meant he'd have to leave too.

When Nadine came back to check on him, there were two people in white coats with her. A man and a woman. Nadine spoke and the other two looked at the paper that had been at the end of his bed. Meryn sat up; they were discussing him—was he going to be moving already?

The new woman spoke to him.

"I can't understand you. I don't know what you want from me." It was pointless even bothering; no one here spoke Decangli or Latin, and they were the only languages he knew. Where was he? And the bigger question, the one he had been trying to avoid, when was he? How many years had passed?

The two in white coats conferred again. They made him do silly things like touch his fingers and thumb together, touch his nose, and hold out his arms. He copied each instruction. But instead of allaying their concern, their frowns deepened. Nadine watched him but didn't interfere. She didn't frown, but she studied him as if she could work out what was wrong if she looked hard enough.

He hoped she would never find out was wrong with

him. None of these people ever needed to know he'd been goblin. While the people in white coats talked some more, he glanced at Nadine, smiled, and shrugged. There was nothing he could to do make these people happy.

Nadine's lips curved, and for a moment her eyes were filled with more than concern.

"Meryn." The man handed him a stylus and a small piece of parchment and asked him to do something, then they waited.

Meryn looked at the smooth stylus. There was no ink to dip it into. He touched the page and it made a mark. The ink was inside. He looked at the people again, and then Nadine. She wanted to know about him. Maybe she could help him. While he couldn't write, he could make maps.

He sketched a map of the place that had been his home in the hope they would recognize it. His hand wasn't steady. It had been a long time since he'd had to perform such a delicate task. To his eye it wasn't too bad; the coast and rivers were there.

More puzzled looks.

Nadine looked closer at what he'd drawn. She brought her hands close and then moved them apart. "Bigger?"

Did he need to draw a bigger map? To include more area? The whole south of Britain? He'd seen the Roman maps of all their lands. Could he draw that and ask where he was?

He mimicked her movement and copied her word, and she nodded, a grin forming.

The two in white coats looked less than pleased that they were excluded from the odd conversation. He didn't care about them and they didn't care about him.

He turned the page over and drew a more expansive map, one that took into account all Roman territory. He made a mark where the Decangli had once ruled. Nadine's mouth formed a quiet *Oh*.

He tapped the place where he'd lived and looked at her, hoping she knew of it.

"Wales," she said

"Wales?" he repeated, but the word was awkward to form.

Nadine took the paper and drew another map, this time the lands he'd drawn were smaller and she added more. She made an *x* where he had, in the place she called Wales, then drew a dotted line and drew another *x*. "Australia."

"Australia." The sounds were strange on his tongue, as strange as the lands she'd drawn. He'd never seen them on a map before. He'd never seen or heard of Australia. He was a half a world away from home. His stomach hollowed out as if he'd been kicked in the gut.

He didn't even try to listen as the three people talked about him. It was no wonder they didn't speak the same languages as him. Why had his cousin done this? What game was Dai playing in dragging him to a place where he couldn't understand the language? Was it punishment for abandoning his duty and king?

Nadine touched his hand. She spoke and indicated to the young man who'd turned on the rain so he could wash. She wanted him to go with the man. He wouldn't fight her. There was no point. He had nowhere to go. Damn Dai. Maybe he should find his way back to the tower Dai had left him in and demand some answers. And then Dai, and Roan, would demand some from him.

How could he ever explain to Roan what had happened? It would never justify why he'd given up and given in. And even if he could, there'd still be reckoning. He was a deserter and a coward, and death at the end of a sword would follow.

He'd find his own way in this strange place. He'd learned the Romans' language, and he could learn this one. Nadine had already taught him his first words.

He clasped her hand with both of his. "Thank you."

She didn't pull away. She said something, but all he recognized was his name.

He nodded and released her hand. Immediately his skin felt cooler without her touch. The stolen gold in his pouch became heavy. Maybe if they hadn't been surrounded by people, he'd have found the courage to hand it back, but even as he thought it, he knew he'd never be strong enough to see the look in her eyes turn cold with hate. He also knew he'd have to find a way, otherwise he'd have to live with guilt. The man he'd been would never have wallowed in doubt. He'd have done the right thing without question.

Now he questioned everything.

He took one last glance at Nadine before going with the young man and doing as he was told. She raised her hand in farewell and he returned the gesture. He almost turned around and walked back to her. He didn't want to go somewhere new without her; she'd made him feel human. He was pathetic. Had the curse stolen his spine as well as his heart and soul?

The screaming in his mind echoed as if there was nothing left of him except this walking body. What was a man without heart and soul? Without king and kin?

Maybe he had died, the goblins had gotten to him and this was the death he had to face—an eternity of never being understood and of never having a peaceful night's sleep. To be endlessly followed by a past he couldn't change. To be a no one. Would the gods be that cruel?

With measured paces, he followed to wherever the young man was leading. They went into a box that moved and then opened somewhere else by magic. No matter how far he walked Nadine's touch lingered on his skin, the concern in her eyes chafed his aching heart, and her golden cross became heavier with each step.

The man took him to a new room. The differences in this room were that there were only four beds and Nadine wasn't here. He was alone…except for the two other people in the room, but they were sleeping. He knew that was what was expected of him. Until when? How long did he have to stay here? Until he could speak the language? Was this some kind of house for the sick and feeble minded?

Maybe this is where he belonged.

Meryn lay down. The bed was well above the ground and narrow, exactly the same as the other one. He fingered the sheets, feeling the fineness of the fabric then pulled them over himself. He wasn't ill and infirm, nor an old man in need of care. Yet his body ached as if the goblin spears from his dreams had pierced him and beaten him down. He was tired as if he'd been fighting all night, confronting an enemy he couldn't defeat. As he lay in the quiet, his head pulsed, the pain radiating around his skull and down his neck. He closed his eyes and sighed as if he could expel the ache with a breath. Sleep tried to catch him, but each time he caught himself and jerked awake. He couldn't rest; he didn't want to relive the deaths of his family. He tried to make plans, but his mind couldn't pin down a thought.

Then he blinked but didn't wake; instead, he was in the Shadowlands.

Goblins skulked through his sleep. They fought each other, drawing thick, black blood. Their weapons gleamed as bright as their eyes. He crept closer to see what they were willing to die for. A dark-haired woman was being held by the goblin currently claiming king-ship. A spike of gold threaded through his nose; gold rings hung in his ears. He swung his sword with one hand and kept the woman in his grasp with the other. This was the prize they'd brought back from the Fixed Realm on the Wild Ride.

She saw him and cried out, in one language and then another. Pleading. In his ears the words sounded the same. Help me.

She didn't want to be a goblin queen. She fought back, kicking and scratching any goblin who tried to grab her. Even the king of the troop hadn't been able to hold on to her. But when the other goblins had swarmed around, she'd understood her fate.

He'd watched. Not because he didn't care, but because he hadn't known what to do. He didn't want to hurt her, but he didn't know how to help her. Help was a concept that his goblin mind couldn't grasp.

Around him, the goblins squabbled and smaller fights broke out over the gathered gold and who would claim the woman. He understood everything, yet no one used the same language. The words off their tongues were languages he'd never heard before living in the

Shadowlands, yet everything made sense. He'd never questioned how goblins knew Decangli...somehow he'd forgotten that was what he'd spoken, as if his goblin mind was too concerned with gold and fighting to think beyond and reason like a man. He stood watching and listening and absorbing.

He recognized the languages the woman used as the two Nadine had used—the one that everyone around him spoke and the other one, the one that was like an echo of Latin too distorted for him to comprehend.

The woman grabbed a knife from the closest goblin, desperation in her eyes. He knew that look—he'd seen it in his wife's eyes just before she'd died. Meryn looked away, unable to watch what happened next. Red blood stained the gray dust. But the goblins still fought, blaming the others for the loss of their prize.

He'd always known he was different from other goblins, that something was wrong with him, but until that moment, he'd been able to deny it and pretend he was the same.

Now he knew why he was different. He hadn't yet completely surrendered his human soul.

He glanced at the woman. She lay unseeing on the gray dust—the curve of her lips and cheek now strangely familiar.

Chapter 4

NADINE PEEKED THROUGH THE WINDOW INTO THE room. Meryn was sleeping, but it didn't appear to be restful; his hands gripped the sheets too tight. What was he dreaming? The same nightmare that had made him call out in her ward? Was it some kind of post-traumatic stress? She bit her lower lip. Something about him wasn't adding up. He could draw a detailed map of Europe but didn't seem to recognize Australia. His reactions had all been normal. And if he was from Wales, shouldn't be able to speak English?

She lingered, watching him for a little longer. There was always something wrong with the really good-looking ones.

She shook her head and turned away. Like she could judge.

In the changing room, Nadine toed off her shoes, stripped off her scrubs, and dropped them on the floor. From her locker she pulled out her running gear, leggings and a long-sleeved T-shirt. After the shift she'd had, she needed to get out and stretch her legs before crashing for a few hours.

She dressed and tied up her sneakers. As she stood, there was no familiar bounce when her necklace should've hit her chest. Nothing. She traced the length of gold chain, but there was nothing hanging from it. Her mother's cross was gone.

"Shit." Panic shot through her system like a drug.

She shook out her scrubs, hoping the cross would drop out like it had last time. She'd pinched the clasp together a number of times with pliers, always swearing she'd take it to the jeweler to get fixed, yet never wanting to part with it to get it mended. When the cross didn't fall out of the fabric, she ran her hands over the cloth, double-checking. Her hands trembled as she kept searching, and her stomach liquefied. It wasn't there.

"Damn it."

Where could it be?

She couldn't have lost it. She'd worn it for twenty years. Her social worker had said that, when they found her, she'd refused to let go of the broken necklace. Her first foster mother had bought her a new chain so she could wear it. Since then she had never taken it off. It was all she had left of a mother she could hardly remember.

How could she have been so careless? If she'd gotten it fixed, she wouldn't be in this mess. Nadine scowled at the scrubs on the floor. Maybe it had gotten stuck in her civvies. She pulled the clothes she'd worn to work out of her locker, waiting for the telltale tinkle of gold hitting the linoleum. Nothing.

The contents of her locker followed the clothes onto the floor. Had she been wearing it when she came to work? Maybe it was at home in the shower or on the bedroom floor? She closed her eyes and tried to think when she'd last felt its weight around her neck but couldn't remember. She was so used to it being there that she paid it no attention. Her left hand curled into a fist as if she could feel the cross's weight and shape in her palm.

She didn't get that lucky. It wouldn't be at home. It would've come off while she was working. Tears welled, but she swallowed and forced them back. She didn't cry. And she wasn't going to start now. If someone found it, maybe they'd hand it in.

Yeah. Like that was going to happen. People didn't hand in lost jewelry. They either kept it or pawned it. She unclenched her hand. She wasn't a child clinging to hope anymore. For too long as a child, she'd imagined her mother and father would find her and take her back. Eventually she'd been forced to face the truth. Her mother was dead and her father was doing time for her murder.

What she couldn't remember she'd researched in old newspapers as a teenager. At the time it had been quite a scandal.

French immigrant killed by Sudanese husband.

Five-year-old daughter the only witness, too traumatized to speak.

No remorse. Husband pleads not guilty.

Wife-killer repeatedly refused parole for refusing to tell police where the body is.

Despite everything she'd read, she still didn't recall a thing about that night. All she had were nightmares that left her terrified of the dark but offered no answers. During the horror of being assessed and bundled off into foster care, her maternal grandmother had done nothing. She'd refused to get the granddaughter she'd never wanted and take her home to France—she didn't want the embarrassment of a brown-skinned child in the family. It was no wonder her mother had left Lyon and come to Australia. How different would her life have been if her parents had stayed in France?

She shook her head. That was another fantasy she refused to dwell on. Her father had taken away everything, and now he was free. As if a twenty-year sentence could make what he'd done all right. And now her mother's cross was gone. It was just going to be one of those days…maybe one of those weeks. Ever since he'd been released, she'd been on edge, waiting for something to happen.

Nadine folded up the clothes and packed them into the small backpack she wore when running. She cast her gaze once more over the floor but no gold glinted. With a heart weighed down by loss, she bundled up the scrubs and dropped them in the laundry. Then she scribbled a note and pinned it to the staff notice board, just in case by some miracle someone found the cross her grandmother had given her mother for her confirmation.

But she wasn't going to hold her breath waiting.

For the benefit of anyone who saw her, she pasted on a smile. She'd learned a long time ago that looking sad drew attention and questions that people then wanted answered. It was much easier to look happy and be left alone.

She slung her backpack over her shoulders and adjusted the straps so it wouldn't move around. At least while she was running she wasn't thinking about anything except her next step. She braced herself for the early morning chill as she left the hospital. The days were getting warmer, lighter, and longer. Spring was in the air even though it wasn't September yet. Just the idea that the winter solstice was behind her was reason enough to celebrate. It would be nearly another year until the anniversary of her mother's death came around.

As she warmed up from a walk to a jog to a run, the chain around her neck bounced without weight. Every step was a reminder of what was missing. She ran along the river without seeing it, up the stairs that connected the city of Perth to Kings Park, through the park, and to the City West train station down the hill. Her lungs burned but she didn't relent. She didn't want to be able to think.

Her feet hit the platform, and there was nowhere else for her to run to. But she didn't stand still even though it was ten minutes until the train arrived. Instead, she paced and calmed her breathing. She'd pushed herself hard and still didn't feel any better. Her hand touched the empty chain, as if she expected the cross to reappear by magic.

This early in the morning, there was hardly anyone on the train, and those who were got off in the city ready to start their days. She didn't miss the early morning crush. It had been hard enough to conform to what everyone called normal hours while she was studying. Having to attend classes during the day and attempting to sleep at night was awful. As a child she'd sleep as soon as she came home from school, wake up for dinner, and then play or read silently until dawn, the lights burning to keep away the creatures that crawled in the shadows and haunted her nightmares. Then she'd sleep until she was dragged out of bed by yet another foster parent who couldn't understand why she was being difficult.

By the time she got off the train and was walking the last couple of blocks home, she'd almost convinced herself the cross was at home, tangled in her bed sheets. The loop had never been quite right since it had been pulled off at school by a child who'd decided to make her suffer for being different. She'd pushed him off the jungle gym and broken his arm in retaliation.

In hindsight, she could've killed him. Maybe murder ran in her blood.

The two kids at the bus stop across the road waved. Their mother would have gone to work already and left them to get themselves to school. At least she'd never had to do that. She'd always had breakfast made for her and someone to send her off each day. Nadine waved back as always. They knew that if there were ever any problems after school, they could knock on her door. So far there'd only been a couple of Band-Aid emergencies.

When she got inside, the house was silent. Gina was having an extra-long weekend away with her just-returned army boyfriend. For today the place was hers. The stillness echoed around her and she breathed it in, searching for peace and trying to rein in the hope that lingered in her belly—her cross was here, it had to be. She dropped her bag by the door and went to her bedroom. The bed was unmade, as she'd left it.

She rummaged through the sheets, then stripped the bed, shook the sheets, and searched the floor. Then she went into the bathroom. The cross wasn't there either and it was too big to go down the drain. She worried her lip between her teeth.

It had been two decades since she'd slept without it and before then her mother had been alive and had read to her every night. If her father was home, and not driving a cab, he sat on the end of the bed and listened too. She couldn't remember an argument between her parents.

Nadine closed her eyes and put her hand on the empty

chain. It wasn't all lost. She still had the original broken chain. She swallowed and tried not to choke on the lump in her throat. That would have to do. But before she could sleep she'd have to remake the bed, shower, and eat.

Dressed in striped panties and a hot pink tank top with her short, wet hair sticking up in all directions, she ate a bowl of cereal. She really couldn't be bothered with cooking, and this had dried fruit in it. It was almost a real meal.

As she ate, she sifted through the mail on the kitchen table. Most of it was junk. Real estate agents cruising for a house to sell. A letter for Gina. And one for her. She stared at the familiar handwriting.

Nadine put her spoon down. She'd already received her birthday letter from her father. What did he want from her now? Part of her hated him for what he'd done; the rest of her couldn't be bothered dedicating the time to hate him properly. She'd never argued that he remain in jail until he died, even though she was given the option every time he came up for parole—it had always been denied because he'd never shown remorse or told police where the body was. However, according to the letters she'd received from the Department of Corrections, he'd been a model prisoner. He'd gotten an education and worked on the prison farm. Good for him. She was still paying off her college debt and would be for years.

She toyed with the envelope for a little longer, as if she could convince herself to read the first letter he'd written to her as a free man.

Usually it was just her birthday and Christmas. When she was little, her first foster mother had read them to her. Later, when Nadine could read, she'd just put them in a box unread. She didn't want to know how much he loved her. If he loved her, why had he ruined her life?

Why had he destroyed the happy family they had by killing her mother?

Her earliest memories were of laughter and singing. Of speaking Nuer with her father and her mother reading fairy tales in French. Not one of her memories involved anger or tears. She didn't trust the only memories she had of her family. How could she?

How could she trust anything her father said?

If he'd pleaded guilty, pleaded insanity—anything— she would've at least had a father. Instead, she was the little girl no one wanted. Too difficult, too traumatized, too anything but loveable.

Her appetite vanished and she threw the rest of her cereal in the garbage. But like every other letter from her father, she couldn't throw it away, so she added it to the collection that lived in a box at the bottom of her wardrobe. Next to the box of letters was the book of fairy tales. Taped inside were the broken chain and a picture of her family.

Her mother on one side of her and her father on the other. Both of them were smiling and in the middle was a tiny version of herself with pink ribbons in her pigtails. She didn't remember the photo being taken. But there was no doubt she was their child. She looked too much like them both. She'd inherited his eyes, a murky mix of green and brown, and her mother's wide cheeks and narrow chin; even her skin was the shade between her pale mother and dark-skinned father, as if she were the perfect blend of both of them.

On the next page, handwritten in French, was the

fairy tale her mother had told her the most—*Le roi des gobelins*, The Goblin King.

Once upon a time, there was a king. He was fierce and brave and handsome, but also just and kind. When his lands were attacked by invaders from over the sea and his brother captured as a slave, he rose up full of fury. But the invaders were sneaky. They didn't want to face the king who was uniting the people against them. So they laid a trap and tricked him and his loyal men with magic. The king was turned into a hideous goblin with a heart of solid gold and banished to the Shadowlands, the place where nightmares are created.

Her gaze skimmed over the familiar script; she knew the words by heart. When she was young, she used to close her eyes and imagine she could hear her mother reading to her like she'd used to. The words blurred, but it didn't matter. Her lips moved as she read to the end, the last line resonated in the air around her.

Love is the most powerful magic of all. Never forget that. If you can love, you can do anything.

Unlike the other stories in the book of fairy tales, *The Goblin King* didn't have a happy ending. The story seemed incomplete. More of a cautionary tale. As a child it hadn't bothered her; she'd believed the Goblin King would get a happily ever after because that was what happened, and she'd go to bed imagining a princess who could break the spell.

Nadine closed the book with a heavy thump. Revisiting her mother's stories was always bittersweet. With the curtains left open so sunlight would spill onto her and wake her if she slept too long into the afternoon, Nadine lay down on the bed, taking the book with her.

At first her dreams cradled her, the way dreams should. Her mother was sitting in the garden; behind her was a fountain and a castle. As a child Nadine had spent a lot of time imaging this place until it was so real she knew each flower, each brick, and every turn of the path. It was her sanctuary. Here she had lived her perfect life with her mother and father, but she'd banished him when she was old enough to understand what he'd done. Sometimes she was an adult walking the palace corridors, looking for something or someone; today Nadine was little again. She skipped along the path and then jumped onto her mother's lap.

Together they read Beauty and the Beast *and then* Sleeping Beauty. *Then her mother flicked back to the first page of the book and read* The Goblin King. *Her silky smooth accent made the story flow, so Nadine could almost see the King who'd been banished to the Shadowlands, a place so gray and bleak only goblins could survive. Even though she knew the story word for word, she shivered as if the sun had gone behind a cloud. She glanced up. It hadn't. There were no clouds for it to hide behind. The sun had vanished, yet it wasn't night. The sky was empty and weird and gray. That wasn't right. There was always blue sky and sunlight here; it was never dark. Everything was always as it should be. The gray bled into the landscape around her, stealing the color from the flowers. She watched them wilt and die.*

Fear gripped her. This was her place; she was in control. She would not let nightmares encroach. Nadine stood and she was an adult again.

"No!" Her voice echoed oddly. She spun to face her

mother, but she was gone. Where her mother had sat on the bench the book lay open, the pages fluttering in an unfelt breeze.

If you can love, you can do anything.

The words spun off the page and danced in the air like black butterfly skeletons. They twirled around her and tangled in her hair. Where they touched her skin, they cut with razor sharp wings. Nadine slammed the book closed before more words could escape. Around her the world shattered as if it were made of glass. The sky began to fall in like shards of lethal rain and the ground cracked like she was standing on thin ice. She screamed as if she was going to fall off the world and cease to exist.

Nadine sat up. Her breath came in short, sharp pants. Terror lodged in the back of her throat, jagged and rusted with age. It had been a long time between nightmares, yet her ears still rang with the sound of breaking glass.

She knew that whatever lay on the other side of the glass in her dreams would hurt her, but she always woke up before she saw what it was. The child psychiatrist had said it was her brain's way of protecting her from what she'd seen the night her mother was killed. Part of her wanted to know the truth; the rest of her was too scared to remember. It was one thing to know her father killed her mother, but another to have seen it. She took a deep breath and flopped back onto the bed and tried to go back to sleep.

But Nadine couldn't close her eyes; the fear was too fresh. Instead, she stared out the window at the blue sky, wishing she could see the sun, as if she needed reassuring it was still there. The blank gray sky of her nightmare had been alien and oppressive. She knew it was the Shadowlands of her mother's story. She shook her head and closed her eyes. When she went back to her dream castle, she'd fix whatever was damaged and everything would be fine.

—∿∿—

Light and noise filled the room. Meryn opened his eyes in time to see someone being wheeled out. The man lay motionless on the bed. Was he dead? Where were they taking the man…and would he be next? When the door closed, Meryn eased up and looked around. One sleeping area had the curtain pulled around. The other two were now empty.

For a moment he sat not sure what to do, only that he had to do something. He wasn't used to sitting still. He slid out of the bed and his feet touched the cold floor. It was smooth, unlike the dust of the Shadowlands. He flexed his toes. He was still in the Fixed Realm.

The door swung open and a woman pushed in a cart. She spoke a greeting.

Meryn copied. "Good morning."

She put a tray of food on his table and swung it around so it was over the bed, as if she expected him to eat in bed like an invalid. He was about to argue, then realized it would be a waste of breath.

He mouthed the words again and committed them to memory. *Good morning.* Not Decangli or Latin. Then what language? And what did the greeting mean? He shook his head. He would learn better with food in his stomach—even if he didn't know what that food was.

On his tray was bread and stuff in a box. There was

writing on it, that he couldn't read, and a picture. So he followed the picture and poured the contents into the bowl and added milk. Then he picked up the bowl and began drinking and crunching through the contents.

He smiled as he ate food he hadn't had to hunt and kill. The skinny deer of the Shadowlands that rotted almost as soon as he killed them were barely a decent feed. The food in his mouth changed taste and texture. He glanced down at his bowl. The milk had curdled, as if he were still in the Shadowlands and being punished for not eating fast enough. He dropped the bowl and everything spilled on the tray.

His throat tightened but the food in his stomach stayed put. He scanned the darkest corners of the room, but nothing hid in the shadows. The spilled milk had only soured after he'd thought of the food he'd scavenged in the Shadowlands. He shuddered. Had the Shadowlands followed him? Or was he still goblin enough that he could sour milk with a smile?

Meryn pushed his tray away, his appetite gone. He didn't know what was going on. Was he man or goblin? He didn't belong in the hospital; he knew that. He wasn't sick. He touched the bandage on his head and pulled it off. The blood was old, but the area was tender. Most of the wound was in his hair and would be hidden from a casual glance. He got out of bed and pulled on his boots.

Had it been the dust still on his boots that had brought his fear of rotten food to life? He rubbed his fingers together, feeling the fine dust between them. It seemed harmless, but he knew better. The Shadowlands bred nightmares from a single thought. His thoughts.

He ripped the blanket off the bed and scrubbed the dust off the boots. When they were more brown than gray he shoved them on. The pale blue trousers were what people wore in bed, not on the street. Once again he looked too different and didn't fit in. The memories of the crowd closing in around him last night were too fresh. He didn't want the soldiers in blue to arrest him again.

He glanced over at the clothes folded on a chair on the other side of the room, then paced over and picked up the first item: dark gray trousers. He shook them out and measured them against his body. They were twice his width.

The next item was a lightweight tunic with fastenings up the front. The last a tunic with the same fastenings but made of a heavy brown fabric. He slipped it on over the pale blue top he'd been given. It was too big but passable.

The person behind the curtain stirred.

Meryn froze. He glanced down at himself. He was stealing clothes like a goblin. No, not like a goblin. Goblins stole gold. He was a man who needed clothing. It still didn't feel right. The curtain moved. Meryn made a quick decision. He strode back to his bed, grabbed his coin pouch, shoved it into the pocket of the brown tunic, and hurried out of the room before the other person could wake and raise the alarm.

He retraced his path from last night to the metal box. He looked at the buttons—arrows pointing up and down. He'd gone up last night, so it was down this morning.

A woman frowned at him. "Are you okay?"

"Okay." He nodded and smiled and hoped he'd guessed right. Then he turned away, hoping the box would open before the other person realized he'd stolen some of his clothes and came after him. He was tempted to tear off the tunic and leave in just the clothes he'd been given, but that wouldn't make things better. The only course of action was to move forward.

The doors opened. There were already people inside. Last night it had been just him and the other man and it had seemed crowded. He forced his shoulders back and got in as if he used magic boxes every day.

"Are you going down?" an older man asked him as he pointed to a button.

"Down," Meryn agreed, hoping that the word meant what he thought it did.

He stepped inside and the doors closed. His heart lurched as the box moved, and for a moment he thought they would fall to their deaths, but the box stopped and everyone got out. He followed the people; then down a short corridor, he saw glass doors and the world beyond. Meryn stepped out of the building and drew in a relieved breath. He'd gotten out.

He tipped his face up. Above him the sun crept higher in the pale blue sky, giving him direction. But where would he go? West to the coast or inland? Did it matter?

Without thought, his fingers found the gold in his pouch, fingering the cold metal as if holding it and cradling it as he once had would calm his mind. His hand closed around the points of Nadine's cross for a second; it was the balm he needed. If he thought of nothing but mindless metal, he might have a chance of holding on to his sanity. It was bitter comfort to know his hope came from theft of the one person who'd showed him some measure of care. He opened his hand. The cross had left marks on his flesh. The figure's agony mirrored his own. An eternity of pain and the knowledge he could've stopped it all. He could've prevented the curse from ever happening if he'd found the traitor sooner. He could have saved his family. And his tribe.

He shuddered and pushed aside the memories of the slaughter. Instead, he tried to remember every word of that last meeting between his king Roan and the druid Elryion. They'd argued about the rebellion; the Romans knew about their plans because one man had betrayed them to the Roman General. Then the druid had cursed Roan and the five men who had dared to stand with him and the rebellion had gone ahead as planned. As a goblin, Meryn had watched it fail. Meryn looked at the gold figure on the cross. If he'd known who the traitor was, he'd have hammered in the nails himself.

~~~

Solomon Nhial knelt on the cold church floor and closed his eyes. With his head bowed and his hands clasped before him, he prayed for the same things he had for the past twenty years.

He prayed his beautiful wife, Michaline, was in heaven where she belonged. As always his chest tightened when he thought of her. The old ache hadn't lessened with time; he had grown used to living with the constant pain and loss.

He prayed his daughter, Nadine, was happy and loved. That her life had been better than the one he could've given her as a single father.

He prayed that they both forgave him for not being there when they had needed him most. He'd been driving

his cab the night Michaline had been killed and hadn't
been able to produce an alibi. The police had been quick
to convict him. They'd needed someone to blame for
such a horrible crime and he was the easy target—and
one they understood. In some ways, Australia was
no different from France. The same biases lived on
people's hearts.

Because of that his little angel Nadine had been left
alone, surrendered into state care. While he'd written
to her, he'd never received a response. He didn't blame
her, and even though it tore at his heart, he suspected she
hated him. For a short while, he'd received pieces of her
artwork sent by the foster parent. He'd kept them all. A
hand print, her wobbly letters as she wrote her name,
and endless paintings all in gray.

Those paintings chilled him more than he'd ever
admit. He knew what it depicted and what he could
never tell the police. His wife hadn't been killed by
a human; her fate had been much worse. Michaline's
fascination with the goblin myths had finally claimed
a price.

He praycd that she hadn't suffered and thanked the
Lord that Nadine had been spared from the goblins let
loose for solstice. Solomon shifted uncomfortably on the
hard floor. His joints weren't as good as they used to be.

He finished with the same wish he always did, that
an angel would guide his steps back to his daughter. It
was true he could never regain the time he'd lost and all
the things he'd missed by not being there for her, but he
wanted a chance to know who his daughter had become.
He had to believe that he would get that opportunity. He
had faith and love and hope. And after twenty years in

prison with men who'd done things he didn't want to think about, that was something.

Solomon kissed the dark ink of the cross tattooed on the back of his hand the same way he always did, and stood. His knees cracked with the movement. He'd gone to prison young and heartbroken and come out an old man with old memories.

For a moment he paused and gazed up at the Son of God, suffering all humanity's sins. Wallowing in self-pity would achieve nothing. While he placed his life in the Lord's hands, he also knew God was busy and helped those who were making an effort. Today he would try to find a job. Tomorrow he would come and pray and then go to the volunteer work his parole officer had arranged. He'd grown used to taking one day at a time and never looking too far ahead. Twenty years was too long to count the individual days when some hours lasted long enough to fill a life.

He pulled some coins out of his wallet and placed them in the dish. There would be someone worse off than him who would need what he could do without. The priest nodded a thank you.

Solomon smiled. It would be easy to be bitter, but as Michaline had always said: love is a stronger magic. It had held them together through her mother's hate, through a move across the globe. Magic or miracle, if it brought his daughter back into his life, he wasn't going to be picky.

Chapter 5

"How safe is Perth?" The news reporter raised her eyebrows as if the higher her brows were the more important the story. "New footage from the city at night reveals what happens when the shops close and the bars and night clubs open."

"For real? Didn't they do this story six months ago?" Nadine shook her head as she dressed in front of the TV to get ready for work. She was about to change the channel in disgust, even though she knew she'd be watching it again tomorrow, but the footage playing behind the woman made her stop.

A man dressed in gray clothes held a sword at a crowd that looked like jackals closing in on a wounded animal. Despite the drawn weapon, she knew who was really in danger. Bullies always hunted in packs and picked on the person who was different. She'd learned that lesson early.

The reporter rambled on about illegal weapons on the street and gave some statistics from the police about seized knives, machetes, and now a sword. All Nadine saw was the naked fear in the man's gray eyes.

It was the man from last week, she was sure of that. Meryn. She'd gone in early the following morning to see him, but he'd been gone. Walked out and left a pile of paperwork behind. Had he woken and been better? Or was he out there now unable to communicate? She bit her lip. He wasn't her problem. No, but that hadn't stopped her from wondering about him and how he was; seeing him on the TV as he had been the night he'd been brought into hospital only spurred her curiosity.

The video footage cut to a knife fight caught on camera outside of a nightclub and was followed by a reminder about a spate of recent bag snatchings and car break-ins around Kings Park. She didn't care about night-club brawls. They were commonplace; Meryn wasn't. There'd been something about him. He might not have been able to speak English, but he'd understood everything else. Few people would've stepped in front of a drug-enraged man, yet he had without hesitation—and offered her his hand. She'd never gotten the chance to thank him. On a quieter night she might have been able to spend more time with him, working out what was wrong and how best to help. Maybe if she had, she could have prevented him from leaving before he was ready.

The reporter concluded that the city was becoming more dangerous as more weapons hit the streets.

"Nowhere is safe," Nadine said to the TV before she walked into the bathroom. Not even people's houses. It didn't matter how well the doors were locked. If someone wanted in, they'd get in. The trick was to not let the fear take control. As long as she wasn't alone at night, she was fine, generally.

She hoped this spate of nightmares would pass once she got used to the idea that her father was free. She brushed her teeth and her hair. When it wouldn't sit nicely, she added gel and made it look like she'd wanted it tousled—as if she'd slept all day and just rolled out of bed.

Around her neck hung the empty gold chain. Her fingers touched the place where the cross should have hung. Her breath caught, but she forced the next exhale and each one got easier. After a week of looking and hoping, she knew it was gone. With only a slight tremble of her fingers she unclasped the chain; there was no point in wearing it. Without the cross, it was just a gold chain with no meaning. Before, it didn't matter how scared she got or where she was, she'd always had a part of her mother with her. Now she was alone.

And an adult. Her mother was long dead. It was time she stopped clinging to fairy tales and wishes and moved on. She put the chain in the box along with the unread letters from her father. The alarm on her watch went off, reminding her she had to leave for work in twenty minutes. She grabbed her bag, determined to be early today.

This time the memory of the man with the sword and gray eyes didn't leave her. She wanted to believe his family had found him and he was with people who cared. But in her heart she knew that if someone had come for him, they would've done the paperwork. He was out there alone, even though someone must know him and miss him. Somewhere, unlike her, Meryn must have a family that was worried about him.

<hr />

Meryn watched the sun rise over the hills in the distance. He doubted he'd ever get bored of seeing the golden light spill over and turn the sky pink. He shoved his hands into the pockets of the stolen *jacket*—he was learning the new words for everything and the way they were put together. He was also learning how the world worked.

His first evening in the park, two men had confronted him with the intention of stealing what little he had. Instead, Meryn had taken their knives and clothes. He'd seen them once in the parkland since then...and they'd seen him, so he was cautious, never taking the same route back to his campsite. They had a look in their eyes he'd seen before on men who didn't like to be beaten and would stoop low to ensure a win next time. And Meryn was sure there'd be a next time.

Their clothes were odd but not uncomfortable, and they fit better than the clothes from the *hospital*. What rubbed was that they weren't his. He had nothing but what he hunted or stole. He'd never begged in his entire life and wasn't about to start now. He was a warrior, a leader of men. His hand fisted around the points of Nadine's gold cross. If he couldn't prove it to himself, how was he going to prove it to anyone else?

Meryn rolled his shoulders and stretched his back. Old injuries that had never troubled him while he'd been goblin were stiff in the cold morning after a night on the ground. After seven nights of watching and learning and listening, he knew enough of the language to get by. Knew enough about the people to know he wasn't fitting in. He was living rough in the forest that overlooked the city, living off the lizards and snakes he caught, and washing in the public restroom.

He took a breath, enjoying the now familiar scent of the grass and trees. He had to find somewhere more permanent to live, some way to earn coin.

For the first time since he was a child, his days were his own. His nights were filled with memories he'd rather forget, and they were getting stronger. His fingers traced a cut on the back of his hand. He'd woken with the wound after fighting goblins in his sleep, as if he'd been to the Shadowlands and back. The implication of that was something he didn't want to think too hard about.

Each day he'd ventured farther from the park, a different direction each time. The forest was hemmed in by roads, traveled on by *cars*. Amazing advancements had happened in his absence. Two hundred years, three hundred years…more? The time was harder to grasp than the language.

Every new word he learned he repeated and tried to use in sentences the way he'd learned Latin. But he had no one to practice with. Back then it had been Roan and he and a few others, all trying to learn something about the invaders. Dai had picked up the language fast and could read and write fluently while he and Roan were still speaking like babies.

He stopped and tried to press down on the sadness that burst like a boil in his chest. He'd lost everything. His wife, his children, his tribe. Gone forever because one man had sold the Decangli out to the Romans. Wanting to know who was almost a reason to seek audience with his king. Almost.

But he couldn't bring himself to admit he needed help. He'd been the one people came to for aid. He would not face his king until he had proven to himself he was a man who could care for himself. Yet he wanted to know what had happened to the other men who'd also worn Roan's curse. Six of them had woken in the Shadowlands, confused and scared. Six of them had witnessed the rebellion failing. But then, instead of doing his duty and ensuring the safety of his king in the Shadowlands, he'd given in to the cold and mindless curse, welcoming it's embrace instead of fighting.

He'd forever live with the shame of being the first to fade to goblin. If the man who'd dragged him free of the Shadowlands truly was Dai, then it meant he and Roan had survived and found a way to break the curse—thus also freeing him.

But while the man looked like Dai and spoke like Dai, the man he'd seen hunting him in the woods wasn't the angry youth he'd known. This man had patience and magic. Had Dai changed so much?

How had Roan changed?

How had the curse been broken?

Where were the others: Fane, Brac, and Anfri? Were they all adapted to this world?

Of course they were. It was only he who'd given in to the curse and become goblin.

He had to prove he was no longer weak hearted and that he wouldn't fail again. Not for them, but for himself. If he couldn't look at himself in the mirror when he trimmed his beard, how was he ever going to look his king in the eye?

Nadine jogged down the path, inhaling the fresh scent of the lemon scented gum trees lining the road. On one side, at the bottom of the hill, Perth spread out along the Swan River; on the other, tamed park was interspaced with buildings. Behind the buildings, Kings Park gradually gave way to wilderness, a sanctuary in the middle of the city that was well used by runners and cyclists on weekdays and families on weekends. Opposite the white building that was a restaurant, she stopped. An old-fashioned wishing well, complete with wrought-iron arches, sat alone and out of place. Most people walked past it without a second glance. She hadn't stopped here for months.

Nadine turned off her MP3 player and pulled out her earbuds as she caught her breath, her muscles easing after the run up the stairs known as Jacob's Ladder that linked the park to the city. Last time she'd been here, she hadn't known what to wish for. The letter from the Department of Corrections had arrived, informing her of her father's imminent release. Even though she hated him for what he'd done to the family, she couldn't wish him ill or ask that he remain in jail forever. That would be a misuse of the power of a wishing well.

A wishing well was for granting wishes and she'd read enough fairy tales to know that wishing misfortune on someone else was a guaranteed way of having bad luck come visiting.

She unzipped the small pocket in her pants and pulled out a gold two-dollar coin. For a moment she just closed her eyes and held the money tight in her hand. Meryn's gray eyes had been with her all night while she worked. She hoped he was okay, half hoped he'd come back. He hadn't. Was it wrong to make a wish for someone else? She didn't know what he wanted. The only thing she could do was wish him well. No one should be lost and alone.

She held her hand out, over the well. The top was covered in mesh to prevent thieves from stealing the money that would eventually go to charity. She let the coin fall. It flickered brilliantly in the early morning sun before splashing into the shadows.

"Good luck, Meryn. Wherever you are." For three heartbeats she waited, as if expecting a puff of smoke and a shimmer of magic. Nothing.

Her lips moved in a quick half smile. Wishing on stars, or in wells, hadn't helped her as a child, yet she couldn't stop herself from believing in magic or hope.

She was sucker for a happy ending and hated depressing news stories.

After stopping, she didn't feel like running again. There was a train every fifteen minutes and it wasn't like she had to get home for anything important. So she dawdled, strolling through the park and looking at the scenery. The morning was too nice to waste, sunny and cloud free. If it weren't for the biting breeze, she could pretend it was already summer.

She noticed a man sitting on a bench. His arms rested on his jean-clad legs and his gaze was on the road. He didn't seem to be aware of the swirl of people passing him. As she drew closer, he lifted his head. His dark eyebrows arched in surprise and then he smiled as if he knew her. She glanced over her shoulder, but no one was there. The smile was for her. She smiled back to be friendly, like she did with most people. Then she noticed the half-healed cut on his head and his eyes. The man did know her. It was Meryn.

Her foot snagged on a tree root and she tripped. Instead, of landing face first in the grass, she was caught by the man with the strange gray eyes. His touch was strong and sure as he helped her back onto her feet. That was the second time he'd saved her; around him she couldn't seem to stay on her feet. Heat crept up her neck. This close, his eyes were dark gray; they seemed to draw her in, but she knew if she fell she'd get lost in there forever. His eyes definitely weren't the empty gray she'd first thought, but they had a faraway touch, as if he'd seen places no person should. She blinked and the moment was gone. He released her arm and she immediately missed the warmth of his hand.

"Meryn," she managed to say.

His smile widened and revealed a dimple in his right cheek. "Nadine. Are you okay?"

He did remember her. She glanced at the wound on his head. It could've done with some stitches, but he didn't look like the kind of man who cared about a scar or two. She glanced at his hands, remembering the nicks she'd seen on his skin. There was a fresh cut on his hand. Did he go looking for trouble, or did it find him?

"Your head looks better." God. Could she be more lame? He looked better, in jeans and a hoodie zipped up against the cold. He'd trimmed his beard and looked, well, like an attractive man she'd stop to talk to if she hadn't seen him confused and disheveled. It was hard to believe he was the same person who looked so lost in the hospital.

"It is. Thank you." He spoke in accented English.

She paused and realized he'd spoken to her in English. The other night they hadn't been able to talk. Her lips curved as a smile began to form. Today she could ask him everything she'd wanted to. Should she? Or should she just walk away?

If she'd been able to stop thinking about him, she wouldn't have dropped a coin in the wishing well.

Besides, he didn't seem dangerous and she was in a public place.

"And you speak English today."

He glanced away before answering. "A little."

"Do you speak French?" She hadn't spoken her mother's language for so long, with anyone, yet she hadn't forgotten. And the other night he'd responded as if he recognized the language.

He shook his head, his brown hair curling just above his shoulders in a fashionable *I don't care about my hair* look. "I've heard it."

"What languages were you speaking? Was one Latin?"

Meryn considered her for a moment. "Latin and Decangli."

"Decangli? Is that from Wales?"

He smiled. He should smile more often. "Yes. You run here?"

"Sometimes." Liar. She ran every day after work. But it was too soon for him to know that, even though she wanted to sit down and get to know him better. "Ahh." She shifted her weight, not sure what to do. "Well, um. I'm glad you're looking better—er—feeling better."

"I am." He paused as if he wanted to say something else but didn't know what.

That made two of them.

"Thank you," he said, filling the silence.

She reached out and touched his arm, a gesture meant to offer comfort. But feeling him beneath her palm, she didn't want to pull away. She wanted to step closer. What she'd thought was simple curiosity, or even compassion, was turning into an attraction she shouldn't have. Her pulse sped up as if she were running.

He moved and caught her hand in his. Skin to skin. His palm rough against hers. She wanted to know everything about him. How he'd ended up in hospital, what he did. Why he was here.

Instead, she drew away, her fingers sliding free of his and craving the contact as soon as it was lost. He was already under her skin. Whatever she was feeling was dangerous, and falling for the wrong man could be fatal. Her mother had learned that the hard way.

"Well, maybe I'll see you here sometime."

Meryn smiled again and the chill left the air. Before she could get sucked into talking to him more, she walked away, but couldn't resist glancing over her shoulder one more time. He'd sat back on the bench and was watching her. She waved and turned away before she was tempted to go back and ask more questions.

He wasn't like other men. There is a reason why, she reminded herself. He wasn't right. Wasn't right or just damaged? She couldn't judge him when she'd been to more shrinks before she'd hit ten than most people saw in a lifetime. At the end of the street she stopped and looked back. He was sitting, head bowed again. Was he praying or thinking?

~~~

Meryn glanced down the road in the direction Nadine had left, but she was gone, back into the endless city. Tomorrow he would wait here and hand back the cross. He couldn't hold her hand and lie to her in the same breath. Today he would learn more words, so he could make her understand him better. So he sat in the pale winter sun and let other people's lives eddy around him.

He lost himself in their discussions. The words were foreign in his ears, even though he understood their meanings. The words he mimicked under his breath were awkward on his tongue. Yet he knew he had to try harder, as this was the only way he would be able to learn the language and be able to speak to Nadine.

He had to try harder to fit in and become a man of the times.

The sun tracked higher. Meryn knew he should get up and do something, but sitting and absorbing had taken on a greater importance than walking around aimlessly. The dark-skinned man he'd seen pulling up plants earlier sat down on the bench. Meryn watched from the corner of his eye as the man unpacked food. He should go and get something to eat and drink. He'd sat here for too long listening and watching. He was about to move when he noticed a marking on the back of the man's hand.

A cross.

He tore his gaze away.

"Would you like a sandwich?" The man mistook his glance as interest in his food.

Meryn shook his head. He wasn't taking charity from an elder; he hadn't sunk that low, had he? His stomach grumbled. It would be nice to try something different—something he hadn't hunted and killed, and he would be able to try out some of the new words racing around his skull. He could have his second conversation for the day; that was enough to keep him seated.

He pulled out a silver coin and offered it to the man. "I'll pay."

The man studied the coin, then looked at him, a faint

frown lined his forehead. Did they not accept silver coin anymore?

"No charge." He handed the coin back. "You might want to hang on to that; it'll buy you a bit more than a sandwich."

Well of course it would buy more than a *sandwich*. It would buy meat and wine enough for several meals, but he had nothing smaller and nothing else to trade.

"I've nothing else to…" He searched for the right word. "Give."

The man shrugged and offered him the box of food. There was fruit and bread. Meryn hesitated.

"Go on, have a bite to eat. You'll feel better."

Meryn blinked in surprise. This man had been watching him. "I'm fine."

"You've been sitting here on the bench all morning. You aren't fine."

"I've been thinking."

"Thinking is easier when you're not hungry."

That was true. Everything was easier when the stomach wasn't making demands. "I can get food."

The man nodded. "I'd like to talk to someone while I eat, and I feel rude eating when you aren't."

Meryn reached over and helped himself to a half sandwich. He didn't examine it too closely in case that was considered rude. So he took a bite and hoped it tasted all right, or at least better than raw lizard or cooked snake. He swallowed. "Thank you. I'm Meryn"

"Solomon." Solomon ate another bite.

Meryn ate even though the questions about the marking on Solomon's hand burned on his tongue. Would it be impolite to ask? Was it a slave marking?

A mark of punishment? Finally he gave in. He needed to understand the meaning of the gold cross he'd taken from Nadine.

"What does the…marking…mean?"

Solomon looked at his hand. "To remind me not to lose faith."

"Faith?" What was Solomon trying to believe in?

"In God."

Which god? What god had the Roman cross as his symbol? "The cross is punishment?"

Solomon looked at his hand, thoughtful for a moment. "Yes and no. Jesus the son of God died on the cross. But he died for all our sins. When all seems lost, if you have faith, you aren't alone."

Meryn had lost faith and hope. He'd lost everything in one night. But instead of having the courage to hold on to something, he'd let go of everything. "I gave up."

"We all do sometimes. Admitting it, facing up to it, is the true test of character."

Meryn wanted to believe what this man said, if only because it gave him a slim chance of redemption when he deserved none. He finished the sandwich in silence. Nadine wore the cross as a sign of faith to her god. What would her god say about him stealing it? Would He understand and forgive? "And if I fail?"

"You try again. And again. Because if you stop, you might as well be dead." Solomon carefully closed the lid on his food box. He looked at Meryn as if he were seeing him anew. "You're not from around here, are you?"

How could he answer without sounding like a half-wit? "I'm a long way from…home."

"Where was home?"

"Wales," Meryn said, hoping that would explain everything that was wrong with him.

"I shall add you to my prayers. I hope you find a new home."

"Your God will answer?"

Solomon shrugged. "He listens."

Would any god listen to him when he'd given up his humanity for so long? "Where are you from?"

Solomon smiled. "I was born in Sudan, taken to France as a baby, and came here with my wife to start a new life many years ago. It didn't go as planned."

Meryn didn't recognize any of the places Solomon listed. Had the world been renamed in his absence? Everything he learned revealed ten new things he didn't know. Would he ever learn everything he needed to survive?

Solomon stood. "I need to get back to work. It's been nice talking to you, Meryn. I hope you find the answers you need."

"How shall I repay you?" He couldn't be in debt when he had nothing.

"God will provide the answer."

Meryn watched as Solomon walked away. He had fewer answers than before. Perhaps he was going to need his cousins' help to rejoin the world after all. With the realization sour on his tongue, he got up, knowing that next time Dai came searching for him, they would have to talk. As he walked, his muscles ached from sitting still for too long. He'd spent too long in one place watching people. He would have to make sure he moved around the park so he wasn't noticed.

Except for in the morning. Then he would wait for

Nadine and he would return her symbol of faith. He took the gold out and looked at it again, this time with a new understanding about the man carved on its surface. He'd died for everyone's sins. Meryn's included even though he didn't know this God? Had Solomon's God forgiven Meryn already for failing his wife and children, his king and tribe, for stealing? Even if He had, would Nadine?

Did he forgive himself?

Chapter 6

NADINE LAY ON HER SIDE WATCHING THE TREE IN THE backyard sway in the breeze. She should've fallen asleep as soon as she'd climbed into bed. Instead, she was almost excited after seeing Meryn in the park. She'd smiled all the way to the train station and then all the way home. The shimmer of tension remained in her stomach like butterflies bumping around in the hope of escape.

She closed her eyes, determined to sleep and not think about Meryn. Would he be there tomorrow?

If he was, what would she do?

She raked her teeth over her lip as she thought. She should avoid him. He was a sword-wielding, mysterious-stranger who'd been delivered to the hospital by the cops. And then there was the nightmare in the hospital. She frowned. What was causing him to wake up so violently, fists ready for a fight?

Were his dreams as dark as hers?

After her mother's murder, she'd stopped speaking. She hadn't said a word for six months in any of the three languages she knew. The psychiatrists said it was normal for a traumatized child. Maybe it was. Maybe it was her way of burying everything she'd seen, except for when she slept and she'd wake screaming silently, unable to remember what had troubled her. Maybe some things weren't meant to be spoken aloud.

But Meryn had spoken English today. Not a lot. Her

frown deepened and drew her eyebrows and lips into the scowl. Why forget English but remember Latin? What had happened to him that was so bad he'd wanted to forget?

She knew that if she saw him again she needed to find out—even if that meant sharing her past. And precious few people knew the truth about her family because she didn't want to be judged by her father's crime. But Meryn was different. Very different.

Once again she walked the corridors of the castle she'd built in her mind as a child. A dress of ice green trimmed in gold swept the floor with each step. Years of stories and imagination had filled its stone walls with tapestries and paintings, candelabras and elegant furniture. It was here she'd escaped to when she couldn't sleep. Here she'd hidden from the world. In her castle, anything was possible and reality became the dream. Today she was alone. There was no ball, no servants, no imaginary parents doting on her.

Nadine's footsteps echoed, flat and heavy, as she wandered through the great hall and up the stairs. When she called out, her voice echoed through the castle. And no one came. That wasn't right. This was her dream and it should obey her will. Her steps became faster as she searched for a way out, but there were no doors. She ran to the window and peered out. The walled garden where she sat with her mother listening to stories was barren land. Gone were the shrubs, flowers, and statues. They'd been replaced with gray dust. Her breath caught in her throat. It was all gone. Beyond the glass pane was a wasteland of gray, flat nothingness.

Her dream was deconstructing, going back to the

emptiness it had come from. She placed her palm on the glass. It was cold, as if no sun had ever touched its surface. She sighed and her breath clouded on the glass as the temperature dropped.

The howls and cries that always haunted her dreams drew closer. She'd always known creatures hid beyond the walls of the palace garden. But she'd always been safe in her castle. Now? Was it safe to hide here when it was changing by itself, unraveling and twisting as if she no longer had any control over the dream?

Without a door, how could she leave?

Something moved in the gray beyond the walls; she pressed her nose to the glass to try to see what was out there, moving in the dust and empty twilight. The shapes became figures, closing in on the castle. A glint of gold caught her eye. It was outside on the windowsill. She glanced back at the creatures. They were coming for the gold. Her fingers scrabbled around the window frame for a latch, but there wasn't one. She couldn't get the window open. She ran to the next one, but a gold coin rested there as well.

Her heartbeat raced, as if she were sprinting. She stepped back from the window, her dress now faded as if it had been washed too many times. The tapestry to her left had lost the bright colors she had given it. The gray was breaching the walls. How long until the creatures reached the castle and claimed the gold?

Why was no one coming to save her? Where was her knight in shining armor to fight off the monsters?

A face appeared at the window.

Golden orbs for eyes, mottled gray skin, a hooked nose, and long pointed ears. A goblin.

Nadine screamed and the glass shattered.

She jolted awake, her heart straining to break free of her body, and sat up. Her bedroom door swung open and she yelped again.

"Geez, I thought you were being killed." Gina stood in the doorway in one of her fiancé's T-shirts that was doubling as a very short nightie.

Nadine pressed her hand to her chest as if she could slow the pounding of her blood. It took another two breaths before she could ground herself back in reality and escape the very real clutches of her nightmare. Never had it been so real...or so terrifying. Her castle had always been her sanctuary. Her dream space was unraveling and she'd been helpless to stop the destruction.

She swallowed down the sticky fear still lodged in her throat. "Just a nightmare." The words didn't come out as carefree as she'd intended.

"They're back?" Gina's forehead creased in concern.

Nadine nodded. Most of the time she was fine. Around the winter solstice she got twitchy, but it usually faded shortly after. This year, her nightmares continued to haunt her.

She blamed her father's release. When he was in jail, the dreams never had that much power and she'd always been able to escape to the castle and hide. But it was no longer safe; it was in the Shadowlands now. It felt like she'd lost another piece of herself and her mother.

Gina sat on the edge of the bed and gave her a hug. She was one of the few people who knew her family's murderous secret.

"This got something to do with your father?"

She was tempted to say no, but how would she

explain the Shadowlands and goblins to Gina? They were her mother's stories. Most people had never even heard of the fairy tale of *Le roi des gobelins*. It was an obscure story, lost in history. She had no idea how her mother had even found it or why it had been her favorite. It was easier to agree with Gina and blame her father.

"I thought I was okay. I mean, I knew he'd get out one day." She shrugged. One day had always been far away, then it had arrived and passed with little fanfare. Or so she'd believed. Obviously it had cut her deeper than she'd thought; only now she couldn't find the wound to stop the blood. She inhaled deeply and tried to force calm. "He sent me a letter."

That terrified her. What did he expect from the daughter he'd abandoned twenty years ago? Why couldn't he just walk away like she had? She'd never encouraged any contact. She didn't know what to say to him...if anything. Would he answer if she asked why? Did she really want to know?

"What did the letter say?"

"Dunno."

"Sweetie, I've said it before, and I'll say it again. You should read them. He's the only father you've got."

"He pleaded not guilty," Nadine said through gritted teeth. "After he killed my mother."

"I know you don't want to hear it, but maybe he didn't do it. There wasn't DNA evidence back then."

Nadine shook her head. He'd never asked for a retrial or a reexamination of evidence. He'd been content to wait out his time with his guilty conscience.

"When my uncle went to jail—"

"He did one year for unpaid traffic fines." It was hardly in the same category as twenty for murder.

Unbothered by Nadine's interruption, Gina continued, "All he thought about was his pregnant girlfriend."

"Yeah, and she wasn't his girlfriend when he got out." She knew the story and had been to enough of Gina's family functions to know that the girlfriend had done him a favor by leaving. The child wasn't his.

"That's not the point. Who do you think your father thought of while he was in prison?" Gina placed her hand on the blanket covering Nadine's legs.

"Maybe my father should've thought some more before he killed my mother." Nadine hugged her knees to her chest. She didn't want to talk about her family anymore. It was easier not to think of them than to try and understand what had gone wrong.

"Where's your necklace?"

Nadine touched her bare throat. "I lost it at work. The cross came loose again."

"Maybe it will turn up," she said with more hope than Nadine felt. It had been a week. It was gone.

"It doesn't matter." But it did. Without it, she'd lost her mother's protection and the nightmares were closing in. When they caught her, she knew there'd be no escape. She forced a smile, as if the goblins of her nightmares had vanished in the daylight streaming through her window, and changed the topic. "So how was your trip down south?"

"Lovely. It was good to get away and be alone." Gina touched her engagement ring absently. Her boyfriend had proposed the last time he was home and Gina had spent an anxious six months waiting for him to come back.

Hell would have to freeze over to keep Bryce from coming home. He was crazy about Gina. The only thing that had stopped them from marrying already was the danger he'd get killed while serving overseas. He didn't want Gina to be an army widow.

"So the wedding is still on?" Nadine teased.

"Of course." Gina said it with a smile—then it faltered. "Bryce and I have started looking at places. I know we thought we'd stay here for a bit until we got sorted, but we want our own house. By not going on a honeymoon, we've got enough for a deposit."

Ever since the ring had gone on Gina's finger, Nadine had known this day was coming. She nodded, unable to speak.

Gina gave Nadine's hand a squeeze. "I'm sure you won't have a problem getting someone else to live with."

She didn't want someone else. She and Gina had done everything together for years. Shared the ups and downs of studying, dating, and working. And now Gina was moving on and getting married. It made Nadine realize what she didn't have.

"I'm sure I won't." The house was in a great location, and not too expensive but too much for her to have on her own unless she gave up on her savings account and her dreams of travel.

"Getting a date for my wedding on the other hand…" Gina raised both eyebrows wanting the latest gossip.

And here it came. No doubt Bryce had a newly single friend. "Do not set me up."

"I won't." Gina held her hands up. "That didn't work out too well last time."

"No, it didn't." Nice enough guy, but he'd thought a

fun date would be going to the drags and racing his V8 on amateur night and then expecting her to be excited when he won. So not happening again.

"Besides, you're seeing Daniel. Did you go on a second date?"

Nadine looked at her friend. How could she say Daniel was lovely, handsome, smart, a doctor, and totally boring? When he kissed her cheek, all she felt was his lips. She'd got more of a jolt from Meryn holding her hand and she hardly knew the man. "There was no chemistry."

"You can't tell that after one lousy date."

"Yes I can. There's got to be…something." Something that made her heart jump. Something that made her want to know more about the man. Something that made her want to risk jumping into a relationship.

Something about Meryn made her want to know him better, even if it was just to untangle the mystery that surrounded him. She just hoped she'd like the answer when she worked him out.

"You're too fussy."

"Selective." She wasn't going out with someone who didn't meet her criteria—even if she wasn't sure what that criteria was.

"Limited," Gina countered.

"Discerning."

Gina raised one eyebrow. "I'm sure you'll find someone who enjoys long runs and foreign films and who doesn't mind a nocturnal wife."

"I'm still looking." She grinned as if she wasn't bothered by her inability to find a partner. But Gina was right. It didn't take long before guys worked out that she was damaged and too much hard work, and then they ran. So she'd stopped trying. Besides, it was better to be single than make her mother's mistake of falling for the wrong man. "You're going to be awake for the barbeque this afternoon?"

She couldn't say no, but she wouldn't be able to drink, and she'd have to leave early to go to work. "Of course. Wouldn't miss it."

―ᨓ―

Nadine picked up a glass of juice and smiled as everyone toasted Bryce's return. The house she shared with Gina was full of people she half knew either through Gina or work. Her friends, the ones who thought they knew her but they'd never even scratched the surface. She wouldn't let them.

On the other side of the yard, away from the men clustered around the barbeque, arguing over the best way to cook a steak, she saw Daniel. Of course Gina had to invite him. She held her breath, not sure if she was hoping her heart would give a flutter of excitement or if he wouldn't notice her. He nodded and began moving in her direction. Damn. Her heart sank.

Maybe it was her heart that was broken, and this was as good as it got.

No, she refused to believe that. She saw the glint in Gina's eye when she looked at Bryce and the way he looked at her. She didn't want to settle because she should or because he looked good on paper.

She smiled as he reached her side, but he didn't try and touch her.

"Big party." He sipped his beer and looked around.

He didn't fit in. He was too…she didn't know. He just didn't fit. It was nothing obvious, and nothing she could put her finger on.

"Yep." Did they really have anything to talk about besides work?

He looked at her as if assessing the odds he was going to get shot down. Which was going to be more awkward: her going first or waiting for him to ask? Definitely the second.

"About the other night," she said. "It was nice, but I don't usually see people I work with." Not a lie, but not a rule she'd always kept either. Where else was she going to meet guys?

He nodded and looked across the yard. "So a second date is off the table."

She sipped her juice without tasting it and hoped the food would be ready soon, so she'd have something else to concentrate on. Maybe she should've stayed in bed until it was time to go to work.

"I think that would be best." What was she doing? There were women tripping over themselves to get Daniel to notice them and she was letting him off the hook. She glanced at him, but he wasn't making eye contact. Instead, he was studying something across the yard.

"Can I ask why you agreed to a first date?"

Ugh, a fair question. "You asked, and I always give people a chance." One chance and only one. But Daniel hadn't put a foot wrong. He'd been charming and funny, and she was turning him away because…?

"Ah, so I failed a test." This time he looked at her, his dark eyes searching for something.

She couldn't lie. "I didn't feel a spark." And once

spoken aloud it sounded really dumb. This was real life not a fairy tale.

"You don't think that can grow?"

She looked at Daniel and then at Gina and Bryce. She recalled the vague memories she had of her parents together and their smiles for the camera. The skin on her hand tingled as if remembering the touch of Meryn's hand on hers. That had been a spark, one that would burn her if she played with it, but it had still been something—and enough to give her hope that she wasn't chasing a dream. "No. It's either there or it's not."

Chapter 7

As dusk fell, Meryn made his way back to his campsite. Most people who came to walk the park's paths or eat at the café had left. He'd been tempted by the food for sale, but he didn't have the right money to pay. After Solomon's reaction to the coin, he'd watched more closely. The people here had colored pieces of paper, not gold and silver. Another reason to find a way to earn some coin—he needed the local currency.

His shelter was sturdy and reasonably weatherproof. While the fire he built to cook his meal on didn't burn all night, he was warm enough—warmer than he had been in the Shadowlands. He put the snake he'd caught that afternoon on to cook. He was getting very sick of reptiles, but there was no large wildlife to hunt. No pig, no deer, not even a hare or rabbit. Plus he needed more than meat; he needed a proper meal, but he recognized none of the plants and he wasn't ready to risk poisoning to find something to go with snake.

Ale would've been good.

He'd even settle for watered Roman wine.

He gave his bedding a shake and checked for spiders. They seemed to crawl into everything. Brown ones, black ones, hairy ones. He hated them, always had. Satisfied he wasn't going to get bitten on the ass, he sat. To one side of his clearing lay a dozen arrows. He'd made them in the first few days, thinking he'd need them to hunt. The sapling he'd selected to be his bow lay waiting for attention. Once he would've spent every spare minute readying weapons and armor. While he would have never fought with a bow, he liked to hunt with one. There was a skill to sighting the target and making a clean shot, one he'd mastered better than most. But there was no honor in picking off men from a distance, the way one would shoot a pig.

A twig snapped and echoed in the silence. Meryn lifted his gaze from the fire and drew the stolen knife. He listened, waiting for the noise that would betray the intruder again. Leaves crunched as they were trodden on. It was too late to throw dirt on the fire; the smell of smoke would linger. His heart thudded almost loud enough to block out the sound of the would-be attacker. As a goblin, a beating heart had never been a distraction.

"Meryn," whispered a voice in the darkness.

Meryn eased up and put a tree at his back and the fire between himself and whoever was coming. At the bottom of his heart, he knew who it would be. Dai. He forced a breath out between his teeth. Better to face him this time than melt away into the woods. Besides, his campsite had been made. Running now would only make him seem a coward.

"Meryn, I know you're here," Dai said in Decangli.

Yeah, he was here. He just didn't know what to say.

His cousin stepped into the clearing. Laying on the palm of his hand was a rough arrow—the one Meryn had made in the Shadowlands and used to shoot Dai when he'd come to drag him back to the Fixed Realm. It had only been eight nights ago, but it seemed like a lifetime had passed.

They assessed each other, as if waiting for the other one to move first. Last time they'd met, Meryn hadn't recognized his long-haired cousin. There was a glint in Dai's eye and a sureness in his step that came from fighting many battles and losing few. Meryn lowered the knife but kept it in his hand, held loosely, ready to react. He hadn't survived as a goblin by being sloppy, but this time he'd give Dai a chance to speak before attacking.

Dai put the arrowhead in his pocket and held out his open hands. "I'm unarmed." A man who could cross between realms at will needed no weapons to be dangerous in a fight. "I came only to talk."

The language of his birth rolled easily through the still night air. Words he hadn't heard in too many years made his heart ache for the familiar. He shut it down. It was gone. All of it. He had to start again.

"Then speak English. I need the practice." Meryn couldn't hide the edge of bitterness in his voice.

Dai inclined his head. "Very well." He switched languages.

"What is it you want to say?"

"The Fixed Realm has changed since we last walked in it as men. After bringing you back from the Shadowlands, I should have…" Dai paused and looked at Meryn. "I should have explained things to you better and made the adjustment easier."

Kept him prisoner until he'd regained his mind more like. "You locked me in the tower." Meryn's voice cut through the twilight, harsher than he'd remembered. He'd had so few people to talk to and the words were strange even though he understood them.

"I was wounded." Dai gave Meryn a pointed glare. "I thought you'd be safe there until I returned. Then we could've spoken."

"I don't know you. Why would I trust anything you say?"

A hurt flickered over Dai's features. "I'm your cousin."

"My cousin was no mage." The trees shivered in the breeze, the leaves rasping like the whispers of the goblins in the Shadowlands. Meryn suppressed the shiver that ran down his back.

Once they'd been close, closer than Dai had ever been to his brother Roan. Now so much had happened in their lives, and not just the time lapse. Could he trust this man when there was nothing he recognized?

What did Dai see when he looked at him? A broken man? A man too weak to resist the curse? He'd commanded an army for his king, and now he lived in a hovel on the fringes of society, playing at being human. In that moment, Meryn hated what he'd become. While his old life was gone, he wanted more than this. Maybe he shouldn't have fled the tower; he could've waited for Dai to return. And then what? Be dependent? At least he was living on his terms.

He looked at the man who bore a vague resemblance to the cousin he'd once known. "What were my children's names?"

"Branna and Gwynedd," Dai said without hesitation. "And my son?"

"I was there when you farewelled your stillborn son. You named him Cathal and gave him your sword."

Meryn's chest tightened for a moment as he remembered the pain that day had brought. Even the small sword had been bigger than the baby that had been born too soon. "Which sword?"

"The one I first used, the one you first used," Dai said softly.

Meryn took a step forward but didn't rush to greet him. The silence swelled like a feasting leech. There might as well have been the whole expanse of the Shadowlands between them.

"It is you then." Meryn tucked the knife away.

"It is. I never intended to keep you locked in my apartment. I just needed to buy some time. I wanted a chance to show you how the world has changed and to help you. I saw you sleeping in the hospital, but when I went back you'd left. Since then you've avoided me quite well." Dai almost smiled. "Why tonight?"

Why not? As much as it rankled, he couldn't adapt on his own. He wasn't going to admit that though. "I thought it time to find out who was hunting me."

"I've been making sure you are okay. There have been many changes."

"I understand that. Why bring me to this land?"

"Our lands are gone, forgotten. The battles, the death—no one remembers. No one remembers Roan standing up to Claudius, the failed rebellion, or any of it. A few remembered the tale of the Goblin King because we made them remember, we kept it alive in the hope of finding a way to break the curse." Dai held out his hand. "Come, I'll show you that our lands are now no different from this place."

Meryn drew back. How could it all be gone when they'd told stories and sung of heroes who'd fought the gods? He looked at his cousin, the offered hand, and knew that Dai would use magic to take him and show

him, or it was a trick and Dai would take him back to the
tower and make him face Roan.

"What do you want from me?" Meryn crossed his
arms. He would not go and bow before his king while
he lived like a beggar. If he was going to face Roan, it
would be as a man with a measure of pride. Right now
he didn't even have that. He disgusted even himself.

Dai lowered his hand. "You can't do this on your
own. I want to help you."

"There is no help for me unless you can silence the
screaming in my mind. Remove the ache lodged in my
heart. Give me back the life I once had." His rank, his
wealth, his family. The things that had made him a man
to be respected.

"I can't undo the past, and only you can accept this
chance the gods have granted us. It's a second chance
at life, Meryn."

A second chance? Did the gods know what he'd
done? That he'd watched the murder of his tribe, his
wife and children, and then given into the curse without
pausing? Was he really worth that trouble? His thoughts
turned to Nadine; she thought he was worth the trouble.
She made an effort when it would have been easier for
her to walk away.

But he wasn't ready to put his hand out and accept
help from the man he'd once trained to use a sword.
He'd do it himself, if only to prove he could and that he
was still man enough to make a life.

"Go back to yours and let me be." In his rough
campsite, eating bloody reptiles while he tried to work
out what he was going to do, he wasn't living; he was
barely surviving.

Dai shook his head. "You can't stay here."

While what he had was luxury when compared to the Shadowlands, it wasn't how people lived now.

"What are you going to do? Drag me back to where you live? Force me to face our king?"

Dai opened his mouth, but no words came out. Meryn realized that was exactly what Dai had planned to do. That he couldn't trust his cousin hurt. Once, trust wouldn't have even been a question. What had happened to Dai while Meryn was a goblin? What had happened to Roan? How much had the man he'd once called king changed?

"I don't need charity." But Meryn missed Roan's company. They'd spent so much time together plotting and scheming. Whatever their relationship had been before, it wasn't the same now. While he remembered the past like it was yesterday, for Dai and Roan it had happened a long time ago. He tried to imagine a city like this one standing where the Decangli had lived and fought and died, and failed.

"Would you have done less for me? You are family."

"My family is dead," Meryn snarled. "I should've died with them."

"But you didn't."

"I became goblin." And that was worse. He lowered his gaze. He wasn't the man he had been. But he did have a second chance to be someone. He just had to work out who that was.

"Come with me, I can tell you everything you need to know and get you set up for this life."

"I'm not a child in need of teaching. I need…" He pressed his teeth together and frowned. What did he need? He was managing, but barely. He'd like a more comfortable life, but what would be the price? He looked at his cousin; it was true he'd be helping in every way if their roles were reversed. However, talking to Dai was one thing, talking to Roan was another. He wasn't ready to explain to his king what had gone wrong.

"I'm not ready to see Roan. I'm still sorting through memories." Plus, if he left with Dai, there was a good chance he'd never see Nadine again. He wanted to be waiting for her at the bench in the morning. There was something in her smile that made adapting to the world a little easier.

Dai regarded him. "Okay," he said slowly.

"That's it? You're not going to tell me why I should leave with you?" Once Dai would've argued for the fun of it.

"You're an adult, you know how to survive in worse places than this." He slid a bag off his shoulder and placed it on the ground. "Food, extra clothes, and a few bits you might like." Dai looked around the campsite. "You are sure you'd rather be here than in a proper bed?"

"The last bed I shared was with my wife. I'm not ready to sleep alone." He'd never lived in a house alone. He took a breath as the memories of his home flooded back.

"You aren't alone, Meryn."

"I am, for the first time in my life." As he said it, he realized what a weight that was to cast off. No battles to plan, no one to train. No responsibilities. No one to run from. No one to kill. No need to do anything. And while he'd struggled with that at first, it was a gift. He didn't want the responsibility of that again.

Dai smiled. "The Meryn I knew would have found a way to fill that time with something productive and of benefit to the tribe."

"That man is gone." Maybe some of the selfish goblin remained in him, because he saw no need to take up the yoke again. He'd be his own man, in every sense of the word.

"I'd like the chance to know this new man."

Meryn looked at his cousin and couldn't deny that he'd like to know more about what had happened. He wanted to hear Decangli spoken again and find out how many years had passed. He wanted to know how the others were living, but tonight wasn't the night. "Thank you for coming."

"I'll visit again."

Dai stepped back, and then he was gone, vanished as if taken by the shadows clinging to the trees. Meryn walked around the fire to where Dai had stood. Faint impressions remained in the dirt but they, and the bag, were the only signs that his cousin had even visited.

Around him, the forest was silent except for the sounds of animals waking. For a man used to the weighty silence of the Shadowlands, each noise made him jump like a nervous colt. Yet it was reassuring. He was surrounded by life. Even the sky was full. Stars dotted the darkness—the first he'd seen in many years and not one constellation he recognized. He was so far from home in every aspect.

Meryn placed some extra wood on the small fire and held his fingers toward the warmth. The pack Dai had left lay on the ground, waiting to be examined. After a moment's hesitation, he gave into curiosity and pulled the contents out. Clothes and soap and other bits…and food in neat little packages. Hunger won and he ate, careful to ration what was there for a couple of days. It was so good to be eating something different, he almost wished he'd gone with his cousin, but he couldn't let his belly do his thinking for him.

When he was done, he took a drink from the bottle of water Dai had included in the pack, then lay down. The ground was cold, but unlike the Shadowlands, it didn't suck the heat from his body. Here he was able to relax. He closed his eyes, knowing that when sleep came his dreams wouldn't be peaceful. The cut on his hand was a reminder that they were more than dreams and he had to be careful.

He listened to the popping of the wood as it burned, the smell so different from what he'd grown up with, and the rustling of the trees around him. The movements of small animals in the night was more familiar than the eerie silence of the Shadowlands, even though he had spent many years there as a goblin. Just being back in the Fixed Realm was bringing back the memories of his life as a man. He ignored the ones that hurt and dragged up the happy ones. He could almost imagine himself home—back in the forests of his youth and the easy summers before the Romans had come and the battles had begun. But even before the Romans had reached the lands of the Decangli, refugees from other tribes had swelled their numbers. The Silures' Princess, Idella, amongst them.

"Come on, Meryn. I won't tell. No one will know." *Idella tugged on his hand, leading him farther away from the fires and the watching eyes of the tribe.*

"I will know. One more day, Idella. Then we will have a lifetime."

She grinned, her teeth white in the moonlight. One of her fingers traced the swell and curve of her breast. His eyes followed as if spellbound. He couldn't resist her. His fingers curled but didn't move from his side. He had asked for this marriage and had sworn not to dishonor her—or his family—before it was formalized. They'd had to wait to see if her father could be reached. Her brother, the new King of the Silures, had sent message that he welcomed an alliance with the Decangli. Some suspected he'd sent his sister away for more than her own safety and Meryn had fallen into the very beautiful trap. He was glad his cousin Roan and future king was only eleven and not yet a man, or he might have lost Idella to a better alliance.

She took his hand and used it to cover her breast. "Can you wait one more night?"

Meryn swallowed; he wanted her now, and he'd wanted her yesterday and every night when he went to sleep. He smoothed his thumb over her pale skin.

She sighed and pressed closer. "One night doesn't matter. We will be married tomorrow."

"Don't tempt me into breaking my promise. I don't want a war with your brother." Yet he couldn't pull his hand away. "Once we are married you won't be able to get rid of me."

He swept her up into his arms and kissed her until neither of them could breathe.

He set her down and drew away before the warmth of her body could tempt him further. "One more night."

She cupped his cheek and turned his words on him. "One more night and then I'm yours."

Idella stepped back as if to rejoin the celebration, one hand going to her stomach as it swelled. She glanced down, then back at him, years adding weight to her stare. "What have you done?"

A wound opened on her neck, blood poured out, and stained her clothes. This wasn't what had happened. They'd gone back to the feast. Their first child hadn't arrived for another two years. Then he realized his dream had skipped ahead. This was the night she'd died.

He tried to reach for her but couldn't move. "Idella!"

Meryn jerked awake. His hand rested on the stolen knife, ready for an attack that didn't come. Instead, Idella stood by the fire, arms wrapped around her stomach, lips moving without sound.

"No." He threw off the clothing acting as a blanket and dropped the knife in the dirt; he would save her this time. He caught her as she collapsed. But as he touched her, she disintegrated, her body becoming dust in his hands. The fine, gray dust of the Shadowlands coated his hands. The dust nightmares were made of. His memories were coming to life to haunt him and remind him of what he'd lost.

He remained kneeling, staring at his gray-coated hands. Idella hadn't been real, just a memory given life by the Shadowlands. The beating of his heart drowned out all other noise. This time it didn't break at the sight of her dying. Grief didn't rip him apart. It should; the devastation should still burn, but what felt like yesterday had happened years ago. The screaming in his head was silent, as if the ghosts of his family had finally abandoned him and left him to his fate. He released a slow breath, grounding himself in the present.

There was no blood on his clothes or skin, only gray dust. Meryn rubbed his fingers together, feeling the fine, cold particles. It was definitely Shadowlands dust, but it shouldn't be here and his dreams shouldn't be forming in the Fixed Realm.

He lifted his gaze and looked around his small clearing, but no other nightmares from his past had joined him. He'd tried to forget her and his children once. Not even being goblin had erased the horror. It had lurked, waiting for him in the shadows, ready to drag him down and punish him for forgetting. Forgetting wasn't the answer. Remembering was. He was happy to dream of Idella, but not like that. He would not remember her by her death, but by her life.

He wiped the dust from his hands on his trousers and stood. Slowly he picked up the knife and returned to his bed, sitting so sleep didn't follow him. The gray dust on the ground shimmered in the moonlight. What new horror would it breed when he slept? Would everything he feared be given fresh life, only to fall apart at first touch and deny him a chance to change the past?

Chapter 8

Nadine jogged slowly along Fraser Avenue. When she saw Meryn on a park bench, a smile broke across her face.

She made her way over and sat next to him. "You look happy this morning."

"You came back." He returned her smile, a dimple forming.

"I was hoping to see you." That was the truth even though she'd tried to convince herself she wasn't looking forward to seeing him again.

He looked at her as if trying to determine if she meant it or was just being nice. A bit of both. She was curious, plus she wanted to know if the spark was still there. It was. When she looked at him, there was a flutter of something that shouldn't exist for a man she barely knew. Barely knew now, but that could be fixed.

"Why don't you join me for a muffin and a coffee?" She tilted her head at the café.

He glanced over at the building and for a second she thought he was going to say no. She was too forward; she'd been told that before. Maybe he was just being polite in speaking to her; after all, she'd seen him while he as in a pretty bad place, but then again, he'd been here waiting. She held her breath for a heartbeat.

Then he shook his head. "I've no money on me."

Ah, so either he didn't want to talk to her or he

really had no money. She glanced over his clothes again. He wasn't dressed for running and he wasn't dressed for an office job either. But he was clean and neat, in jeans and a long-sleeved T-shirt, but he could be one of those people who refused to let others see the real mess and who carried on as if everything was fine regardless of the cracks. And something had cracked for him to come into the hospital—but back then he'd actually look disheveled.

Now he looked like everyone else until she looked in his eyes. There was an edge and a hurt she should be wary of, but there were people in the café, and it wasn't like she was going anywhere alone with him. Besides, if he'd meant her harm, he wouldn't have helped her twice.

She stood and held her hand out to him, offering him the assistance this time. "My treat."

He paused for a moment as if reluctant. She could almost see him battling with his pride. This was a man not used to needing help and almost resenting it. Who was he and what had happened?

His fingers closed around hers and a jolt of electricity ran under her skin. There was something there—enough for her to continue believing that she was right: the spark couldn't be grown over time. It was there or not. But just because it was there didn't mean it had to be acted on. Meryn was a handsome stranger. His dark hair was pushed back of his face, the ends brushing his shoulders. Beneath the fabric of the long-sleeved T-shirt, she could see the curve of muscle. She was willing to bet that if he stripped off the shirt, he'd be lean and fit. She suppressed the smile that wanted to form at the idea. She shouldn't be imagining him without his shirt on. Maybe once her curiosity had worn away there'd be nothing left. *Yeah, professional interest*. She didn't believe it, but she refused to let herself think it could be anything else. Anything else was dangerous.

"Thank you," he said simply as he stood. He didn't release her hand as they walked to the short distance to the café.

While she could've pulled her hand free, she didn't. She didn't want to. She liked the touch of his rough palm against hers and the light pressure of his fingers. She couldn't remember the last man she'd let hold her hand. They tended to lead her around like they were showing off what was on their arm. But Meryn wasn't like any other man she'd known.

"Can I ask a question?" She glanced at him, aware of the heat seeping from his palm and into hers.

"You don't need permission."

Maybe not, but there was an air about him like he wasn't used to being questioned about anything. "Why do you speak Latin?"

A frown crossed his face for a half second before he answered. "I had to learn."

She waited for more but he didn't give her anything else. Where did he go to school to learn Latin? Or what had he done that made it a requirement? She tried to study him without staring. He waited for her to ask another question or continue the conversation. How much could she ask before he would think her rude? She took the gamble and asked the question she needed answered.

"What was wrong with you the other night?"

Meryn stopped walking and looked down at his feet. "I am sorry about that."

"Don't be sorry." She turned to face him. "I just want to understand and make sure you're okay. You had the nurses quite worried." He'd had her worried, especially after he'd wandered off.

"I am okay. My wife…" He stumbled if he were trying to find the right words.

His wife, of course he would be married. The slap of jealousy caught her off guard and left a sour taste on her tongue. She pulled her hand from his. What had she been thinking?

He made no effort to take her hand again. "My wife was killed. I couldn't think past the pain and memories."

"Oh." She touched his arm, but it was such a pathetic gesture. She knew how those memories could creep up and ruin a day. Was that what his nightmare in the hospital had been about? No matter how curious she was, it wasn't right to ask how she'd died. "I understand."

He looked at her as if there was no possible way she could have any idea what he was going through. Most people wouldn't. Unfortunately, she wasn't most people.

They walked into the café in silence. At the counter she ordered two coffees and two muffins. She got the triple chocolate one, because if she was going to eat a muffin for dinner, she was going to enjoy it and not even pretend to be healthy. Meryn went for the smart choice, blueberry.

She went to pick up the tray and carry it to a table.

"Let me. It's the least I can do." He picked it up and followed her to a table that caught the winter sunlight and had views over the Swan River.

They sat and she stirred two sugars into her coffee.

He did the same and then tasted it carefully, as if he was expecting it to be scalding hot. Which it was. Nadine broke bits off her muffin as she considered the man opposite her. She was sure she could talk to him forever and never understand everything. How many questions could she ask before he started asking some about her? What would she do then? She swallowed and reminded herself that she was perfectly capable of having a conversation with a good-looking man without making an idiot of herself.

Her gaze landed on his hand as he tore off the top of the muffin and ate it. One hand was marked with a healing cut, but there were other fine, white scars that lined the backs of both his hands, and his knuckles showed signs of damage.

"How did you get these?" She touched his hand, unable to resist, her finger tracing an old scar.

"Fighting." He sighed. "Soldiering."

She'd guessed right at the hospital; he was ex-army. That explained the look in his eyes like he'd seen too much. "But not anymore?"

"No. Not since Idella's death." Every word was weighted as if just speaking about it was raw.

Idella. That must be his wife's name. It was a pretty name; no doubt she'd been beautiful. Meryn would've had his pick of women, especially once he was in uniform. Although she couldn't quite picture that and she didn't know why a soldier would need to speak Latin.

Nadine's clothes began to stick to her as her body cooled. She felt plain and sweaty in her running clothes, so she changed the topic. "You're from Wales; do you have family here?"

He nodded and sipped his coffee, his nose wrinkling as if not finding it to his taste. "Yes. Cousins."

So he wasn't really alone, not like her. Maybe they were helping him—by leaving him alone to sit around the park?

"Do you see them?" Or was he really struggling to get through this without help? No one should have to work through something as big as the death of a loved one on their own. She'd had shrinks and foster parents, and while she'd resented their enforced help at the time, in hindsight, she could've been a real head case without it.

"It's complicated." He shrugged.

Wasn't it always with family? "If there's anything you need…" She let the rest of the sentence drift as his face hardened. That was obviously a raw nerve.

He took a moment, then smiled. She noticed there was no dimple this time—he was forcing it. "Thank you for the offer, but for the moment, I am okay. Life is simple when there is nowhere to be and no one to answer to."

"True." She couldn't imagine a life without work and responsibilities. It was her way of proving she was better than her father and more than her mother's death. Sometimes it was almost as if people had expected her to be useless and achieve nothing. They made the excuses for her and she'd always had to disprove them.

Maybe Meryn had the reverse problem; he'd lived up to expectations and done everything by the book, and now death had brought him to a point where he was free from conforming. She looked at his shoulder-length hair. If he'd dropped out of the army when his wife had died, how long ago had it happened? Had it been the anniversary of her death that had driven him to such despair? Would that happen every year?

Of course it would. She still had nightmares after twenty years. Something like that left a scar; it was just a case of how well that scar healed and how well it was hidden. She was an expert at that.

Meryn wasn't.

But it was too soon to dig deep.

"So, ex-army, you've moved to Perth, have some family here…any plans?" She tried to keep it light and hoped it didn't sound like she was looking for information. This wasn't a first date, as such, more like a test run to see if she'd actually like more. Yet her stomach was tight and she was forcing bits of muffin into it.

Meryn looked her in the eye. "I'm having some time off. I've spent all my life…in the army…it's nice to have the time to do nothing. What do you do when you're not working?"

Nadine took longer than needed to finish a mouthful. "I run, watch TV." As she spoke, she realized how super boring she sounded. She needed a cool hobby. "The usual. Because I work at night and sleep during the day, it kind of mucks up my social life." There, it was out; she was already telling him that she was unavailable most of the time.

"But you like having breakfast out…or should you be home sleeping?" He picked up his coffee and watched her as he took a sip.

She wouldn't be doing much sleeping. There was something in his eyes that made her forget that she'd just finished work and was in her running gear—instead of dressed up and presenting her best side. Maybe they were past that. She'd seen him at a low; what did it matter what she wore?

"Both." She smiled and raised her eyebrows.

He smiled, and for a moment, she glimpsed a heat in his eyes most men kept well hidden. But Meryn didn't seem to hide behind what was proper. It was nice not to have to work out what were glossy lies for the first date. She already knew, even if she didn't know the details.

She put the last piece of muffin in her mouth and wished they came in bigger sizes so she could have a reason to stay longer.

"Did you want to meet again tomorrow?" The words were out before she'd thought them through. Did she want to meet him again tomorrow? And if she did, at what point did simple coffee become more? Tomorrow it wouldn't be pre-date coffee; it would actually be a date…wouldn't it?

He nodded slowly as if considering. "I'd like that."

She met his gaze and saw the gray of his eyes soften. The little spark in her chest was fanned by that look and caught hold to become a little flame. Her lips parted, but she couldn't take the invitation back and she didn't want to, even though she knew it was wrong. It didn't feel wrong; it felt fun, as if she were on an adventure and she didn't know where she was going.

Her fingers brushed the back of his hand, then he turned his hand over so the tips of their fingers touched before she pulled her hand away. For a second she was tempted to lean in and kiss him, but she stopped herself. He hadn't given her any indication that he was interested in anything else than coffee—even if she saw it in his eyes. And she had the feeling that when Meryn said coffee, he'd actually mean coffee.

Nadine pressed her lips together and glanced down, but still the heat crept up her cheeks. The desire to kiss him had snuck up on her and now couldn't be dislodged. It wasn't just kissing him that was on her mind. Did he hide other scars under his shirt? She looked up and realized he was watching her with that look in his eyes. On another man she would've called it lust, but with Meryn that label seemed too casual.

She wasn't thinking about coffee.

It was time to go before she did something dumb.

She swallowed and found some composure; men never unraveled her and got beneath her skin. Wasn't that what she wanted though, someone who made her feel alive?

"Okay, I'll see you tomorrow." she said as she pushed her chair back and got up.

So did Meryn. He moved easily, each movement the bare minimum required. There was nothing flashy to draw attention. He did that by existing.

"I'll walk you down the road."

"You don't have to."

"I have nothing else to do."

She nodded. Okay then. As he passed the garden bed, he stopped and picked a flower, a pale blue sprig of something. She watched, then her eyes widened as he went to tuck it behind her ear. She let him.

His hand brushed her cheek, a move that was almost accidental. "Thank you for breakfast. It was nice to have someone to eat with."

Nadine smiled, but her heart was breaking for him.

He was lonely. While she'd been assuaging her curiosity, he'd been enjoying having someone to talk to. Next time she'd let him ask some questions—it was fast becoming a proper date. The thought made her heart beat a little faster even though she knew anything she felt for Meryn was dangerous.

Meryn turned away instead of watching her leave. He enjoyed spending time with her, even though he couldn't tell her the truth about his life. He wanted to. The truth hovered on the tip of his tongue every time she asked a question, but instead he bit it back and told a half truth.

What could he say without her running away screaming?

If he told her about goblins, she'd think him mad at best and a threat at worst. If he talked about his life as a Decangli warrior, she wouldn't believe him. He was a man without a past and that was just as bad. How long until Nadine saw through his answers and realized how much he wasn't telling her?

How long until his own dishonesty poisoned their fragile friendship?

He scuffed his boot on the path and kicked a stick out of the way. He forced out a breath. He didn't want to see distrust and fear in her eyes when she looked at him. He wanted to see more of those glimmers of heat, the ones that flickered before she looked away and smothered them. It had been a long time since anyone had looked at him like that. It raised a heat in his blood that he'd thought was killed with his wife.

Lust for a woman, not soulless gold. The need for more metal had consumed him with its cold burn in the

Shadowlands so that he almost hadn't recognized true desire. A smile formed as he thought of her and his flesh hardened. It cut and hurt the way he thought it would. His love for Idella was still there, and always would be, but Nadine was a living, smiling woman. One who smiled at him.

Considering he'd been with Idella for eight years, he'd almost forgotten what courting meant. He owed Nadine more than a simple flower. He still had her cross, and it was becoming harder and harder to find a way to hand it over. To do so now would reveal he was nothing but a thief and a coward.

Which was exactly what he had been when he'd first been pulled from the Shadowlands, and now? Maybe he still was, since he couldn't bring himself to hand back her jewelry.

He took the long route back to his campsite, but he wasn't listening to anything people said as he walked. A growing sense of dread filled his stomach, smothering the desire that had lifted his spirits. He could never tell Nadine where he lived. He could never have her share a meal with him, not after sharing breakfast with her in the café. The small fragment of shame that had lingered at the back of his mind took hold and grew, reinforcing what Dai had said.

People didn't live in the scrub. They didn't hunt for lizards and snakes and then sleep under the stars, hoping it didn't rain. He was failing simply because he was refusing the help Dai offered. His pride was getting in the way. He swallowed down the bitter realization.

He either had to give up on the hope of courting Nadine or take what Dai was offering.

What strings would come attached?

He didn't want his old job back; he didn't want to be second to the king. He still didn't want to see Roan.

If he'd been half the man he used to be, he wouldn't have hesitated. There would've been no doubt in his heart. Now he second guessed everything. If he turned away from Nadine now and never looked back, that would again prove he was too weak to even risk failure.

"Damn it." He was caught; every choice seemed to reinforce he was afraid to make a decision. He was like a child who couldn't make up his mind.

He stepped off the path and took a circuitous route back to his campsite. He never took the same path or entered at the same point. And he was always careful to leave no tracks. The two men he'd taken the clothes from had followed him more than once from a distance, and each time he'd lost them easily by leaving the park and walking along one of the busy roads that framed the park. He hoped they didn't realize he lived here. But again, he knew he was pushing his luck.

At the edge of the clearing he stopped, his chest tightening at the monstrosity hanging over his rough shelter. His campsite was as he'd left it, except for one thing. The gray Shadowlands dust that had been mingling with the dirt had now reassembled and a large black spider with a slash of red down its abdomen dangled from a web.

It wasn't real. It couldn't be. The body of the thing was as large as a man's head.

Meryn took a step back.

He'd seen plenty of these spiders hiding under things. Red meant danger, so he was guessing they were

poisonous, but none that he'd seen so far had been this
size. The strands of web were so thick they could have
been used to weave cloth. And the spider was…

It was as if it was someone's worst fear had grown to
enormous proportions. His fear. He'd been killing them
and growing more paranoid with every branch he'd
lifted and every shake of his bedding.

As he watched, the spider seemed to grow a little
larger, as if feeding off the fear. A bead of cold sweat
rolled down his spine. No spider in nature was like this.
This was a creature born of the Shadowlands.

It was because of him it had life. Somehow he'd
dragged the Shadowlands with him and his nightmares
were coming to life—the curdled milk, Idella, and now
this. Each one was growing in strength and becoming
more dangerous.

He glanced at his hands, unwilling to take his eyes off
the spider for long in case it scuttled off. It was much
better to keep an eye on the threat. Was he still connected to the Shadowlands, or was it part of him? Why
couldn't his hopes and dreams come to life? Why was
it always the bad things that came back to haunt him?

Because that's what the Shadowlands was—the
place of nightmares. He picked up the sapling he'd been
hoping to make a bow out of. He had to banish his fears,
kill anything that appeared out of the gray dust. He had
to find a way to be free of the Shadowlands before
it smothered everything he dreamed of. His fingers
gripped the wood like a sword ready to run the spider
through and end its life. Once again he was fighting
for survival. If he let that thing live, it would kill him
with one bite and anyone else who had the misfortune

of crossing its path, and it would grow, swelling and feeding on fear.

He gritted his teeth and rammed the stick through the spider's body before he could hesitate further. Its legs flailed and it twisted as if trying to reach him; even now it grew. He tried to tamp down the fear but failed. Fear had a place; it kept people alive, but it couldn't rule. In this changed world that's what he'd been doing. He'd been afraid to do anything in case it was wrong.

Instead of fighting against it, he took a breath and refocused. He let an image of Nadine form and fill him mind. She smiled at him as she sipped her coffee. Her green-brown eyes lit from within.

The spider twitched and then broke apart, showering dust over everything. He dropped the stick and brushed off his hand. A gray smudge remained.

He watched the dust to see if it would do something. The sun tracked higher but nothing happened. He squatted down to see if anything tiny was happening—he had no idea how long that spider had been growing, only that thinking of something good in his life had helped kill it. Maybe the dust was dead now…maybe, but he doubted it. Nothing was ever that easy.

No, it would wait for him to dream again and latch on to another fear and become something else. He needed to become someone better. In his eyes, his campsite became shabbier and more pathetic.

He hung his head. As he'd told people before, sometimes it was harder to be humble and accept help than it was to continue, but in the end, the reward would be greater. Taking his own advice and finding it less than palatable was something he'd never counted on.

He knew Dai would return sooner rather than later, and when he did, Meryn would have to accept the help that was offered.

The night was colder, the weather shifting. He could feel the change and see it in the clouds that formed. Meryn chanced putting another piece of wood on the fire. There was no one around to see, but the tension that wrapped around his shoulders and back increased. He was taking risks he shouldn't, just to be comfortable. The flames flickered enticingly and he edged closer, the heat warming his skin but little else.

Something moved in the scrub. Meryn cracked open his eyes, but otherwise didn't move. The knife was by his side, a burning branch was ready to be brandished and shoved into the face of an attacker.

Meryn's nose twitched as the delicate scent of cooked and seasoned meat—something other than reptile—drifted through the night air. Even though he'd eaten, his stomach grumbled.

"Meryn, are you here? I brought some dinner." Dai spoke English without being asked.

"Where else am I going to be?" Meryn couldn't hide the resignation in his voice.

Dai walked into the clearing, a bag in one hand and the arrowhead in the other, and that odd glimmer in his eye. That was how he was locating him, with magic, and Meryn was willing to wager that the arrowhead he'd made had something to do with it.

Dai took a seat on a nearby log and began unpacking the food.

"You came alone." Meryn had almost expected Dai to bring Roan with him to force a confrontation.

"I thought it best after last time. I wasn't sure how I'd be received." Dai gave him a pointed look.

Dai was trying; it was he who was behaving poorly. "Thank you for bringing dinner. It is food of this country?"

"Of the time. Chicken and fries."

Meryn looked up from the food and at his cousin. "How many years have passed since I was a man?" How many years had Dai and Roan and the others lived in the Shadowlands waiting for the curse to break?

Dai didn't answer straight away. The trees whispered in the breeze and sent a shiver down Meryn's back. He knew many years had passed. One hundred, two hundred? More?

After several heartbeats Dai spoke. "Nearly two thousand," he finally said softly.

Meryn blinked, sure he hadn't heard correctly. Two thousand years? How was that possible? He couldn't grasp a number that big—not as years anyway. He was used to seeing thousands in an army. A full Roman legion was close to six thousand men. But two thousand years? A man could live forty lives in that amount of time. Idella would have been reborn and lived many lives in that time. While she had lived and loved other men, he'd spent that time killing for gold with cold, gray hands and an empty head and heart.

The reality sunk in leaving him cold. He forced himself to speak. "What of the Decangli?"

"Wiped out that night. The men were killed for supporting the rebellion." Dai watched him as if waiting for him to give up and turn gray again.

Meryn drew in a breath of cool air. That was to be expected. He'd watched the battle, remembered the men had proceeded with the plan, even though some bastard had whispered the plan to the general. "The families were killed too?"

Leave no one alive to raise another rebellion. The Romans were brutal, they fought for an Empire so big, so vast it would take a lifetime to travel from one end to the other.

Dai nodded. "What happened to you that first summons?"

The muscles in Meryn's jaw worked. They didn't know what he'd seen or why he'd let the curse take him into its cold embrace. Maybe now it was time to share— not because he expected sympathy, or forgiveness, but because he wanted Dai to understand.

Meryn reached out and picked up a handful of fries. They were hot and salty and oily, but not unpleasant. He chewed while Dai remained silent, waiting for an answer.

"Idella was calling out for me. I appeared in our home. She wanted me to help her." He closed his eyes. The memory was so fresh, but it was old, thousands of years old. "There were legionnaires in our house, attacking her and scaring the girls. When she saw the goblin I'd become, she screamed and I could do nothing to help. I couldn't move as my family was cut down."

"I'm sorry you had to see that. But it was not your hand that killed them."

"My hand would've been quicker." He didn't blame himself; he blamed the traitor. That man was responsible for the death of all the Decangli.

"And bloodied," Dai said as he pulled a leg off the chicken and passed the rest to Meryn.

"Your hands?" Meryn took the chicken and pulled off a chunk of flesh. It was hot and smelled better than

anything he'd eaten for too long. There'd been something about the way Dai had spoken that suggested he'd
seen his own horror that night.

"They aren't clean. That night, I was summoned by
Claudius…" Dai stumbled over the name and Meryn
knew why. There were things Dai had never told Roan,
fearing it would spark a rebellion before they were ready;
in the end, it hadn't mattered. "He gave me a choice. My
sister's life in his hands or her death by mine."

"Then there was no choice. You couldn't have let
your sister live the way you had." Dai had been a slave
and hostage ensuring Roan's good behavior. He'd
weathered all kinds of torture at the hands of the Roman
general. Any man who treated another so poorly was
barely better than an ignorant animal.

For several heartbeats neither of them spoke. They
ate in silence surrounded by the memories of the life
they'd once shared. It was becoming too easy to fall
into old habits and trust his cousin. As much as Meryn
wanted to keep his guard up around Dai, he longed to be
surrounded by familiar faces again.

"Roan would like to see you."

Meryn had known the request would come, and he
knew he couldn't avoid his king forever. But he could
delay a little longer, until he worked out what he was
going to say. "Tell me of the others. How do they fare
in this strange world?" Meryn asked.

Dai's shoulders dropped and he tossed a bone into the
fire. "Brac died in battle with the druid. We gave him a
warrior's funeral in the Shadowlands. Fane took his own
life soon after." Dai shook his head. "He was too young;
the Shadowlands were too harsh."

"And Anfri?" It had been Anfri's role that Meryn had taken over when Anfri had decided he was too old to advise the new, young king. He'd wanted to step aside officially, thereby making it appear to the Romans they had fresh leadership. It had worked. Even before Anfri had stepped aside, Meryn had been working with him, learning how to keep the king in people's hearts.

"He faded only days before the curse broke." Dai looked up, his face hard, revealing the pain of every death. "After you succumbed, we all swore to die before becoming goblin. We didn't know breaking the curse would free the faded." Dai forced out a breath and shook his head in regret. "Roan shot Anfri."

"Roan couldn't shoot an arrow to save himself."

Dai's lips twisted with a grin that didn't fit the conversation. "With a gun, a new, more dangerous weapon than a bow. I'll show you one; you would appreciate its simple lines and accuracy, and I have no doubt you'd be an excellent marksman."

"So there is no one except us and Roan left." The last three members of the Decangli. "What of the Romans?"

"Ah, they crumbled about four hundred years later."

That was the first piece of good news Meryn had heard all night. It gave him a small measure of satisfaction. He ate a little more even though his stomach was full and he'd probably regret it with an uncomfortable night's sleep. "How did the curse break?"

"Love. A woman called Eliza summoned Roan and somehow saw through the curse. They're married now."

"He finally found a queen."

"Not a queen, a wife. Things are different now. We have to adapt and survive."

That was something Meryn was very familiar with. "I've been surviving for a very long time. Running with goblins has made me weary." That was the truth. He wanted more than mere survival—he wanted to live, even if he wasn't sure how to do that in this world.

Dai pulled a black leather square from his pocket. "This is a wallet; it's got money and your identification in it." He handed it over for Meryn to examine.

"And who am I now?" Meryn opened the wallet. It was full of the paper money he'd seen people using, each one marked with squiggles he knew was writing. He wished he'd had the time to learn to read while he'd been planning battles and trying to keep the Decangli from being trampled by the Romans.

"Meryn Knight, thirty-seven, ex-army, security expert. Your family was killed a year ago. Since then you have been recovering."

Night. That fitted after all the years he'd spent as a goblin. They were creatures of the shadows and darkness.

Meryn closed the wallet. He wasn't thirty-seven; he'd been twenty-four when cursed. Nadine had assumed he was ex-army because he'd done a lot of fighting; it had been easy to let her hold on to that belief. Security expert? Well, he knew how to plan battles. He looked up at his cousin. "You have a lie?"

"I do. I am Dai King, thirty-two, language researcher."

"King?" Dai would never have been king. If Roan had died, that would've fallen on Meryn's shoulders and Dai would've still been a Roman slave.

"Roan picked the name, not me." There was an edge to his voice like he wasn't thrilled either.

"Who picked my name?"

"Me. I kept as much of your life as I could and made it into something modern people would understand."

The wallet was heavy in his hands. It would make life easier. This was the help he'd been needing, but it was too much; there were too many notes. He couldn't take it all from his cousin. "I can't accept the money."

"It's yours. All the gold that Roan and I and the others horded has been divided equally. There is enough for you to live very comfortably." Dai pulled out a key from a small pocket in the bag. "I have arranged a house for you not far from here, so you can come to the park every day."

Meryn stared at the key but didn't take it. Help was one thing, but Dai was rewriting his life for him, showering him with gifts that would be far beyond his ability to ever repay. "It's too much." He'd be indebted for the rest of his life—and probably his next one too.

"It's not safe to sleep out every night, Meryn. Plus it's winter and there are storms forecast."

Winter but milder than any he'd known. But he knew Dai was right; he'd already reached the same conclusion. He couldn't keep living in the woods. When he didn't respond, Dai pressed the point.

"At least let me show you where it is, please." Dai was asking, not ordering.

"Very well," Mcryn said through gritted teeth, then realized how ungrateful he sounded. Two thousand years and their roles were reversed. Once it had been Dai resenting Meryn's help even as he needed it. "Thank you for the gifts and organizing the house; it must have taken a lot of effort and coin."

"After everything you did for me, I am glad to be able to return the favor."

"It is returned, in full," Meryn said without looking at him, as his eyes were burning. But he wouldn't let the tears of gratitude fall. "Right, show me this house."

They packed up the remains of the chicken, and Meryn ate the last of the fries and the sweet tasting coleslaw. Then Meryn put the wallet into his pocket and together they walked along the paths to the high-rises that overlooked the park.

"Over there?"

"The white building, ground floor, number two." Dai pointed to the symbol on the key tag. "Would you like me to show you around?"

Meryn couldn't deny that part of him was curious about the kind of houses people now lived in. What kind of house had Dai arranged for him? Yet he had to retain a shred of dignity. "No. I can do that myself. I'm not a child."

Dai handed him the key with a smile, as if he understood that some things needed to be tackled alone. For a moment they both stood there, the silence expanding.

That house was a place he could take Nadine without embarrassment. It was somewhere safe to sleep without fear of attack.

Could he make himself into someone else the way Dai had and the way Roan must have? Did they have two thousand years of memories locked in their heads? Was it even possible for a man to remember that much? Then again, there wasn't much to remember about the Shadowlands, just endless gray broken by the occasional twisted tree. Surviving as men there must have been harsh. He swallowed the bitterness at the back of his throat. He should have been with them instead of running with the goblins for two thousand years.

He had no gold to share with them. He had nothing except what he was given. His fingers curled around the key. While he wanted to investigate, he couldn't. Not with Dai watching his every move.

"Can I tell Roan you will see him?"

That was the unspoken cost of the house. Dai didn't want money; he wanted Meryn to return with him to see Roan. "I am not ready to see him."

Dai nodded, his gaze on the ground. "There is only so much I can do, Meryn. I have given you everything you need to fit in, to live in this time." He lifted his head and looked at Meryn. "There is no going back, no changing of the past, only this. And it's weird and strange and some of it will take a while to get used to, but we're Decangli—we don't quit when it gets hard."

That was a line Meryn had used many times when trying to keep hope alive in the tribe. Back then he'd believed it. Now?

If he quit trying, he might as well crawl under a log and die, but that didn't mean he was ready to move into a house and start faking his new life.

"I'm not quitting; I'm taking my time. You've had two thousand years; I've had less than ten days." Meryn turned and walked away, half expecting Dai to follow.

When he glanced over his shoulder Dai was gone, as if he'd never been there. Meryn opened his hand to check the key was real, that he hadn't dreamed the whole conversation. The metal glinted in the moonlight; for a heartbeat he was tempted to try the key in the door of the house, then he shoved the key into his pocket.

After three paces he turned around and walked toward the building. In the shadows he fumbled with the gate before getting it open. Once through the gate he stood in a small courtyard. There was a glass door on one side. He walked toward it, but there was no lock, only the smooth, cold surface. He frowned, unable to work out how to get in. He gave the door a push but nothing happened. He pressed the small red light, but nothing happened. He swore under his breath.

This was a job for daylight.

Maybe he should've let Dai show him in, maybe this was why Dai had grinned, because he'd known that it wasn't as easy as putting a key in a lock. He'd prove to Dai he could get in…in the morning. He'd spend all day if need be.

He walked back to his campsite, wishing now he was sleeping in the house, but he was tired and he didn't want to linger around the building at night in case someone rang the police. Another night in his shabby shelter with stolen clothes for blankets. What did Dai think of him living like this? He shook his head and busied himself building up the fire and changing from the good clothes Dai had given him to the other stolen ones and jacket he'd taken from the hospital. Then he lay down ready to sleep. Despite his full belly, it didn't come quickly. He was too aware of his hovel, of the night animals calling to each other, and the key and wallet in his pocket.

His mind rebelled at the idea of using the key Dai had given him, even as his body craved the comfort of warm water and a bed. And not just for sleeping.

How far had he fallen? How far did he have to climb before he would once again be the man he once was? If he were a new man, instead of holding on to past glories, what would he do? He would take the help offered and climb faster, instead of stubbornly insisting he navigate the cliff face by himself.

He was climbing, his fingers scrabbling for a hold on the cold, gray stone. He adjusted his weight and reached for the next handhold, his fingers curled with the strain. He risked a glance down. The goblin that had been following him, hunting him, had begun climbing.

He had to reach the top first.

Without giving himself time to rest or consider what would happen if his hands slipped, he pressed on. The muscles in his arms and back burned. Sweat trickled down his spine like cold droplets of rain.

When he didn't think he could go any further, his hand closed over the ledge. With a grunt and the last of his energy, he hauled himself up onto the top of the wall. It was two paces wide at the top. He took his bow off his back and pulled out an arrow. He carefully sighted on the goblin still climbing after him. He grimaced and paused. It didn't feel right to pick off an unarmed target. And yet if he waited, he knew the goblin would win.

He looked over his shoulder at the castle. He wouldn't be able to climb down and reach the safety of hall before the goblin caught him. He used his sleeve to wipe a trickle of sweat out of his eyes and re-aimed. The goblin was closer; he could see the scar slashing down its cheek, drawing its eye down and twisting the side of its mouth. He knew this goblin. He'd caused that injury. The creature's lips drew back in a snarl. Meryn drew the bow and looked down the shaft to the side of the goblin's neck. One shot was all it would take.

Shapes emerged out of the dust. He blinked, but it

wasn't an illusion. More goblins were coming, drawn to the castle. He loosed the arrow. It flew true and the goblin fell off the wall, but ten were coming to take his place. He didn't have enough arrows for them all.

Why were they coming?

For him?

He slung his bow over his shoulder and began a rapid descent, half climbing, half slipping and sliding, cutting open his hands and leaving crimson stains on the wall. His feet hit the dust, the impact reverberating through his body, but he didn't pause. He sprinted across the space between the wall and the castle. A broken fountain without water and a bench sat in the dust. This must have been a garden once. He could almost see it, the grounds neatly laid out. The sound of his footsteps changed and he glanced down. The dust had been replaced with a paved path, but he didn't have time to examine how that was possible. He glanced behind him to see the goblins coming over the wall.

His heart lurched; there were too many of them. He looked back at the castle. On every windowsill was a gold coin, as if the occupant was intentionally attracting goblins. Who would do such a crazy thing?

And he was caught between the castle and incoming goblins. He had no choice but to reach the castle and pray the walls would offer safety.

At first he saw no door, but as the path formed beneath his feet a large timber door formed in the wall. He didn't waste time knocking, just pulled on the handle, let himself in, then slammed it closed, and dropped the bar. For a moment he leaned against the door and caught his breath.

Outside the yelling grew louder as the goblins drew closer.

If they found him, they'd eat him. He had to get rid of the gold.

He looked up at the sound of soft footsteps. Halfway down the stairs was a woman in a pale green dress that swept the floor with every step. His heart stopped.

Nadine.

"You came." She ran toward him and threw her arms around his neck.

The weapons he'd been carrying clattered to the floor as he returned her embrace.

"The gold. The goblins." The castle began to shake with the footsteps of a goblin army.

She silenced him with a kiss, her lips pressing hard against his. Before he could enjoy the taste of her mouth, glass shattered.

Meryn's eyes opened with a snap. He lay still, his heart pounding hard and lust coursing through his blood. Something had woken him—something more than a dream kiss. Soft rain pattered on the leaves, but that wasn't it; something else filled the night. His heart refused to settle even though wariness replaced desire. Slowly, he slid his hand to his knife.

Around him the forest was quiet. As quiet as nature could be. Across the other side of the barely glowing coals, a pair of yellow eyes appeared. Meryn watched. A shuffle and a grunt and the eyes drew closer. The outline became clearer. Meryn blinked, not believing what he saw. It couldn't be a goblin. Not here. Not now. It was the wrong time of year.

The goblin grinned. Its mouth twisted as if it could

hear Meryn's thoughts and taste his fear. His stomach tightened. His dream had crossed the boundary and reformed in the Fixed Realm, again. The goblin drew his knife and crept closer. The scar down the side of his face was pale and white.

Meryn adjusted his grip, ready to fight back. He'd killed this goblin in the Shadowlands, and again in his dream. He could destroy him again—but in his dream there'd been more than one; there'd been an army. What of the others that would follow? Around him the bushes rustled as if a hundreds of goblins were materializing. For the first time since being in the Fixed Realm, he longed for the safety of four walls, but he knew they wouldn't stop the goblins—not when it was him dreaming them into existence.

If he dreamed them here, he could will them away.

With his gaze on the goblin and his ears listening for others, he eased up slowly. How could he banish a nightmare?

The goblin stepped over the coals.

Meryn forced himself to remain still, ready and waiting.

A point in his pocket dug into him. Nadine's cross. Gold. Was the goblin coming for the gold? There was no way he was letting this creature take it; it was Nadine's. The goblin faltered. Meryn let his thoughts fill with Nadine again. If his fears fed the nightmares, maybe his hope could banish them.

At first nothing happened. The goblin remained still, watching him.

He was used to putting his faith in weapons and plans, not wishes. But he knew the power of nightmares and also of dreams. Nadine was in the dreams he wanted for his future. Her kiss lingered in his mind even if he couldn't taste her on his tongue.

He wanted to find love again and be seen as a man, not a goblin.

He wanted to be free of the Shadowlands once and for all.

A breeze swept through the clearing with a hiss, making the trees shudder. The goblin screamed as if in agony, then raised his knife, intending to stab Meryn in his bed. Meryn twisted and deflected the blow. He kicked the goblin in the chest; it felt real enough beneath his boots. The other nightmares had crumbled when he touched them. This one was different. The goblin fell back into the coals. He howled in pain, his fingers curling as he scrambled to get up.

Meryn placed his knife to the goblin's throat. "I defeated you once, and I will defeat you every time. I do not fear you. Be gone and trouble me no more."

He drew the blade across the gray skin. Black blood stained the knife. He expected the body to turn to dust the way the others had, ready to reform another night. It didn't. Meryn stood up and looked at the body of the goblin. He wiped the blade clean on his trousers.

How was he ever going to explain his nightmares coming to life to anyone?

What would Nadine say?

The body remained there instead of disintegrating. Very odd. He frowned. If he was free of the Shadowlands, maybe the dust had lost its power and the goblin was trapped here. He'd killed his nightmare. He gave the body a nudge with his boot. It didn't move. He couldn't leave it. He used a branch and shifted the body off the coals enough that he could get the fire going properly. Everything was damp, so it took a while to find dry twigs and bark to feed the coals, but once they took hold, they couldn't be stopped. In seconds, the goblin's body was consumed, leaving only harmless ash.

He didn't want to risk another nightmare, so he sat up the rest of the night, thinking of Nadine and the kiss.

Chapter 9

MERYN WAS TIRED AND HIS BONES ACHED. IT HAD continued to rain—not heavy enough to seep into his shelter, but enough to make everything damp. After the goblin had attacked he'd been unable to go back to sleep, partly because he was waiting for another nightmare to spring to life and partly because his body knew there was a bed waiting for him. While he sat there awake and listening to the soft patter of rain, he hadn't been able to stop thinking about what Dai had said. Did Dai really think he was looking for a reason to quit? After surviving as a goblin and then as a human in the Shadowlands, any life he had in the Fixed Realm was easier. But then Dai had never had to adjust to being human again and all that entailed.

He touched the key in his pocket and looked up at the white building. Like most of the buildings, it was lots of houses stacked on top of each other. How many other people lived in there? Even as he looked at the building, he smiled. Dai had found a house that was near the park; he was making it as easy as possible for Meryn to walk in to his new life while still being somewhere familiar. The park was on his doorstep.

The bench where he waited for Nadine wasn't far away. He glanced up at the sky; it was mostly blue, but even the patches of gray clouds had more depth than the Shadowlands ever had. She'd be here soon, and after yesterday he didn't want to be late or, worse, miss her. Today, he could pay for breakfast. And when the money in the wallet ran out, how was he going to get more? Dai had said that he had more. Was it in the house? Meryn frowned and pushed aside the thought.

He walked down the road to the bench and saw Nadine already there. She stood when she saw him, a smile on her lips. His mouth remembered the kiss, but last night had been a reflection of his desire, that was all, no matter how real it had felt at the time. He'd rather dream of Nadine than goblins any night. He'd rather be kissing her in daylight than just in his dreams. She was unlike any woman he'd ever known, but like many he had known, she had spirit—a gleam in her eye that suggested she'd have made a fine Decangli woman.

A pretty smile on a bold woman and he'd do whatever was asked of him. He wasn't that different than the man who'd fallen for Idella so many years ago.

She watched him walk over. "Do you live nearby?"

"In the white building." He was grateful to be able to answer without lying or admitting he was living in the park.

Nadine raided her eyebrows. "Lucky you. River views or park views?"

"Ground floor. My cousin arranged it for me." And it felt good not to lie, even if he was leaving out bits and pieces.

"Still, some cousin. He must think highly of you."

Dai had once. It was hard to say if he did now. Maybe Dai was acting to clear a long held debt, or maybe he was acting out of respect and love, or maybe on Roan's orders. At the moment Meryn didn't care.

"I think he knew that I'd like to be close to the park."

"You like being surrounded by nature."

"It's peaceful."

"Yes, it's why I run here. Running along the paths in the morning, it's so quiet."

Meryn smiled. "Did you want to get coffee? I have my wallet with me today." And he wanted to repay her kindness and test out his knowledge of modern money.

She bit her lip and his heart sank. She was going to say no. He'd misread her friendship as attraction.

"I want to, but I have to go and collect bridesmaids' dresses. My friend Gina is getting married in a couple of days." She looked at him again, her gaze skimming over his face and body.

What was she looking for?

Then she shook her head even though she was grinning. "I don't even know your full name."

That he could answer, thanks to Dai and his creative lies. "Meryn Night."

"Nadine Gilbert." She put out her hand and he clasped it without a second thought. "Pleased to meet you."

"But we have already met." The heat from her skin warmed his hand

"Ah, but now I know who you are."

"No. Now you know my name."

She laughed. He'd forgotten how beautiful the sound was. Her eyes lit with happiness like what he said was funny. Had he misspoke? Translating between Decangli and English wasn't easy.

"You're right, I don't know everything about you. But I'd like to." She looked him in the eye as if daring him to refuse.

He wouldn't say no to anything she asked. He'd raced to her aid in his dream, even though a goblin army was on his heels. He'd never let goblins take her. "I'd like to know more about you."

She gave the slightest flinch as if that idea was painful. He doubted her past was as bad as his…then he wondered how he was going to talk about the life he'd had without mentioning Romans and the Decangli. He was going to have to think about it. But he wasn't going to let it stop him from making sure he'd see her again.

"Breakfast tomorrow morning?" She'd invited him last time, so it seemed only fair he put out the invitation this time.

She nodded. "That would be nice. Until tomorrow?"

Then he realized he was still holding her hand. He shifted his grip and brought her fingers to his lips for lightest of kisses. "Until tomorrow," he echoed.

Her lips parted and the look in her eyes changed to something more dangerous. She stepped closer and raised her free hand to cup his jaw. Her thumb brushed his cheek. His hand had found its way to her hip, as if he could keep her close. She didn't resist; she leaned in. Her breath on his skin heated his blood and hardened his flesh. Lust had never felt so good. Goblins didn't know what they were missing by craving only gold. He'd trade it all for one night with Nadine, to be the man she wanted in her bed.

Of course, if she knew the truth, it would be over. He turned his head at the last moment, so her lips touched his cheek. He couldn't kiss and lie in the same breath. It had been easier in his dream.

She drew back, her smile gone. "Too soon?" Her fingers began to loosen so she could pull away, but his hand wouldn't release her.

"No." He shook his head. He wanted her kiss. "Unexpected."

He touched her face, caressed her cheek, and traced her lower lip with his thumb. He wanted to kiss her, to see if she tasted as sweet as she looked. To enjoy it without goblins interrupting. He sighed. "Nadine…"

There was a tightness in his voice that he didn't expect. He didn't know how to tell her that she'd be the first after his wife, or that it had been years and years and years, not the one year that Dai had made up. He didn't know how to tell her that it was her who made it easy for him to become a modern man. That it was her kind touch that made him realize he was still a person capable of love. She made him want to be better, more than his past, more than the curse. If not for her, he might have been content sitting in the bushes whittling useless arrows.

He wanted to tell her that after all this time he wasn't entirely sure how to move forward without screwing this up.

She gazed at him without moving. "Just kiss me." Her words were little more than a whisper.

That was an order he couldn't disobey. He leaned in and placed his lips to hers. Her mouth was soft as he'd expected, as it had been last night, her lips opening as she tilted her head. His tongue darted along her lower lip, tasting her mouth the way he'd wanted to before the goblins had attacked, and she returned the gentle touch, seeking more. While his heart pounded hard, as if he was running into battle ready to claim her, he drew back. Standing here when she was about to leave to get dresses wasn't the time or place to go further.

He swallowed the raging desire she'd woken.

Nadine blinked and sighed. Her tongue traced her lip as if she couldn't get enough. "You know how to leave a woman wanting more."

"I want to make sure I see you tomorrow." He'd also like to see her in a dress—even though he liked the tight fitting pants she wore to run in. They showed off every curve of her legs.

"You will…and by then I'll know more about you. Everyone can be googled," she said with a wink.

He had no idea what she'd just said, only that she was somehow going to try and find out more about him. He hoped Dai's lie held up to her scrutiny. "I hope you like what you find."

"I hope you like what *you* find."

"I don't have google." Was that even correct? He was heading into territory that could reveal just how little he knew about her world.

"No Internet?"

Whatever that was he didn't have it. Meryn shook his head.

"Ah, well then, you will have to wait until tomorrow to find out more about me." Her lips curved in a grin that was clearly designed to tease and encourage and torment him until tomorrow.

One day wouldn't kill him. He released her hand slowly, letting his fingers glide over her skin. "I'll look forward to it."

She stepped back, her gaze never leaving him and

that smile on her lips that made him want to step forward
and prevent the distance from widening.

Nadine looked at Meryn for a moment longer. What
was it about him that kept drawing her back when she
should walk away? She didn't need someone else's
problems—and he obviously had a few—or someone
as damaged as she was. None of the reasons she came
up with dampened her interest. It was definitely his
eyes. They trapped her. One moment full of heat that
threatened to burn her, the next empty, the next full of
sorrow. She'd seen the same sorrow in her eyes when
she was growing up until she'd learned to hide it. For
a few minutes with this man, she hadn't had to. Until
now she hadn't realized the weight of the mask she was
hiding behind.

Before she gave in to temptation and demanded
another kiss, she turned around and walked away. She'd
never been kissed like that before. Most men swooped
in and took it as a victory and one step closer to scoring.
Of course, most of the men she'd dated were younger
and hadn't been married and widowed.

Huh, maybe that's all it was. She was appreciating
the maturity.

She stopped herself from glancing back and took a
calming breath, but it didn't quell the excitement. This is
what had been missing with Daniel and the others. She
pulled her smart phone out when she turned the corner
and typed in Meryn Night, and got a corrected search
for Meryn Knight. She accepted the first link to a news
story from last year.

His home had been broken into while the family
was there. His children and wife had been murdered in

front of him. The killer had never been caught. Meryn had gone AWOL and was discharged from the army on medical grounds. There were no pictures and no information on what he'd done in the army. That usually meant one thing—Special Forces. They were meant to be the toughest. He must have done and seen all kinds of things, but he'd never expected to have to confront them in his home.

No wonder he'd reacted badly to the anniversary of his wife's death. Her feet stopped. He'd hesitated before kissing her. Her fingers touched her lips. Was she the first since Idella?

The more she knew about him, the more questions it raised. And when she had all the answers, would she lose interest?

Was she making her mother's mistake and falling for the wrong man? She made herself walk on toward the train station. She wasn't falling anywhere, tripping into his arms didn't count, and neither did having coffee…the kiss on the other hand…she wanted more of them. She wanted more of him. But that was lust, not love. When she fell in love, and most days she wasn't sure it existed, it would be with someone safe and sensible.

Just like Daniel.

But safe and sensible wasn't what she wanted. She wanted Meryn.

Chapter 10

THE RAIN STARTED AGAIN. NOT HEAVY, BUT ENOUGH to soak him through if he remained outdoors. Meryn ran his fingers through his hair and walked back toward the house. The taste of Nadine's lips lingered on his mouth, tempting him with something he'd thought was gone for good. Once, he'd have never thought he'd be able to live without Idella; it was why he'd given in to the curse, to block out the pain. But he was alive, and the heartache no longer tore at him. She was in his heart, not forgotten—never that—but he needed more than memories. He wanted to have a proper life, a full life.

He touched Nadine's cross in his pocket. Again he hadn't found the words to tell her he had it. Would he ever? Had it passed that point, or would she value honesty and understand what he'd been when she'd first seen him?

He had nothing to offer her. No standing, no house, and no job. No woman would see him as a husband worth having.

For the second time in his life, he cared what someone else thought of him.

He wanted to be able to provide for any family that might come along. Thoughts of his daughters filled his mind—their laughter and their peaceful sighs as they slept. He wasn't sure he could take the pain of losing children again.

One step at a time.

He had to have a house first.

In daylight, it was much easier to open the gate at the entrance to the tall, white building, now he could see clearly how it worked. The small courtyard was paved and held a few potted plants. On the other side was the smooth glass door that had no lock. How was he supposed to get in? He stared at it, but it wasn't just the lack of a lock that stopped him from going in. Using the key and accepting the house felt like failure. The gold Roan and Dai had hoarded had bought this. Their gold, not his. He'd done no work to achieve this.

It was a gift.

It felt like charity.

He'd have done the same for either of them if the situation had been reversed, but the thought didn't ease his conscience.

Desire still warmed his blood and thoughts that had never crossed his empty, goblin mind now taunted him. He glared at the door. Rain trickled down the back of his neck. He wasn't getting any drier standing outside. He swore a filthy oath in Decangli. Life had been much simpler when he'd held a sword and commanded an army.

He had to find a way through the glass door before he could even find which house was his. He walked up to the door and pulled out the key, hoping there'd be a clue. On the tag there was a squiggle. *Number two*, Dai had said.

That squiggle was probably a two, which meant all he had to do was look for the matching symbol. He could do that. Reading wasn't that hard after all. But there were no other markings that indicated how to open the glass door.

While there was no lock, there was a small red light. He went to press it again, this time it went green and the door clicked. It hadn't done that last night. He glanced at the key in his hand. A key that worked without being placed in a lock. He knew it wasn't magic, but it seemed close enough. He gave the door a tap and it swung open. With a shrug he went in.

The symbol on his key matched the one on the door to his right. This door had a lock, so Meryn pushed the key in and gave it a twist.

The door opened and he gaped in astonishment.

It was a house inside the building. He'd been expecting a single room, but it was huge, far bigger than the house he'd once had. He shivered, unable to stop the reaction as his body adjusted from the cold to heat. How had Dai arranged this? How much coin did a house like this cost? Roan must have hoarded a massive pile of gold while cursed.

Meryn swore again, cursing Dai and his interference in the same breath as he thanked him. With a wrench of will he crossed the threshold and shut the door. He pulled off his dirty boots and padded through the house. Beneath his feet the tiles were cool and smooth. The room he was in had lounges and tables and chairs. He walked through the house, not sure what he was looking for or what he was hoping to find, just curious. Aside from the size and some of the furniture—what was that large black rectangular thing that the lounges faced?—it looked much like the houses he remembered, somewhere to cook, somewhere to eat—he kept walking—and somewhere to sleep. The bed would have easily fit his whole family. His children's laughter echoed in his skull. For a heartbeat he could see them running through the house, pushing past him to play on the bed. He turned away.

To the side of the bedroom was another room filled with white tiles and shiny steel. Hanging from rails were sheets of thick white fabric and a huge bath took up a corner. His lips curved. A bath, a proper bath, a real soak, not just a quick scrub in the restroom.

This was exactly what he wanted. He got the water running but didn't bother waiting for the bath to fill. The idea that he could fill a bath so easily and then have it to himself was decadent.

He stripped off his trousers and stepped in. The water swirled around him and he leaned his head against the edge and closed his eyes. For a long time he didn't move, couldn't move as his muscles relaxed for what felt like the first time in more years than he could count. He was safe here. No one would find him camping in the park. No thieves would come and destroy his things. A sigh escaped.

He hadn't been truly safe since he was a child, before the Romans came. After the invasion it had been battles, then battle planning as he'd risen to role of Roan's second—a job his brother Drem had envied. Drem had always been wheedling for more information and a chance to show Meryn up. Maybe brothers didn't get along until they were forced to. He'd never seen eye to eye with Drem about anything. Drem had just wanted the prestige that went with the role without the hard work—the long nights, dinners with a general he'd rather kill, and all the while plotting, planning, and praying.

It wasn't a job he'd wish on anyone. There'd been times

when he and Roan would sit in Roan's house and neither
of them would speak, neither of them willing to voice
how dire the situation, yet neither having a clear solution.
The plan for the rebellion had first been voiced by Dai. A
whisper of an idea that they had spent months working on.
It had unraveled faster than he'd ever thought possible. If
not for the curse, he'd have died that night with the rest of
the Decangli.

Meryn reached out and turned off the tap before the
bath could overflow. Then he took a breath and sub-
merged himself under the hot water. He ran his hands
over his hair and face and resurfaced with a gasp.

With his body warm and relaxed, curiosity rose up
like a hunger that needed to be sated. People didn't
appear to live that differently from how they had when
he was born. He'd recognized furniture, and yet, his
fingers ran along the smooth white surface of the giant
bath, everything was different. The bath was carved out
of a solid piece of something. He gave it a rap with his
knuckles, but it didn't sound like stone.

With a grunt, Meryn hauled himself out of the bath.
At the bottom lay a film of fine gray silt, the last few
grains of the Shadowlands washing free. He pulled the
plug and let the water go, watching the last of the dust
that nightmares were made of disappear. He dried off
and examined the towels before hanging them back up.
They were so soft…and white. People really had a thing
for white, a color usually reserved for druids. He paused
with his fingers gripping the towel. What had happened
to the druid who'd cursed them?

Next time he saw Dai he would ask.

He walked slowly back through the house, pausing

to touch things and examine them more closely. On the pale, polished wood of the dining table was a sheet of paper covered in black inky scribbles and a piece of gold jewelry. A bracelet shaped like a torque. He touched his neck. He knew the real reason he didn't want to see Roan. He didn't want to become Roan's second again. He was done with fighting and giving orders.

He'd given up the night he'd turned goblin. He was done and he just wanted to live. Looking his king in the eye and saying that was going to be impossible.

His fingers traced the shape of the bracelet. Dai had obviously left it for him, but for what end? Only the king had worn gold…had he hoped that gold would appeal because of the time he'd spent as a goblin? If anything it repelled the man. But an overwhelming urge to try it on flowed up his hand. He couldn't resist the compulsion, as if he were once again goblin and driven by the lust for gold.

The bracelet fit snugly on his wrist.

The ink scribbled on the paper became words he could read.

He yanked off the bracelet and let it fall to the floor with a hollow chime. "What magic is this?"

His Decangli words echoed around the house. The bracelet didn't respond. The answer was on the paper. Meryn picked up the bracelet between two fingers, as if it were a critter that would bite. Again the compulsion to put it on ran up his arm, but this time he could fight it. The bracelet obviously held a powerful enchantment.

He looked at the sheet of paper, but words didn't form. He leafed through the papers hoping one would make sense. None did. Many were blank. With a snap, he put the bracelet back on, sure he was going to regret the decision. Druid magic had only ever brought him grief. The black lines became letters and words he understood. They formed in his mind with magic.

Meryn,

So that was what his name looked like in script.

My heart is gladdened you are here. I imbued the gold with magic to help you read, a skill you will need. I can't help you with writing. That is something you will have to practice.

That is what the blank paper and the pen was for. Meryn shook his head. Learning to write was not essential to survival.

There is food in the kitchen and clothing in the wardrobe. The details of your life in this time I have written for you over the page. I have used as much truth as possible. I won't press you further. I understand how hard this is for you. When you are ready, there is a phone in the kitchen. Press 1 and the green button. I've programmed in my number.

By the way, this is written in Latin so no one else can read it.

Don't wait too long. There is much news to share.

Your cousin,
Dai

The words clawed at his mind as he struggled to take them in. He pulled off the bracelet. It spun on the table before falling over. Meryn rubbed his temples. The words on the page no longer made sense. But he knew the first one was his name and the last one that of his cousin. The lines made letters. And made sense. He could see them repeated in other combinations. Despite the throbbing in Meryn's head, he picked up the bracelet again. Would he be able to read everything in the house?

He found food and made himself something to eat. Then he gathered up his damp and dirty clothing and put them in the small room behind the kitchen where a white box proclaimed it was a washer. He'd wash his clothes later; he'd seen clean clothing in the bedroom. After touching the fabrics and investigating all the drawers he pulled on a clean shirt and trousers, too loose but he belted them, and after a few good meals they'd fit fine. But there were no shoes. Not a single pair. He'd found undergarments and socks, but no shoes. He was going to have to put his old boots on.

An idea began forming. He opened up the wallet and looked at the money, this time reading the denomination on the notes and memorizing them. Out of curiosity he read the identification card also tucked inside. *Meryn Knight.* The meaning of his surname became clear, and he smiled at his own misunderstanding. Dai hadn't been referring to Meryn's years as a goblin when choosing his name.

Then Meryn took the bracelet off, not wanting to risk losing something so valuable. He hadn't ventured back into the city after that first night. He closed his eyes, remembering that he'd passed many windows filled with

many things. Would shoes be one of them? He opened his
eyes. He had nothing better to do today. He shrugged and
put on a jacket, much like the ones he'd seen other men
wearing, and hoped that it wouldn't start raining again.

Meryn went down the hill and into the city. This time
he wasn't half crazed and confused by the world as much
as his memories. The speed of the cars didn't worry him,
and the maze of streets made sense, a neat grid cast into
shadow by the tall buildings. He tilted his head and gazed
up—taller than trees, their windows like rows of blank
soulless eyes, yet he knew people would be up there.
Doing what he didn't know. If they lived up there, where
did they work? Where were the farms? And if people
worked there, what job involved staying inside? They
couldn't all be scribes, mapmakers, or weavers.

As he moved deeper into the city, the buildings
changed. They were still tall, but at street level there
were shops and places to eat. Merchants still existed,
selling their wares. The tension in his muscles eased
at the recognition of the familiar. Not everything had
changed and some of the items for sale as he passed
the windows he recognized: glass ornaments and beads,
cooking implements, clothes, and jewelry.

He paused to stare at the gold, but its lure no longer
shone for him. It seemed gaudy, the yellow too bright,
the gems too colorful as if the shopkeeper could tempt
the unwary into spending too much coin in his store. A
small row of crosses hung at one end of the window.
None of them were like Nadine's. Her cross was a
souvenir he'd didn't want. But until he found a way to
return it, he was stuck with the cross. It was like an evil
reminder of what he'd been for two thousand years.

He walked on, taking in as much of the city as he could, listening, looking, learning, and wishing he had risked wearing the bracelet, so he could read all the signs that hung above every shop. A brightly lit shop made him stop. Inside were shoes. Hundreds of them on display. Men's, women's, and tiny shoes that could only belong to children—not winter boots for keeping their feet warm and dry, but dainty little slippers and sandals. His daughter Branna would've loved them.

His gaze tracked back to the side of the store that seemed to be devoted to men's shoes, duller and bigger than the female side which seemed to be made of pointed and spiked shoes. He'd only ever seen Nadine in the white shoes everyone seemed to wear while running.

He glanced at his own feet, then back at the shoes in the shop. He hadn't had a new pair of boots in two thousand years, so he went inside. Meryn's gaze flickered over the shelves—shiny black shoes and ankle boots with pointed toes. He wanted something else…His gaze landed on a pair of canvas lace up shoes that looked a little like runners but were covered in checks.

"Can I help you?" A woman in a red shirt walked over to him.

"I'd like these." He picked up the shoe and hoped the other one wasn't far away.

"Converse. Very popular at the moment. What size are you?"

Meryn raised his eyebrows. "I don't know."

The woman studied his feet for a moment. "I'll get a ten and we'll go from there." Then she disappeared through a door.

Did he have enough money to be buying shoes?

Doubt wriggled like maggots in his stomach. He had no idea what a fair price was. When he looked closely at the shoes, he saw labels with squiggles on them that he couldn't decipher. Next time, he'd wear the bracelet.

"If you take a seat, you can try them on," the woman said behind him.

There was no harm in trying them on and then finding out if he could afford them.

Meryn sat and pulled off his boot while the lady opened a box and drew out the shoes. The woman laced the shoes with the speed of someone who did it many times a day, her eyes on his boot while her hands worked. For the first time in his life, an insidious, creeping embarrassment crept through him. He had always taken care of himself and his family…and his king and tribe.

The lady handed one shoe over. For a moment Meryn just held it. The shoe was so different from what he was used to. Lighter for a start. The lady waited, her eyebrows arched.

"Thank you." He put the shoe on and laced it up.

"Stand up and I'll check the fit."

This time he did as he was asked without pausing.

She pressed the end of the shoe. "They're good. Any smaller and they'd rub. What do you think?"

Meryn studied his feet; one in an old boot, one in a new black-and-white check shoe—one foot in the past, one in the future. He couldn't straddle both worlds. If he was going to succeed in the Fixed Realm again, he had to put both feet on that path and move forward without looking back. But what was in front of him?

What did he have here that was worth living for?

What did he have that was worth dying for?

The only answer he had was in the shape of Nadine. Her ready smile, guarded eyes, and long legs…he cut off the thought before he imagined just how nice her legs would look wrapped around him. To have her, he had to fit in and be a man of this age.

He asked how much they were, then added up the notes in his wallet. He had more than enough money. "I'll have them."

He walked back up the hill, happier than he'd been in days. He had a house and was dressed in clothes of the day. He could speak English and read with the help of magic. In a few short days he'd come so far. He was beginning to feel like he did belong. Before he went back to his house, he needed to collect the rest of his things from the campsite. He stepped off the path and walked toward his campsite, an old Decangli song on his lips.

As he drew closer, the song died. The scrub around his campsite had been disturbed. He circled around, drawing the knife, ready to fight off anything wanting to attack him. Nothing charged him and there was only silence, not even the birds were singing. He braced himself for the worst, expecting goblins lying in wait or more giant spiders.

His camp was empty, but not the way he'd left it. His stomach sunk like a rock in a pot. It wasn't just the scrub that had been disturbed. The shelter he'd built had been torn down. The clothes he slept in had been defecated on, the fire pit kicked and coals and ashes were strewn all over the ground. No animal or nightmare creation had done this.

A man had.

He examined the footprints left in the wet earth. Or rather two men. And he knew which men: the thieves he'd taken clothing from had returned the favor.

"Damn it."

He'd been careful. Made sure he wasn't followed. Approached the camp from different direction so no clear path was left. And yet they'd still found his camp. If they'd found it once, they'd find it again. And he didn't want to be here when they came back. Especially if they brought friends. Men like that always hunted in groups because they didn't have the guts to act alone.

What if they had come while he'd been sleeping?

What if they'd attacked with friends? How many of them could he have fought off? Two untrained men wasn't hard—a handful or more, they won by sheer numbers. He'd been lucky. He could've been sitting by the fire when they found the camp. He turned and went looking for his cache where he hid his valuables.

As he walked, he scanned the ground for signs of disturbance. The scrub seemed to be untouched, but he wouldn't let himself hope. Not yet. He moved a few branches cautiously—but the rain had sent most spiders scurrying for better shelter—and pulled the bag out from under the log. A few woodlice and snails clung to the fabric. Aside from the bugs, his bag that contained spare clothing and what was left of his food was fine. He released a sigh as he brushed the critters off and slung the bag over his shoulder.

The rain that had been holding off began to fall, light and cloying—the kind that was like mist—until it continued and soaked through everything. He jogged through the park, keeping alert for the men who'd sought to hurt him. No doubt they wouldn't be satisfied with what they'd done.

Rain slicked his hair back and glued his clothes to his skin. Rivulets ran between his shoulder blades, down his spine, and into the back of his pants. While rain was part of living, he wouldn't miss fighting in it, or holding secret meetings in weather too bad for the delicate Romans to venture into. He was looking forward to being in the nice warm house and sleeping in a bed...even if it was alone.

Chapter 11

"YOU MADE IT BACK!" BRYCE HUGGED GINA.

"Careful of the dress." Gina kissed him and pushed him away.

Nadine tried to inch past, carrying the pale-pink bridesmaid dress. Fortunately, Gina hadn't gone for some awful meringue concoction. Instead, the bridesmaid dresses were simple and just below the knee. Something she should be able to wear again, in theory.

"I was beginning to think I should send out a search party." He tried to unzip the bag that was protecting the dress.

"Ugh, there was a car accident. People can't seem to drive in the rain." She smacked his hand away. "You can see it in a couple of days. I hope the rain has passed by then."

"I'm sure it will," Nadine said. She'd checked the forecast at least a dozen times. Now all she wanted to do was go to sleep. It was way past her bedtime and she had to work tonight.

"Can I at least see what the bridesmaids are wearing?" Bryce asked.

"Guys, I'm going to bed." She took a couple of steps away and almost thought she'd made it.

"Who are you bringing to the wedding, Nadine?" Bryce asked.

No one. She frowned and turned back to face him.

Tall, rugged, he looked like he could survive just about anywhere with a box of matches and a Swiss army knife. He could probably kill someone a dozen different ways with the same items…and Meryn could probably do the same.

"Not one of your mates. I'm kind of seeing someone."

Yeah, she kind of was. It felt nice to say it. Gina blinked and then stared like Nadine had sprouted horns and a tail or something. Bryce raised his eyebrows.

"Who?" He crossed his arms.

"Someone. He's British ex-army."

"Really? When did this happen? Where did you meet him? How come you never told me?" Gina's voice rose with each question.

"I met him two weeks ago and we sort of ran into each other again. It's only been a couple of dates." Not even dates. Date maybe, if she included buying him breakfast.

"You have to bring him." Gina nodded and smiled.

Bryce was looking at her, studying her. "He got a name?"

"I can't bring him. We're still getting to know each other. And yes, he has a name, but I'm not going to tell you so you can go do nefarious background checks."

Bryce put his hand over his heart. "Me?"

"Have you kissed him?" Gina asked.

Nadine shook her head but heat crept up her cheeks.

"You have. Please invite him. I want to meet him. The guy who you dated more than once—that's almost a record," Gina said with mock shock.

"It's him or my friend Blue." Bryce smiled, teasing.

Nadine knew she wouldn't be allowed to keep Meryn

a secret from her friend forever, but she'd hoped to keep it under wraps for a little longer, until she was sure there was something to talk about.

"Neither." Nadine lifted her chin ready to stare Bryce down.

"What did he do?"

"Don't know." Meryn hadn't said, just that he'd been a soldier.

"Why'd he get out?"

She almost mentioned Meryn's wife, but at the last moment decided she couldn't reveal that piece of information that had been told to her in confidence. "Personal reasons."

"Do you know them?"

"Yes. This isn't twenty questions."

"Are you sure you won't tell me his name?"

"I don't need you to look out for me." Yet a part of her was glad she had friends who actually cared.

"So you'll bring him, so we can meet the mystery guy?" Gina hooked her arm through Bryce's.

"I'll invite him, but he might have plans." Or he might run a mile, or she might forget to mention it, and thus save any further complications.

"I'm so glad you decided to see me, Mr. Nhial." Andrew Timms extended his hand to Solomon.

Solomon shook the offered hand and received a luke-warm, half-dead response. Since Mr. Timms didn't have the strength in his hand to shake properly, it was unlikely the lawyer had the strength of will to do anything that required a modicum of effort. His initial appraisal lowered.

"I always give a man a chance to speak."

"Which is exactly what I'd like to give you. I've read your case, the police reports, and I believe a gross miscarriage of justice occurred."

Solomon nodded once. He knew justice hadn't been dealt, but he doubted very much that Mr. Timms knew what had really happened. He doubted Mr. Timms had ever given goblins a moment's thought.

Mr. Timms continued with his sales pitch. "The detectives who took your statements have recently been convicted of corruption and falsifying evidence."

Solomon knew that. The prison had buzzed with people seeking retrials, claiming they'd been set up even before the detectives had been convicted. The conviction this week had been the lead news story, taking over from a football scandal and a well-known lawyer who'd been caught embezzling funds.

"There was no evidence at the scene of my wife's murder." None that made any sense and none that would exonerate him.

"There was blood."

"My wife's blood."

"It was never DNA tested. The killer's blood could be there. The other substance, the black oil, could be tested more thoroughly." Mr. Timms paused and looked hard at Solomon. "Despite the fact you had no alibi for the night, you have always maintained your innocence. Don't you want to be vindicated?"

Solomon glanced at his hands, but only for a second; Mr. Timms was the kind of man that shouldn't ever be left unwatched.

"The night my wife was killed, my daughter was

left alone until I finished my cab shift. I was the prime suspect from the moment I rang the police. All I wanted then was someone to listen and let me look after my little girl. My girl is now an adult. I'm an old man. Rehashing history isn't going to bring back the lost twenty years of my life." He'd never given up on seeing Nadine again. He still hoped, now that he was free, she'd call or write. If he gave up, he might as well stop breathing.

"But everyone will know that you are innocent."

"Only if you're successful." Solomon's voice was quiet and steady. The lawyer was hoping his case would raise his own profile.

"We have a watertight case. Once the media gets involved, everyone will be talking about the corruption, racism, and failure of the legal system."

"The legal system didn't fail; it did the best it could at the time. I know how guilty I looked. I know there was no other suspect. So unless you know who killed my wife, I don't think you can help me."

"You don't want your case reexamined?" Mr. Timms asked as if he wasn't sure he'd heard correctly.

"No." There was no point. Michaline's killer wasn't of this world. He'd seen the goblin army chase down the dark streets as if the gates of hell had opened and let the demons out for the night—evil beasts ridden by twisted, damned souls. His wife had been obsessed by all things goblin and witnessing the Wild Ride on winter solstice was the highlight of each year. She would have watched it that night, and he was sure she'd been taken by it.

His fingers traced the crucifix tattooed on the back of his hand. *Thank you, Lord, for sparing Nadine*.

Mr. Timms leaned back in his padded leather chair, a sly glint in his narrowed eyes. The man was more slippery than wet soap. "Did you actually do it, is that why you don't want the case looked at?"

Solomon looked at the lawyer. He had nothing more to say to the man who was seeking to use the misfortune of others to build his career.

"Good day, Mr. Timms." Solomon stood. Sometimes the past was best left in the past. Digging it up would take everything he had left. Faith, hope, and love.

Chapter 12

MERYN WAS EARLY. HE'D GONE TO BED BEFORE IT was dark and woken before it was dawn. His heart pounded as he'd reached for the light, half expecting his nightmare to be in bed with him. But there'd been nothing there, no blood and no dust and no body. His dream had remained inside his head. The small measure of relief that brought wasn't enough to erase the fear that flowed in his veins. It hadn't been Idella dying in his arms; it had been Nadine. And once again he'd been helpless to do anything. He'd ended up sitting at the dining room table, tracing out letters and trying to learn how to write his name until daylight. Now he was hoping, praying to any god who cared, that Nadine would show up and his nightmare hadn't harmed her.

He walked past the bench and along the road, unable to be still and do nothing but wait. He watched the shadows shift on the sundial as the sun broke free of the hills in the east and climbed higher, pushing away the clouds. It was still overcast, and there'd be more rain. But for the moment, everything was fresh and new and glistening.

He turned and strode back to wait for Nadine. He didn't just want to know she was unharmed; he wanted to see her again, kiss her again. Beautiful, kind, and interested in talking to him. She was different from the women of the Decangli. Nadine hadn't been hardened by war and invasion. Yet, in her smile, there were secrets she didn't want to share. That alone made him want to coax them out of her in soft whispers as she lay in his bed.

He didn't sit, as the bench was wet, but he didn't have long to wait. Nadine ran toward him, a smile forming on her lips. He let the tension he'd been holding close ease. His nightmare had been his alone. The concern that his nightmares might harm another faded. Like any other person, his nightmares lived only when he slept. He had broken the connection to the Shadowlands.

"Meryn." Nadine came up beside him, her eyes bright in the cold. She pulled things out of her ears and bundled up the white cord.

They were almost the same height. He was maybe three finger widths taller. The space around her neck was still empty. Where the cross should have hung between her collarbones, there was nothing but smooth, tawny skin. His fingers twitched as he wanted to touch the bare piece of skin, but he didn't let them in case they traveled too far.

He needed to find a way to return her cross. When he'd taken it, he'd been hoping to become goblin again; with every passing day he was glad it hadn't worked.

"Good morning." He smiled, glad she'd come back after yesterday's kiss.

She stepped closer, and her eyebrows raised a fraction as if she were waiting for something. Her lips curved and parted as if she was daring him to kiss her again, only this time without her asking first.

And if he was wrong?

Her chin tilted and she held his gaze. He wasn't. A woman didn't look at a man like that without having something on her mind. Their lips met. Gently at first, to test her desire, to see if this was what she really wanted, and then to test his own. As a goblin, women were only short-lived queens and gold was always valued more. But at that moment he didn't care if he never saw gold again. The very human heat of desire flooded his blood and slid through every nerve, tempting him with sensations that he'd thought lost.

He cupped her cheek as he learned the shape of her mouth—cautious, as if he'd forgotten what true tenderness was after centuries of fighting just to stay alive. Her hand slid around his neck, her fingers threading into his hair. Nadine wasn't shy about what she wanted. Her lips parted and her tongue darted over his lip. Smooth like silk, enticing and teasing, seeking more. He returned in kind and the game fueled the fire, hardening his flesh and knotting his stomach with desire. He didn't just want sex for the first time in centuries; he wanted Nadine.

With a last caress, he drew back and her fingers trailed along his shoulders before falling away. He missed her touch immediately.

She gave a little sigh, but she was smiling and her brown eyes shimmered with desire. She wanted him as much as he wanted her. He drew a sharp breath as he realized that what he felt was moving beyond friendship, or even attraction.

Nadine took his hand. "It is a good morning, but it's not going to last. There's another storm front coming."

"I thought as much." A winter with permanently blue skies and mild weather was too much to ask. They started walking toward the café.

He could almost hear the questions forming on her

lips about whatever she'd found out about him. He decided to make the first move and bring it into the open, instead of leaving it to fester.

"So what did you learn about me on the Internet?" He still didn't know what that was, but it was obviously a place where knowledge was kept—a very big place if it contained records on everyone.

"That you were in the army. That you were married. That after…after Idella you went AWOL and were discharged." She turned her head to look at him as if hoping he'd fill in a few more details. "You're not working now are you?"

"No." He didn't know what he could do. The only job he'd known he didn't want and he was pretty sure swords were obsolete—he hadn't seen one since he'd been here. "I moved here for a second chance, a clean start without being surrounded by the past. It followed."

She probably thought him weak for still being haunted by his wife's death, but the pain had faded, as if the passage of time had dulled the edge.

Nadine stopped walking and turned to face him. "I know you've probably heard it all before, but I *do* understand what you're going through. I know what it's like to lose someone you love."

He frowned. Had she been married before?

"My mother was killed twenty years ago. I didn't speak for months after she died. The psychologist said I'd suffered a great trauma." Her free hand fluttered to her neck, as if she expected the cross to be there. "I still have the occasional nightmare. So I get that it still hurts."

The cross he'd stolen was somehow connected her to

her mother. The guilt he'd been carrying burst like a boil and left a bitter taste in his mouth. "Does it get easier?"

She shrugged. "I think you learn to live with it. It's always there and never goes away, and the scar becomes a part of you."

"I'm sorry you had to grow up without a mother." He was sorry he'd taken her cross, not that he could ever say that. How could he give her back her cross without Nadine hating him? He knew if he kept it he'd hate himself and it would be there between them, like a poisoned blade every time they spoke, every time they touched, every time they kissed.

"I had plenty, lots of foster parents."

Foster parents? "What happened to your father?"

She glanced up sharply, her lips pressed tight as if she didn't want to talk about it.

"I shouldn't have asked." Meryn backtracked, but he wanted to know about Nadine, how she'd grown up, what she'd done. What she liked to do when she wasn't running or working.

"It's okay, you would've found out eventually." She glanced away as if she couldn't look at him while she told him. "My father killed my mother. He spent twenty years in prison. He's a free man now, but I still have the nightmares of breaking glass and endless screaming."

Meryn touched her cheek, but there were no tears to brush away; it was just a fact of her life. Her scar. "You were there?"

She rested her head against his hand. "I was, but I don't remember anything. Whatever I saw, I've suppressed, according to the shrinks."

Shrinks? They were obviously people who offered

advice. What would they say about him? He couldn't imagine a man who would kill his wife in front of their child.

Nadine took a breath. "Were you there?"

Meryn nodded. "I was too late, and I couldn't do anything but watch as they killed my daughters first, and then Idella and the baby she carried."

"That's awful and you remember it all."

"Every scream." He looked away. "I was numb for a long time trying to hide from it, but that didn't help." The lie slid out so easily because it was almost true—if by numb he meant goblin.

She covered his hand with hers. He wanted her to know the truth and understand the kind of life he'd lived before, but he couldn't. He felt the weight of the past around his neck.

He touched the torque he'd worn since accepting the responsibility of aiding Roan. He couldn't tell her, but he could share it with her. She saw the gesture but said nothing, waiting for him to explain.

"It was a gift, many years ago." He pulled it off and handed it to her. "From a life I no longer have."

She ran her fingers over the smooth metal, her fingers tracing the heads of the wolves as the faced each other on each end. "It's beautiful."

He rubbed the back of his neck, not missing the weight or what it had meant. Nadine went to hand the torque back to him. He looked at it, and then at her and her bare throat. It was a fair exchange. They would each own a piece of the other's past.

"Keep it," he said with a smile.

Nadine gasped. "Oh, I couldn't."

Meryn lifted it from her hand and placed it on her neck. His fingers brushed against her skin for a moment, but the contact simmered in his veins stronger than any yearning for gold. It had literally been centuries since he'd even thought about having a woman. Yet around Nadine, he knew the feeling and welcomed it. He'd had his heart cut out once, but he wasn't afraid to risk it again. A life without love wasn't worth living.

—m—

Nadine let the torque settle around her neck. The metal was warm from his skin. Her fingers touched the wolves. Were they snarling or grinning? She couldn't be sure; she hadn't been able to study them and taking it off now wasn't the right thing to do. "Why wolves?"

"Pack animals." His fingers traced up her neck, caressed the curve of her jaw. She turned her head into his touch. His hands were roughened yet gentle.

"You miss your old life."

"I can miss it all I want, but it won't change anything. It's gone." He sounded resigned. "I have to appreciate what I have now." He placed a kiss on her lips that left no doubt how much he appreciated her in his life.

Nadine had exactly the same feeling. She looked forward to seeing Meryn each morning. His stubble grazed her cheek, but she liked that he wasn't clean-shaven and smooth-skinned.

Her stomach did a little spin and she knew this was growing faster than she thought possible. Maybe that was a good sign, and it meant everything was good. Or maybe she was jumping blindly off a cliff and she should have let Bryce do a more detailed search on who Meryn was. No, she couldn't go through life researching boyfriends. It took away the fun and the thrill of discovery.

She smiled against his lips and drew back. "I need that coffee." And the sugar fix.

This time Meryn pulled out what looked like a new leather wallet and paid.

Her hand fluttered to the torque as they walked to a table in a sunny corner—the same one as last time. The torque had to be valuable. Had his wife given it to him, was that why he wore it? It was an odd piece of jewelry, but then he was Welsh, so maybe he'd been into all that Celtic revival stuff, the crafts and reenactments. She glanced at Meryn and tried to imagine him in a plaid cloak, brandishing a sword. It wasn't that hard. That first night he'd been wearing a cloak, and the cops had taken his sword.

He caught her staring. "Do you not like it?"

"I do, but won't you want it back?"

Meryn looked at her as if he was seeing her in a new light. "No. Seeing it on you makes me happy." He smiled and the dimple formed in his cheek.

Nadine sat, stretched out her legs, and rested her elbows on the table, determined to continue getting to know Meryn while her coffee cooled. Only this time she wouldn't ask questions that came with loaded answers.

"So, what did you do in the army?"

"Battle planning, strategy."

"Officer?"

He looked at her for a moment.

"Or will you have to kill me if you tell me?" she said with a smile.

"I was high ranking."

And he'd fallen about as far as anyone could. He'd had everything and in a few violent moments it had been taken. She knew that feeling, even if she didn't really remember what it had felt like to have a real family. She had impressions and memories, but how could she trust them when all she remembered of her father was laughter and joy?

She took a bite of cake. She probably shouldn't be eating cake this early in the morning, but it was the end of the day for her. Cake for dinner was probably just as bad. Last time it had been a muffin; around Meryn she was developing bad habits. She glanced at him but he didn't seem to care what was appropriate breakfast food as he sampled his cake, white chocolate and berries.

Who made the rule that cake wasn't breakfast food anyway?

Around Meryn, rules didn't seem to matter, although he must have obeyed and followed orders once. "The army won't take you back?"

"No. I broke, Nadine. I'm still mending. I like spending time with you, but maybe I am not the man you want to be around."

But she did want to be around him. She bit the inside of her lip. Should she ask? What was the harm? What if he said no? She took a breath. It was short notice, but it would be nice not to go to a wedding alone. It was more than that; she wanted to go to the wedding with him. Be seen with him—and see her friends' eyes widen in disbelief.

"Are you doing anything tomorrow?" Her heart raced, and it had nothing to do with the coffee or the run she'd done. Tension crawled down her back as he frowned. "It's okay if you are, it's nothing."

"I'm free—what am I agreeing to?"

"It's Gina's wedding. Would you like to come as my date?" That wasn't so hard, was it? She wanted to wilt. That one little question had sucked up all her courage and strength of will.

"I'd like that very much." He reached out and touched her hand for just a second. "Thank you for inviting me."

Nadine let out a relived sigh. "Right, it's at ten in the big rotunda. I'll have to meet you there, as I'm a bridesmaid and have stuff to do, but afterward, there'll be a lunch and drinks." And she was talking too much. He'd already said yes.

For a few minutes they ate in silence, as she realized she didn't know the basics about him. "Can I be nosy?"

He took a drink of his coffee. "If I can be."

Her heart gave a nervous stutter, but he already knew about her mother, and she couldn't ask him questions without giving something back. Maybe getting to know someone wasn't that hard...all it took was the right person to make it easy. "Okay. How old are you?"

"Thirty-seven. You?" He took a small spoonful of cake, watching her as he ate.

"Twenty-six." She wrapped her hands around the cup and let the heat soak into her skin. It wasn't the kind of heat she wanted to be feeling. She wanted skin on skin. "You saw action in the army?"

He nodded. "Do you like being a nurse?"

"I do." She broke of a small piece of orange and almond cake and chased it around the plate before stabbing it. "I broke my arm when I was eight. No one believed me at first." Her crying at night and being unable to sleep was nothing out of the ordinary. "When my arm swelled up, I was finally taken to the hospital. The nurse there was so kind. She didn't think I was weird or strange."

"I don't think you're strange."

"That's because you don't know enough about me yet."

"Try me."

"I can't sleep at night because I'm scared of the dark." She put the piece of cake in her mouth and waited for him to speak, sure she was never going to see him again after this and yet enjoying being able to talk freely.

"It's not the dark you need to be scared of, but the things it hides."

She forced herself to swallow the lump of cake. Was he being serious or making a very dry joke? She couldn't tell. "Thanks, that makes me feel so much safer."

"My eldest daughter, Branna, was scared of the dark. She always found a way to creep into our bed." Meryn's gaze flicked between her and his cake as if he were debating a more serious question.

"You look like you want to ask me something weighty."

Meryn nodded. "You would've been very small when your mother died. Do you remember her?"

Apparently he wasn't worried about sticking to the safe questions. Geez, they hadn't even covered favorite bands, movies, they'd gone straight for the deep and meaningfuls. What did she tell him? That she remembered her mother's cries for help, her orders for Nadine to run and hide? Then the raw screams of terror when she realized no one was going to help her as she was dragged out the window. For the first time she didn't feel like a freak. Meryn would know exactly what she meant.

"Bits. She had long black hair that she used to let me play with and fill full of clips and hairbands, and she had beautiful blue eyes. I wanted blue eyes like hers when I got older. I hated mine because they are the same as his. I have the eyes of a killer."

"You have beautiful eyes."

Nadine smiled and focused on drinking her coffee as her cheeks heated. She wasn't used to be being complimented. He had nice eyes too, gray but not cold. She put her cup down and finished answering the question. "Mostly I remember her reading to me. She always read me fairy tales before bed. I still have the book. She wrote her favorite in the front: *Le roi des gobelins*."

Meryn blinked, sure he'd misheard, but he hadn't. *Gobelins*. Goblins. The language was too familiar. The words the woman had called out as she'd fought against the goblins that had abducted her from the Fixed Realm, her long dark hair tangled in the fists of the *gobelins*, as she'd called them. He looked at Nadine and saw too many similarities in the shape of her face and the curve of her lip. Was the woman he'd seen kill herself in the Shadowlands Nadine's mother? How long ago had that been? He had no way of measuring the time. Or was he grasping for connections?

Nadine sat up straight, her eyes wide. "You know it? No one else has heard of it. My mother loved *The Goblin King*."

He didn't know the fairy tale. He knew the reality. "Maybe not the same one," he said slowly. This was dangerous territory.

"I'll tell you my mother's version." She rushed on as if eager to share what she knew. "Once upon a time there was a king…" She recited the story without break. Each word and each inflection well used, like a bard that had told the same tale many a time. Like all good stories, it never grew tired.

Meryn didn't speak. He didn't know what to say. Their story had survived as a children's fable. Had Dai been responsible for this version?

"Is it the same as the story you know?" Her eyes were bright as if she was hoping he would agree.

He took a sip of the hot coffee. "Not quite."

"How is it different?"

Meryn swallowed down his doubt about sharing. "The men were wrongly cursed by a druid. And at the end they got free." Would Nadine believe he was one of those men? No, loving a fairy tale was different from living it. If she knew he'd been a goblin for so many years, she'd be horrified. Yet he didn't want to keep lying to her. He wanted to be able to talk about his life freely.

Nadine leaned forward, her eyes lit by curiosity. "How?"

"The king found love." A love strong enough to overlook his hideous goblin visage in the Fixed Realm. Love was something Roan would never have found as King of the Decangli. He would have married for alliance to strengthen the tribe, the same way Meryn had in marrying Idella. But Meryn knew how lucky he'd been to find love while still doing his duty to the tribe.

She leaned back and laughed. "That's the beauty of fairy tales. Love is always perfect. The reality sucks."

"You don't believe in love?" Love was what made live worth living.

"Falling in love with my father got my mother killed."

"Love doesn't kill." He was sure of that. A man

would do anything to protect his family. He glanced at his hands. He'd done everything he could—but the curse had bound him tighter than any rope. "But losing it hurts."

"You still love your wife?"

He was silent for several breaths. "Yes." It was the truth. He would probably love her forever. She was his first love and he hers. He was learning to live with her memory and the pain it caused. When Nadine looked at him he felt like he had a chance to be happy again. "But it's not the same as it was, and never will be."

Meryn took another taste of his drink and pretended he liked it. "Can I ask about your father?"

He needed to know if what he suspected was the truth, or his mind making desperate connections between the woman in the Shadowlands and Nadine.

She shrugged. "There's nothing to say. He went to prison, and I haven't spoken to him since."

"Not once?" He would do anything to hear his children speak again, if only one word. One sleepy sigh. One smile. Nadine's father had lost his wife and child to the goblins.

"He ruined my life."

"He's still your father," Meryn said. She couldn't understand the agony the loss of a child caused a parent.

"He pleaded not guilty and was given a life sentence."

"If he pleaded not guilty, maybe he isn't guilty." If the goblins had taken her mother, then her father was innocent, his life and family ruined by the selfish whims of goblins. How could Meryn have ever thought giving in was a solution? But he hadn't been thinking. He'd been out of his mind with grief. No one would have been able to stop him from fading. Dai understood that; did Roan?

Nadine put down her cup and crossed her arms. "You don't know anything about it."

"I know what it feels like to lose a family, to lose children who barely had a chance to live." His voice was rough as the hurt resurfaced, but it didn't drag him down and suck him under this time.

She scowled at him and he knew he'd exposed a very tender wound. When Nadine finally spoke, it was soft and firm as if this was the end of the conversation. "It's not the same." She stood.

Meryn pushed his chair back and got up, determined not to let her walk out while she was mad at him—it was much easier to never come back. "No. You still have a chance. I lost everything. I think of my kids every day, I think of the things I could've done differently to save them, I think of the things I could've done better as a parent. I spent so much time away from them. None of it changes what happened. Nothing ever will. Maybe he has the same thoughts." She opened her mouth, and Meryn held up his hand and continued. "You don't have to like them or agree with them. But you will always be his daughter, regardless of what happened to your mother."

She pressed her lips together and looked at the ground before looking back at him. In that moment the anger that tightened her features had softened, a little. "I'm not used to people defending him. Most people see the color of his skin and assume he did it."

What did the color of someone's skin have to do with guilt or innocence? "You assumed he did," he said softly, not wanting the argument to flare up again, yet needing it resolved.

"Everything says he did. What am I supposed to believe, a vague hope that he didn't and he's wasted all that time behind bars?"

Meryn looked at his hands. They still carried the scars and callouses he'd earned over years of handling weapons as a man. The ones he'd gained as a goblin had vanished, as if the time he'd spent in the Shadowlands had never existed. The knowledge of what he'd seen and done hadn't. He was sure he'd seen Nadine's mother die in the Shadowlands.

He wanted to be able to tell her everything, yet he knew that wasn't possible.

"I think everyone deserves a chance to tell their side, and that sometimes, if they are really lucky, they get a second chance." He took her hand. She was his second chance. A chance he'd never dreamed of.

She stared at their hands for a moment before looking up. Her eyes were shiny, but she was smiling. She shook her head. "Do you always believe the best in people?"

"No." He'd seen evil at work in the Fixed Realm long before he learned how callous a goblin could be. "But people should have the opportunity to speak before being condemned."

Would she let him speak if he tried to tell the truth and explain her mother's tale was real? It was a risk he wasn't ready to take yet, and he hated himself in that moment. While she was being open, he was still hiding and he could feel the gulf between them widen.

Nadine stepped closer, her body only a hand span

away from his. "I'll take that under advisement." Her hand trailed up his chest and landed on his shoulder.

His muscles tensed beneath her palm as their gazes locked. For a moment neither of them moved. Then Meryn lowered his mouth to hers in a soft kiss.

"So I'm still invited tomorrow?" he said against her lips.

"Mmm." She drew back, the heat in her eyes setting his blood alight. "I look forward to seeing you in a suit." She winked, then pulled her hand free of his and started walking away.

He watched her go; this time she turned and waved. He was sure she knew what she was doing to him. And he was enjoying it.

Chapter 13

MERYN'S WORDS ECHOED IN HER MIND. *MAYBE HE isn't guilty*.

Maybe it was time she faced the past and put it in the ground for good. On the train ride home she replayed every memory she had and tried to force the memory of that night to the surface, but all she got was breaking glass and screaming.

When she got home, the house was silent. She let the tension in her shoulders ease. After a shower and changing into pajamas, she took a deep breath and pulled out the box of letters and also the folder full of newspaper articles that she'd printed from the Internet as a teenager, when she'd been trying to understand everything she'd been told for the past decade. Back then they hadn't helped. They'd left her more confused about why he never fought to be free. Why plead not guilty but then never ask for a retrial or a lesser sentence?

What had her mother thought when she began seeing Solomon? Did they sneak around, or were they open? Michaline must have seen something in him to love, to risk her mother's wrath and travel halfway across the globe.

Despite the drama and struggle that must have been for them both, she only had vague happy memories of a childhood cut short by screaming and breaking glass. In her mind, the glass shattered again and again and again. In her nightmares, the glass shattered, spilling onto the floor. Why would her father break the window to get in?

He wouldn't break the window—unless he was trying to make it look like someone else had done it.

For a moment she didn't move. Couldn't move.

Maybe he wasn't guilty. Her heartbeat slowed as she considered the possibility seriously. She ignored the box of letters from her father and took out a folder. Carefully, she flicked through the old printouts. The headings were different when read with an adult's eye, especially one open to the idea that not everything was as it seemed. Instead of seeing the scandal of a black man killing his wife, she saw the racism. She saw police looking for a quick conviction in a case with no real evidence and no motive. While the media had fed off the story, there was very little fact, just endless speculation about how Michaline had died and where her body was. She had never been found. Nadine bit her lip.

She glanced at the shoebox of letters on the floor. Twenty years' worth of birthday and Christmas letters, except for the first few they were all unread. Would the answer be in there? What could he tell her that would make up for the years of being the unwanted child? So unlovable even her grandmother hadn't come for her and her father hadn't fought to get free.

She had wasted so many wishes and prayers on the hopeless dream that her parents would reclaim her and everything would be okay, until eventually she had given up. Somewhere between the ages of eight and nine, she'd realized this was her life now. Her mother was dead and her father had done it. Everybody said so, so it must be true. After that, she'd sworn she'd never read any letter from him, yet here she was.

Because of Meryn. He didn't take the same opinion as everyone else. That was why she liked him. He wasn't like everyone else. He was different and didn't care. He could've lied about everything but hadn't. Meryn woke something inside her; he made her want to believe in fairy tales again, that evil could be defeated and that everyone got a happily-ever-after. He made her want to believe in love again and that there was a prince waiting for her if she wished hard enough. Because of him she was braver.

Nadine picked up the first letter. It had been written while her father was still awaiting trial, someone had read it to her as the envelope had been opened.

> *Dearest Nadine,*
>
> *I'm very sad I couldn't go to Mummy's funeral. I know you are sad too, but we will be together again soon.*
>
> *All my love and prayers,*
> *Dad*

She blinked back the tears that formed. She hadn't really understood what was happening, why her father wasn't there, or why her mother wasn't coming back. She'd been interviewed and asked to draw pictures. They wanted her to do something. And she had been unable to do anything. The next letter had arrived two weeks after her birthday. By then she knew that her grandmother wasn't going to take her in and she was going to be left in the care of strangers. Her father must have known as well.

> *Dearest Nadine,*
>
> *Happy Birthday! A big six-year-old. How is school going? The pictures you sent me are very beautiful. I love the castle. Is that you in the window?*
> *It is good news you are staying in Australia. It means we can still be close. Be good for your foster mother.*
>
> *All my love and prayers,*
> *Dad*

She'd never sent him anything. Her foster mother must have sent him some of her schoolwork and drawings. That would have stopped when she'd refused to even be read the letters.

But like clockwork, his letters had arrived on her birthday and at Christmas. When her pictures stopped being sent he never mentioned it. No letters begged for her to come and see him, and none proclaimed his innocence. Tears trickled down her cheek and splashed on her hand. All were about how much he loved and missed her. He'd never stopped loving her, even when she'd stopped loving him.

She swallowed, even though her throat was blocked with years of unshed tears. Maybe if she had been able to remember what had happened that night her father wouldn't have been found guilty. It was her fault.

She'd always known that. It was why she'd refused
to see him or read his letters. She was afraid he would
blame her—yet not one letter pointed the finger at her.
He hadn't just lost his wife that night; he'd lost his
daughter too.

Her eyes closed in sudden understanding. Her heart
swelled and made breathing impossible. Meryn had lost
his wife and children; that was why he'd reacted so pas-
sionately about her cutting off her father. She was alive
and still had a chance to speak to her father. For Meryn
that opportunity was lost.

Had her father ever thought she was lost to him?

She reread through the letters but found nothing. The
letters he sent to her were hopeful…even the last one,
sent after he'd left prison.

> *Dearest Nadine,*
>
> > *I hope you are well and that you are happy.
> > I am beginning my life again. I realize you
> > may not wish to contact me, but if you choose
> > to, I would very much like to hear your voice.
> > If not, I shall write again for your birthday. It
> > is hard to believe twenty years have passed and
> > you are no longer my little girl.*
> >
> > *All my love and prayers,*
> > *Dad*

She stared at the phone number at the bottom of the letter. One phone call and she would know the answer.
And then?

Then she would be free and maybe the nightmares would stop. Her smile didn't banish her tears, but she didn't care. She got up and went to find the phone.

———

After a fitful sleep, Nadine turned off her alarm and lay still for a moment longer. Her stomach was knotted. It was nerves, she knew that, but she didn't know how to settle them.

When she was younger, she'd imagined what it would be like to see her father again. At first it was excitement and a happy reunion; as a teen she'd thought she'd be cool and aloof to prove he couldn't hurt her and she didn't care.

Now she had no idea.

The phone call had been hard to make. Neither of them sure what to say, only that maybe meeting in person would be easier—of course he'd waited for her to suggest it, but she'd heard the happiness in his voice and it had made her sad that meeting her in a public place for a few minutes could make him feel so joyous. Had he had nothing to be happy about in twenty years?

Probably not. What a waste of a life.

Nadine sucked in a breath and got out of bed. She dressed and went into the living area, hoping Gina was home. She was painting her toenails with her foot propped on the coffee table.

Gina lifted her head. "You ready to do this?"

"As I'll ever be." After calling her father she'd phoned Gina. Of course Gina had to go with her.

Gina wriggled her toes and nodded. "I'm dry enough to travel." She looked at Nadine. "How about I drive?"

Nadine handed over the keys without argument. It

wasn't long before Gina was parking the car a short way away from their meeting spot, a popular coffeehouse.

"Are you ready to do this?"

Nadine bit her lip and nodded. She'd been waiting most of her life to re-meet her father. "What if he's horrible?" she said quietly.

It was the one thing that had been tormenting her since calling him. Maybe she was rushing this, acting on impulse before thinking things through.

But then she thought of Meryn and the look in his eyes when he talked about his children. He'd give anything to see them one more time.

"Then you don't have to stay." Gina twisted in the car seat to look at her. "One cup of coffee. Hell, you don't even need to order. Just get a glass of water. I'll sit where I can see you. It will be fine."

It'll be fine.

If she told herself that enough times maybe it would be. She was down to half a glass of water. He was late, by five minutes—but that was better than early. At least she'd had time to get seated, and try and put on a calm face, instead of revealing the stressed-out crazy person running around inside her. She glanced at Gina, but Gina was flicking through a magazine and enjoying a giant iced coffee.

How much longer should she wait? Maybe he'd gotten cold feet. Was this as hard for him as it was for her?

"Nadine?"

Her head snapped up and she was looking at an old man with graying hair. His skin was darker than hers, but his eyes were the same. A muddy mix of green and brown. He'd always said they were from his missionary father—the only thing he'd gotten from him.

What did she call him? He wasn't Daddy anymore, but Solomon seemed too cold and impersonal.

"Hi." Her cheeks tightened with a nervous smile and her eyes darted once again to Gina, who was now taking a long drink from her iced coffee. "Have a seat. Umm. Did you want to order anything?"

"I'm good, thank you for asking." He sat and scanned her as if looking for something he recognized. "You…you grew up."

Nadine nodded, her throat suddenly tight.

"I'm very grateful you called. I never expected it." Solomon clasped his hands and rested them on the table.

"You wrote every birthday and Christmas." And every time he must have hoped for a reply.

"I never stopped caring about you. I didn't want you to think I'd forgotten you."

"I hated the letters. They reminded me of what had happened." Her voice wavered and she had to blink back the tears that burned her eyes. She wasn't going to cry in front of him. Cool and composed. This was a simple meeting to find out some details.

Solomon lowered his gaze to his hands. A cross was tattooed, prison style, on the back of his left hand. "I'm sorry. I wanted to do the right thing."

"I grew up being told you did it, the newspapers said you did it, but you maintained you didn't."

"I love Michaline. I love you. If I had been there—"

"So you weren't there?" Most nights it was just Nadine and her mother while Solomon drove a taxi. He used to tell her tales of all the movie stars and princes and princesses he drove around. And she'd believed him.

"I was looking for fares. I wish I'd given up and come home sooner. I would've done anything to protect her and you."

She watched him as he spoke. He didn't seem to be lying. But then he'd had two decades to perfect the lie. No fares meant no alibi. These days there was GPS tracking and no doubt of his whereabouts; there would also be more extensive forensic testing. How different would her life have been? She squashed the thought. Musing about the past wouldn't change it, no, but it could be reexamined.

"You didn't do it?"

"I came home and found you under the table crying. I rang the police. That was the last time I saw you." His face crumpled for a moment before he regained his composure. He was fighting to stay calm, just as hard as she was.

"Why not reopen the case and prove your innocence? Why serve all those extra years?" Why leave her adrift in foster homes?

"Why? Would it bring your mother back? Would it give you back your childhood and the family you deserved? I know the truth and I don't need the rest of the world to understand."

"*I* need to understand."

"Nadine, if I'd asked for the case to be reexamined everything would have been dragged out again. The lawyers would've dragged you into it because you were the only witness. The media would've ripped into your life." He shook his head. "I couldn't do that to you. I won't do that to you."

She bit her lip. "You never asked for a retrial because of me?"

"What else could I do?"

She didn't know. If he was guilty, it was a good excuse. If he was innocent, it was the ultimate sacrifice. There was no way for her father to prove he didn't kill her mother without everything being scrutinized. She'd never liked being the center of attention. Only a handful of people knew about her life.

"I don't know." She wanted to believe him, but there was something…something he wasn't saying, but she couldn't accuse him of anything based on a vague hunch.

Solomon pursed his lips and nodded. "You have a good life now?"

"I'm a nurse."

"Well done. I'm very proud of you."

It was all too late. He should have been there when she graduated. She glanced up at the ceiling, trying to clear her eyes of the tears trying to form. "You got your horticulture degree."

"Your mother always wanted me to do what I loved, instead of driving cabs."

She knew the story of how they'd met. Her mum had been a teacher at a school and her father the gardener. Their relationship had raised eyebrows and been a scandal in her grandmother's social circles. They'd married in secret, and when her grandmother had found out, she'd disowned Michaline. They'd come to Australia to start a new life.

"Do you have children?" Solomon asked hopefully.

Nadine shook her head. How did she tell him that because of him she'd been afraid to put her heart on the line?

"I don't expect to be part of your life again. But I would like it if we could keep in touch."

"Birthdays and Christmases?"

"I'd like that. I realize it must be hard for you to trust me after everything. I just hope you can eventually forgive me for not fighting to clear my name."

"I'm sorry I said nothing." If she'd remembered what had happened, she might have been able to keep her father out of prison.

"You were a child. I was told how traumatized you were; they tried to use that against me. It's why I let the thought of a retrial go. I couldn't put you through more when it was obvious you didn't remember."

The breaking glass was all she saw. Surely the police must have wondered why he'd broken a window? They must have questioned the lack of a body. "I still don't remember."

"It's okay. You aren't to blame. The animal who took your mother is."

"Do you know who it was?" And if she knew, what then? Would that prove her father was innocent if she could blame someone else?

Solomon looked out the window then back at her. "No."

That wasn't the entire truth. Was that his secret? Was he protecting someone? Suddenly she didn't want to be sitting here with him even though they were surrounded by people.

"Okay." Aside from knowing why her father had never fought the conviction she had no other answers. "I should probably get going."

"Thank you for seeing me. I appreciate how difficult it must have been for you."

He was still concerned about her, even though he'd served twenty years for a crime he probably didn't commit—but knew something about.

"Thank you for coming." It seemed so formal and awkward. "Maybe we can meet again some time." Or maybe not. Maybe just the odd phone call until he told her what he knew.

"I'd like that." Her father stood. "I do some volunteer work at Kings Park if you're ever there."

Nadine's heart jumped but she said nothing. She didn't want to share that she ran there. Not yet. It seemed too personal to let him in on her routine. Should she find a new running route? But that would take her away from Meryn. "I'll keep that in mind."

"That would be nice." He smiled. It was the one she remembered from when she was little and he would build a block tower just so she could knock it down. "Take care, Nadine."

He walked out of the café and left her sitting with too many questions and not enough answers or time or tears. If she could remember what happened that night, she'd know if her father was innocent and what he was hiding. Without those memories, all she had was his word. Was that enough?

Chapter 14

MERYN READ THE INSTRUCTIONS AGAIN. THEY WERE perfectly clear on how he should operate the phone, but they didn't tell him what he should say. He forced out a short sigh. Dwelling on what might happen wouldn't change anything. Sometimes the only thing to do was act. He dialed the number before he could talk himself out of it again, and waited while the phone made chirping noises.

"Meryn." Dai's voice floated near his ear like magic. He knew it wasn't; it was just another piece of technology he'd have to learn how to use properly and eventually understand.

"Yes." What did he say? Take me to Roan? The pause extended into an awkward silence.

"Would you prefer me to come over and talk face to face?"

It wasn't the use of the phone that was the problem. Meryn blinked slowly as he pulled together what was left of his pride and courage, ready to sacrifice them before his king. He had to do this, so he might as well just get it done. "It's time I saw the king—if he'll see me."

"He's been waiting. Less than patiently."

That sounded like the Roan he knew. The air in his apartment swelled and sighed, then Dai was standing in the living room with a phone in his hand and an unnatural gleam in his eye.

Meryn stared at his cousin. It never seemed real that Dai could vanish and appear at will. A thought slid across his mind and caught, offering a glimmer of hope. Could Dai bend time so he could go back and give Nadine the cross? Go back so he never stole it?

"What else can you do?"

Dai slipped the phone into his pocket. "It's not what I can do. It's more of what I'm allowed to do. True magic is very rare now and fewer believe."

"Can you change the past?" Meryn put the phone on the table.

"No, and I wouldn't try. One change would have ripples that could cause damage never intended. It's not worth the risk. Besides, the past is what made you. Changing it would change you. Even *I* don't want to alter that."

Meryn nodded. If he changed the past he might never meet Nadine. He had to keep moving forward. "Will you take me to see my king?"

"You don't have to call him king."

"Until he tells me otherwise, he is still my king." And Meryn had no idea how much Roan had changed.

Dai offered his hand. "Come."

Meryn eyed Dai's hand. "We will travel by magic?"

"That's how I got here. It's not that bad and easier than driving a car."

Meryn took Dai's hand not sure what to expect. The ground vanished then slapped the soles of his shoes as he landed. His stomach bounced at the sudden shift in location. The dizziness and gut lurching was the same as being pulled from the Shadowlands. It took a couple of deep breaths to overcome the unnatural sensations of traveling via magic.

In a blink he'd gone from his house to the entrance of a palace—white tiles and walls, sparkling lights, and a grand staircase. Meryn let his gaze drift over the interior. This was truly a residence fit for a king.

"You'll get used to it." Dai kept his hand on Meryn's shoulder as if expecting him to fall over.

Meryn rolled his shoulder, throwing off the touch. No. He wouldn't be getting used to it. Men didn't pop in and out of air on a whim like gods.

"I'm fine," he lied as his stomach twisted into another knot. It was fear. And like any warrior about to face battle, he ignored it. It was there to let him know he was alive and that was all. Would it have been easier to see Roan at the park than coming here? It was never going to be easy; however, he was glad he'd waited until he was ready. If he'd stayed in Dai's tower and re-met Roan while he was half goblin and confused, all he would've seen was pity in Roan's eyes, and possibly disgust. This way they met as men.

"I thought we'd agreed that you'd knock." A man's voice rolled down the stairs.

Dai walked over and rapped on the wall twice. "I brought a guest."

Footsteps followed. Then a man in a paint splattered T-shirt and black multi-pocketed pants came down the stairs. Roan's feet were bare. No torque adorned his neck and no sword hung at his side, yet he was obviously a king. His king.

Meryn knelt and bowed his head. He didn't even have his sword to lay down before him because he'd lost it his first night in the Fixed Realm. Next to him Dai didn't move. Once Meryn would have stood and looked

Roan in the eye, but he'd been a different man then. One worthy of a king's friendship.

"Meryn, cousin. Rise," Roan said in Decangli, his footsteps drawing closer.

Meryn lifted his head but remained on his knees. "I would if I were worthy to stand." He'd seen men ask for forgiveness for lawbreaking and beg for leniency, yet he'd never suspected it would one day be him. He'd never pitied supplicants before, and he wasn't going to start now with himself. He swallowed, then forced out the words. "I abandoned my duty when I was most needed. I understand the nature of my crime and also the penalty. I accept your decision as law."

Once spoken, the burden he'd been carrying became lighter. He couldn't change the past—no man could, not even Dai had that power—but he could make reparation. And this was a start.

"That first night in the Shadowlands was hard on us all. I know what you saw and I'm sorry for your loss, for all the lives lost because of the rebellion I led."

"We all supported it." Dai spoke softly.

"But I had the final say. I have to live with that. There wasn't a day I didn't wonder if I could have done something differently. We all have to live with regrets. We don't have to let them rule us." Roan held out his hand. "You're forgiven."

Meryn looked at his cousin's hand. "You forgive me that fast?"

Roan squatted down. "I forgave you years ago. Thoughts of you kept us going when fading to goblin seemed like an easy way to end it. Your sacrifice gave us the strength to fight the curse." Roan's jaw tightened as if he were remembering those that didn't survive. "If you hadn't lost heart, we'd all have lost our souls to the curse." Roan stood, his hand outstretched. "Get up, Meryn. Here I'm no one's king."

Meryn took Roan's hand and rose. Almost as tall as Roan, it had been a long time since they'd been anything but king and council.

Roan drew him into an embrace. "It's good to have you back." Then he released Meryn, but Roan's gaze lingered on his cousin's face. "You did bring the Shadowlands with you."

"It was all I saw for too many years." The dullness and nothingness had gotten caught in his eyes and in his soul. But no more nightmares had crept out since he'd killed the goblin. He glanced at Dai, wondering how much Roan knew.

For a second, Dai's eyes glimmered with magic. "Meryn's ties to the Shadowlands are gone." He gave a small nod as if to reassure Meryn.

But Meryn already knew that connection was gone; he'd severed it with hope and the dreams of the life he wanted. While he might still have the occasional nightmare, at least they wouldn't follow him through into this world.

The three of them stood silent. With two millennia between them, no one knew where to start. Did Meryn want to know everything they had done? Would they want to know what he had done as a goblin? All that was best left well alone.

But it should've been six standing here reunited.

"Dai told me Brac, Fane, and Anfri didn't make it." None of them should've died. Their deaths, the

deaths of all the Decangli, were the traitor's fault.
One man had condemned the whole tribe. "I know it
will change nothing, but I would like to know who the
traitor was."

A look passed between Roan and Dai. Meryn's gut
tightened. He wasn't going to like the answer.

"It was Drem." Roan said. "Dai saw his body in the
general's quarters that night."

Meryn lowered his gaze to the floor, the betrayal by
his brother twisting in his gut even though it had happened so long ago. "I should've known."

Maybe if he'd been paying more attention to what was
going on and less attention to Idella and the baby—no,
he couldn't think like that. Every second he'd had with
her had been worth it.

"None of us did," Dai muttered.

Roan cut in, "We've had a long time to get used to
these things, Meryn. Drem was his own man, however
poor his choices; you aren't responsible for his actions.
We have made a memorial for Fane, Brac, and Anfri if
you'd like to see it?"

Meryn nodded and Roan let them out into the garden. Beneath a little house wedged up in a tree was a
plaque. Meryn stared at the metal as the engraved letters
un-jumbled. Reading, even with magic, required effort.
Three words. The names of the three who didn't make
it and who had died in the Shadowlands. Meryn closed
his eyes for a moment. *May they find peace in the hall
of the gods and a new life on the other side.*

"We buried their torques and swords. Ours too. No
one has swords these days."

"I'd noticed." No one carried weapons; it was odd.

Being weaponless was akin to being naked. "Mine was taken."

"I can get that back," Dai offered.

"With paperwork, not magic." Roan lips were smiling but his words were firm. Dai's magic use wasn't well accepted.

Dai smiled. "Yeah, yeah, of course. How about a drink for the dead?"

Roan glanced at Meryn. "You're staying."

Meryn nodded. He could stay for a while, but he had to be back home by morning for the wedding with Nadine. "I would like to sleep in my own bed."

In Dai's hands three beers appeared. He handed them out. The bottles were icy against Meryn's palm. He copied his cousins as they twisted off the tops and then sat on the grass.

"For the fallen, all of them," Roan said. He raised his drink and then took a long swallow.

Meryn and Dai did the same. Meryn coughed on the cold liquid. It wasn't what he was expecting. "What is this?"

"Beer, hundreds of different flavors, these days. You should try the wine. Much better than the Roman swill." Roan took another drink. "For a while there I didn't think we'd ever see you again."

"Particularly after you broke my sliding door to get out of my apartment."

Meryn winced; Dai had kept nothing from Roan. "I didn't know what was going on. I barely knew who I was when I was pulled out of the Shadowlands."

"I know," said Dai. "I checked on you in the hospital. What I saw filled me with doubt about how well you'd heal. You were tied to the Shadowlands after living and breathing it for so long."

"It's good you are well again; we lost too many." Roan's gaze was on the plaque.

It was such a small reminder of what had happened. The Roman coins in Meryn's pocket became heavy. He'd carried them for so long, as if in his heart he knew they had meaning even after his mind forgot. He couldn't spend them in this life, but the gold and silver could be put to use. He took out the coins and handed them to Dai. "Do you remember how Idella and the girls looked?"

Dai nodded. He should. Idella had looked after Mave, Roan and Dai's younger sister, and Dai had been a frequent visitor.

"Can you make the coins into something to honor them?"

Dai closed his eyes. For a few moments nothing happened, then the metal began to quiver. How much power did Dai have to melt gold and silver without heat? Enough to make the world bend to his will? In Dai's hand a gold disk formed. At the center, in silver, was a pregnant woman, each hand held by a little girl. "Will this serve?"

Meryn studied the image. He touched his wife's face, the likeness as he remembered her. "Add Mave, she was part of the family "

The surface of the metal behind Branna shimmered and an older girl appeared in silver. Dai met Meryn's gaze. "Thank you. She ought to be remembered."

Meryn inclined his head. Had Dai ever had a chance to really grieve after his sister's murder or had he always been wary of spilling the secret of her death? He touched the golden disk again. His family was long gone, living only in his mind. While he would always have his memories of Idella, he wanted a woman of flesh and blood, not whispers and shadows.

"It wasn't your fault." Roan put his hand on Meryn's shoulder.

"I know." Meryn let the disk go.

With magic, Dai stuck the new plaque to the tree. The past was there for all to see. It was a pity the future wasn't so clear, but he saw a glimmer when he was with Nadine.

Meryn raised the beer. "To Idella and the girls, I hope the lives they've lived since have been filled with joy."

Roan and Dai raised their bottles in salute before taking a drink. If they drank for everyone who'd died the night of the failed rebellion they'd be here all night and unable to walk in the morning.

Meryn switched the bottle to his other hand, his skin like ice. Sitting with his cousins felt so familiar it was almost as if no time had passed, and yet so much had. He stared at the tree, but the loss no longer cut him. The wound had healed so only the scar remained. Idella would want him to live, but tonight was about catching up with the past. Tomorrow he'd face his future.

"So, what did I miss while I was running with the goblins?"

Several beers later they were lying on the grass, looking up at the stars. Eliza had come out and introduced herself by bringing food and water, should they choose to start sobering up. The stars weren't spinning. He hadn't had that much to drink, but he had eaten well— toasted sandwiches; dips; crunchy, salty biscuits; and three types of cheeses. Even the Romans would be impressed with all the different foods available now.

He smiled to himself. While Dai and Roan hadn't told him everything that had happened over two thousand years—that would take a very long time—he'd got the short version with just the highlights and lowlights, including the death of the druid that had cursed them and how Dai had met his partner Amanda.

"How is the house?" Roan asked.

"Good." It was; he liked it very much. It was also reassuring to know that Dai lived somewhere else— Roan didn't expect them to all live together. Meryn glanced at Dai. There was one thing that still puzzled him about the house. It had been filled with everything he might need and more clothing than he could wear in a month if he wore something new every day. "Why were there no shoes?"

"I didn't know your size. I thought about putting some in there but in the end I figured one of us would take you shoe shopping. Probably not Roan, as he thinks all clothing can be bought at the army surplus store."

"I like boots that are comfortable and that don't fall apart. Besides, Meryn has shoes." Roan pointed at the black-and-white checked shoes.

Dai sat up and peered at Meryn's feet. "You do."

"I took myself shopping." Both of his cousins looked a little shocked. Meryn bit back the smile. "I'm managing fine."

"I can see that." Roan propped himself up and finished the last of his beer. "Another round?"

Meryn was tempted to say yes, simply because he was actually enjoying himself. But he didn't want a hangover tomorrow when he was accompanying Nadine to her friend's wedding. He pushed himself up. He was cold from lying still, but it was still warmer than the Shadowlands. "Not for me."

"Somewhere to be?" Roan asked, dusting grass off himself.

"Someone to see," Dai corrected.

Was he that transparent? Did it matter if they knew? "I have met someone. We see each other when she runs at the park."

"Ah, and you don't want to sleep late and miss her." Roan smiled.

"No, tomorrow her friend weds and she asked me to go with her."

Roan raised his eyebrows and even Dai looked surprised. Had they really expected him to be more dependent?

Dai looked at Meryn's feet again. "Well, there are suits in the closet, but you can't wear those shoes to a wedding."

"What shoes am I supposed to wear?" Would he have time to buy a new pair in the morning?

"Shoes that match a suit. Black, uncomfortable, with no grip on the sole," Roan said.

"Then why do people wear them if they are so impractical?" He'd seen men in the pointed toes shoes, and women in the spiked heels. Would Nadine be wearing shoes like that? He tried to imagine her dressed in something other than her running clothes and failed. He liked the close fit of her running clothes, the way they gave a suggestion of what was beneath without revealing anything.

"Because they look good. I think you're about my size." Roan looked at Dai. "Grab the ones I wore to get married in."

Dai closed his eyes. "Got them." A moment later they were sitting on the grass in front of his cousin. Dai shook his head as if trying to clear it. "No more beer, or no more magic tonight. The two still don't go well together."

"I can drive Meryn home." Roan stood and offered Meryn his hand. This time Meryn took it without hesitation.

He'd only been in a car when the police had arrested him, and he'd been too confused to enjoy it. He opened his mouth to speak but Dai mouthed *no*.

"It's okay. I have to get home too. I'll just have a couple of painkillers, a bit more to eat, and I'll be fine." Dai gathered up the beer bottles by hand.

Meryn picked up the food tray and they walked into the house. There was a light on, but the rest of the house was silent. No doubt Eliza had given up waiting for Roan and gone to bed. In the kitchen they packed away. For a moment there was a silence. Not uncomfortable, but a pause as if no one really wanted the night to end even though it must.

Roan clasped Meryn's free hand. "You are always welcome here."

"Thank you, for everything. I'm glad I came. I'd forgotten how good it could be to do nothing but talk." For a change, they hadn't discussed ways to kill the General and get the Romans off their land.

"Missing the old days?" Roan raised an eyebrow.

The people but not the life. He'd known it was precarious while living it, yet looking back he saw that they'd been clinging on with fingernails that were breaking from the strain. "No." And he meant it. "Another time."

"Don't wait another two thousand years." Roan released Meryn and nodded to Dai.

Dai took his arm and in a blink they were standing back in Meryn's house, the lurching sensation of his stomach was the only sign they'd moved. A few more drinks and maybe he could've convinced himself he'd imagined the whole thing, except that he was holding a pair of borrowed shoes.

His cousin didn't release him straight away. "Going to a wedding with a woman you hardly know…are you rushing into things? After what happened…?"

He probably was, but it felt good to be alive and he wanted everything that entailed. "I know enough about her."

"And what does she know of you?"

"Nothing, except the loss of my family." Did he tell Dai Nadine already knew about goblins? "You know our story survived as a children's tale?"

The corner of Dai's lips turned up at the side. "Yeah, I had something to do that. People were forgetting about goblins, so I wrote a few pieces, both fact and fable."

"You didn't want us to be forgotten."

"I wanted to warn people that the danger was there even if they didn't remember. Goblins still ride at winter solstice, stealing gold and women. These days, people forget to leave a token piece of something gold and they forget to stay indoors. The damage they blame on storms or vandals."

"I can barely separate one wild ride from another. They blur."

Dai shrugged. "I've forgotten more than I can remember. The human brain wasn't made to hold so many memories."

"Best to make new ones then." And push out every memory he'd made as a goblin.

"Yeah. Good luck tomorrow."

"Why would I need luck?" He'd be accompanying Nadine. It wouldn't be difficult. Yet his stomach still bounced and he couldn't blame either the alcohol or the magic. He'd be meeting some of her friends, and they'd be looking at him to see if he was worthy of Nadine. Once, that would never have been an issue. He was cousin to the king and had rank of his own. Now? What Nadine saw was what she got.

"Women, weddings." Dai was smiling as if remembering. "I'd best be getting home. Amanda is staying over and she'll be waiting."

"Thank you for coming, for everything."

"Just call." Then Dai's eyes shimmered like sunlight on water and he was gone.

Meryn dropped the shoes on the floor. His house was empty and dark. He wished he wasn't going to bed alone.

Chapter 15

THIS WAS A FANCY WEDDING ON A SHOESTRING BUDGET. Neither Gina nor Bryce had wanted to spend thousands for the wedding when they wanted to buy a house. Nadine straightened Gina's dress and gave her a thumbs-up. Gina smiled but she was starting to look a little nervous. Her eyes were a little too wide and her smile too bright.

"You'll be fine." Nadine gave Gina's hand a squeeze.

Her friend nodded. "I didn't think I'd get the jitters. I mean we've been together for years. Nothing is changing except a piece of paper."

"But you have to get up in front of all your friends and admit that you love him." The idea of making such a public declaration made Nadine's stomach tremble.

"Not helping." Gina checked her nail polish again. It wasn't damaged, as Nadine had opened every door and done anything that might chip a nail since putting on the final coat this morning. In a day it would be off, as Gina went back to work. "Is your man here yet?"

Nadine tried to give a casual shrug. "I haven't had a chance to look."

"Send my sister to me. You go find your guy…and make sure you introduce me after."

"You sure?"

"Tell her to bring Dad. No doubt he's talking Bryce's ear off and I want to get this done so I can enjoy the rest of the day." Gina smiled. "Thank you, I couldn't have got here without you."

A lump formed in Nadine's throat. It hadn't always been easy for Gina while Bryce was away, but Nadine didn't think she'd done anything special by being there. Gina would've done the same for her. "You'd have been fine. You're meant to be together."

"You'll have to fight my sister for the bouquet."

Nadine laughed. She wasn't even going to try. "I'll get her. Be patient."

With that she walked out of the catering tent where Gina was waiting as the staff set up the canapés and nibbles for afterward. About fifty people were gathered, talking in clusters. Her stomach tightened and her heart beat a little faster, but she refused to search for Meryn until she'd completed Gina's requests. Spotting Gina's sister and cousin was easy—like Nadine, they were both in pink, mid-calf dresses. She sent them to Gina, then set about separating Gina's dad from Bryce.

Bryce looked uncomfortable in his suit, even though he was smiling and talking like nothing was wrong. Why did people put themselves through this?

Only after she sent Gina's father to her did she allow herself to scan the crowd for Meryn. Her heart was like a butterfly beating its wings to escape. Maybe she should've looked for him first. But she doubted seeing him would have calmed her nerves—and she couldn't blame all of them on the wedding.

She was going to have to introduce him to her friends. How would they judge him? And they would. They'd try to work out what he saw in her, what she saw in him.

They'd want to know what he did and what he'd done. What was she going to say? What was he going to say?

This was a bad idea. She shouldn't have invited him. It was too soon.

Then she saw him walking across the lawn in a charcoal suit and white shirt open at the neck. She was pretty sure her heart stopped. He was flat out the most handsome man there. Where Bryce and his army mates looked like they wanted to get out of their suits as fast as possible, Meryn looked comfortable, almost relaxed. While he hadn't shaved, his beard was little more than stubble. His hair was combed back but curled against the collar of the suit jacket.

No one would think he worked in an office; he didn't have that look about him. Nadine took a few steps toward him and noticed other people were watching. They didn't know him, but they had realized she did and that was enough to spark some interest. She smiled and ignored them all. Let them wonder for a few more minutes.

Meryn's gaze flicked across the gathering before landing on her. He grinned, the dimple forming. Then he covered the last few steps took her hands and kissed her cheek before she had time to react. It seemed so normal; he was doing everything a boyfriend should. She breathed a little easier. What had she been worried about?

He kept hold of her hands, his fingers around hers. "You look very beautiful."

She blushed and tried to brush away the compliment. "It's the first time you've seen me in a dress."

He glanced down her body, obviously and admiringly. "It is." He looked back at her face. "But that doesn't change your eyes or your lips or the way you smiled when you saw me."

His gaze darted over her shoulder and she turned; Bryce was walking toward them. Oh, bugger. She was hoping there'd be no grilling until after the wedding. Keeping hold of Meryn's hand, she turned to face Bryce. Meryn's fingers laced with hers.

"Meryn, this is Bryce, the groom. Bryce, this is…" She glanced at Meryn. Was he her boyfriend? Maybe. If she said it, would he run? Probably not. "My boyfriend Meryn."

Her boyfriend. Meryn knew enough about the world to know what that meant and he liked the idea of being her partner…something less formal than marriage, but more weighted than friend. It also meant Nadine wasn't seeing another man.

Bryce put out his hand. "Please to meet you. Nadine has told us very little."

Meryn shook Bryce's hand. "Not much to tell." Meryn smiled; there wasn't much he could say.

"You're ex-British Special Forces, so I guess we won't be talking about where you may or may not have been, or what you haven't done." Bryce smiled but there was something in his eyes, and Meryn realized he was being assessed for suitability.

Nadine had mentioned the lie about his life. What else had she said? He glanced at her, but she was giving Bryce a look that would have wilted any other man. At least he had an excuse for not talking about the battles he'd fought. "I saw my share of action. You?"

Bryce nodded. "Why did you get out?"

It was a loaded question. One Meryn couldn't lie

about. Nadine's thumb brushed against his skin as if to reassure him. "My wife and children were killed." He took a breath; he didn't like admitting it, but at the same time he had to, so he could move on. "I couldn't keep it together."

"Sorry, mate. I didn't mean to pry." Bryce shot Nadine a look that needed no words. It was a-thanks-for-letting-me-walk-into-that-trap glare.

Nadine smiled sweetly, obviously used to Bryce. Meryn was glad she had friends who cared. At the same time, he was glad Bryce didn't know what Meryn had been or what he'd done.

Some murmurs came from the people who'd gathered for the wedding and another man walked up and slapped Bryce on the back. "Minister's here. Want to get this show on the road?"

Bryce looked at Meryn again. "Since you've done this before, any advice?"

"Make the most of it." It was all he could say. He had no regrets about his life with Idella. And no amount of wishful thinking could change the past. All he had was the future—one that was looking brighter with Nadine at his side.

Bryce left with the other man. Nadine turned to Meryn. "That went okay. I was dreading what he was going to say."

"Why would you dread it? He's a friend, isn't he?" Or had there once been something between Bryce and Nadine? They walked over the grass to the rotunda.

"He likes to act like my big brother."

Meryn nodded as if that explained everything. He scanned the gathering, part of him remembering what his wedding day had been like. Compared to these people he'd been so young. He hadn't felt young at the time. He'd already been fighting. Every man who could lift a sword was needed. By the time Roan was made king, Meryn had two children and the care of Roan's sister, Mave.

"I need to go to Gina now, but I'll catch up with you afterward." Nadine placed a soft kiss on his lips before turning and walking away. He watched for a couple of heartbeats before turning his gaze to the front where Bryce and three other men stood. Nadine and two other women in pink joined the men up front.

Her gaze slid to him and he was trapped like a bee in honey. He knew that look. She was trying to picture him standing up there with her. For him it wasn't hard to imagine, but imagining it and living it were two different things, and he wasn't sure that was what he wanted. Not yet. He hadn't been in the modern world for very long and there was so much he hadn't told her.

But if he told her the truth, he knew she'd walk away. While he could never have his old life back, he wanted the same fullness. To be useful, productive, to love and be loved. He couldn't live any other way.

While he watched the ceremony, he could feel the sly glances of the other people. He ignored them, for the moment he could. As the last few words were spoken and the vows were sealed with a kiss, he drew in a breath and prepared himself for the questions that would come when Nadine introduced him to her friends. He had so few answers to give.

So he lied to her friends when they asked him what he did, their smiles not hiding their curiosity. They were judging him and by extension Nadine and he didn't want to let her down. As she laughed and chatted he also knew she deserved someone better, a man who could tell her the truth about his life.

Nadine knew she couldn't get away without introducing Meryn to Gina, but with all the people there wanting to wish the bride well, the meeting was little more than a kiss on the cheek and Gina mouthing something Nadine pretended not to understand. She knew Gina would eventually get around to pressing for more answers, but for today it was over. She took Meryn's hand and they walked out of the catering tent.

He'd done a very good job of being the perfect boyfriend, but she could see the tension in his stance and the way he forced a smile and answered only when directly asked a question about himself.

Clouds had drifted across the sky, so while the sun still shone, the day was duller. They stopped at a park bench and Meryn sat. Nadine hesitated; she didn't want to get her dress dirty. Then, he drew her onto his lap, his hand on the back of her hip and the other on her knee. It was somehow so intimate despite the public place.

She relaxed into his embrace. "My friends are nosy."

"It's fine." He shrugged.

"No, it's not. You came because I asked, but you didn't really want to be here." She'd inflicted all her friends on him all at once. That was surely breaking some rule of successful dating. But he was still here, he hadn't run...yet.

He was silent for a couple of seconds. "I wanted to be here with you. I didn't expect the wedding to raise so many things."

She bit her lip. He was talking about his wife.

"It made me realize what I'd had, what I don't have, and what I want." His thumb made small circles on her back. The heat of his hand seeped through the thin dress fabric and warmed her blood. He was talking about her.

She tilted her head to look at him, her heart beating a little faster. "And what do you want?"

"You." He kissed her. His lips brushed hers, gently at first, before his tongue swept over her lip. She opened her mouth, hungry for a taste. Maybe it was the wedding, but right then he was all she wanted. She wanted more than a kiss. She wanted to know what was beneath his clothes. She wanted to feel the hardness that was forming against her leg inside her.

She gasped at the sudden rush of lust, but instead of drawing away, she sank deeper into the kiss. Her hand ran up his chest and traced bare flesh at the neck of his shirt. His fingertips touched her inner knee, circling and moving higher millimeter by millimeter, as if he was thinking about sliding them higher. She moved, eager for his touch, but he ended the kiss, his breath lingering on her lips, teasing. She gripped the collar of his shirt and drew him close again. Her tongue seeking out his, kissing him until she couldn't breathe.

A groan rumbled in his throat and his hand locked over her thigh. She wanted more than this, and yet she couldn't. Not here, not now. She swallowed and pulled back, trying to regain some composure. The heat in his eyes was a mirror of her own desire.

Meryn spoke; his voice was rough with lust. "When I'm with you, all I think about is that moment. I forget everything else. But today I realized that I don't have anything else to give you." She opened her mouth to argue, but he placed his finger on her lower lip. "I saw the looks when I said I wasn't working."

She flicked her tongue over his finger, tasting his skin. "I don't care. You'll get a job."

"I don't need to work. But I like to work."

That was the first time he'd alluded to having wealth, even though she'd suspected it. What would she do all day if she wasn't working? She'd be bored. She'd have to do something. Is that what he meant? But how did that change things between them? "What are you saying?"

"I don't know." He shook his head and he smiled— really smiled for the first time since meeting her friends. "Just that I want you, probably more than I should."

"That makes two of us." Her pulse gave a flutter of excitement and a grin curved her lips. "If I didn't have a wedding to get back to, I'd be asking to see your house." Her hand traced down his chest and moved lower to brush his hard-on, leaving no doubt what she was hinting at.

His hand slid another couple of inches up her thigh. "If you didn't have the wedding to get back to, I would accept." He claimed her mouth again, but only for long enough to seal the offer they both wanted to accept but couldn't act on.

She tore herself away before she forgot that she had to be sensible and responsible. Meryn made her forget that there was a world that had expectations.

"Maybe tomorrow? I have to work tonight, but in the morning you could make me coffee?" The words tumbled out before she could sensor them. She didn't want him to say no…it was already bad enough she'd suggested it outright. She wasn't usually quite this forward.

Heat flared in his eyes. Gray had never looked so dangerous and tempting all in one breath. And yet there was something else there. A longing that couldn't be explained. Was she pushing too hard? Was it too soon since the death of his wife—or worse—was she rebound-girl?

She pushed down her doubts. He was old enough to know what he wanted and so was she, and right now she wanted him more than she'd ever wanted anyone else.

"Let's see what tomorrow brings," he said. Not a no, but not a yes. He was giving her the chance to change her mind come morning.

But she wouldn't change her mind, and maybe she would fight Gina's sister for the bouquet. Just because she could.

Chapter 16

NADINE STIFFENED AT THE SOUND OF SIRENS ABOVE the storm. Who was out on such a wild night? She was glad she was at work and not at home. Storms made her anxious at the best of times. The roaring wind, the growling clouds, and the flashing of lightning got into her blood so she couldn't sit still. Stupid, but her mother's stories of the winter solstice Wild Ride were more vivid during a storm. Her hand went to her bare throat. Solstice was past; tonight it was just a regular storm.

Nadine pulled on gloves and pushed goblins from her mind as a new patient was brought in. She had to think of work, not fairy tales and monsters. Or weddings. Or what was in store for the next morning. Meryn was everything she'd never looked for in a man and hadn't known she'd wanted. But was it too much too soon?

She worked on autopilot, the hours slipping past. By morning, the storm was over and the city was washed clean. But the rain had left a trail of devastation. There were suburbs without power and some houses had lost their roofs. Nadine ran along the Swan River as usual, but today it was swollen and brown, palm leaves littered the grass where they'd been torn down by the wind.

As she neared their usual bench, excitement built in her blood. He wasn't there.

Had he been affected by the storm? She couldn't even call to ask if he was okay. Though the surrounding buildings didn't seem damaged.

Damn. She walked a little up the road, annoyed with herself and with him. If he wanted her half as much as she wanted him, he should've been here. Had he changed his mind? Her pulse thudded in her ears, but she couldn't just stand around. She threw off the doubts and eased into a jog. She'd check the bench again after she'd looped through the park—then, if he still wasn't there, she'd look up his phone number and find out what was going on. She hesitated, her steps slowing—she could do that now, work out which apartment was his and knock on the door…yeah unless this was his way of saying no, too soon. It had certainly felt like he was interested yesterday. She'd give him a few more minutes and give herself a chance to settle. One quick lap along the paths and then back.

She gave a quick nod and took off with a new set of goals in place, but she was hoping he'd be waiting when she got back, that she'd get to see where he lived and ask for his phone number instead of looking it up. She didn't want them to be over because she'd pushed too hard. Her heart hiccupped. She'd just introduced him to everyone. It was going to be fine. She hadn't imagined the look in his eye or the feel of his body.

The park was still and silent as she ran along paths slicked with rain and littered with leaves. The air was clear and damp. Usually she'd find peace, but today her thoughts tumbled around as if caught in rapids that wouldn't release them. A jogger passed her and waved. Few people were out this morning, as if they

expected another deluge, but the sullen sky was done
for the moment.

In the daylight it was easier to push aside her belief
of goblins riding in the storm clouds and terrorizing the
streets. An easy smile formed. Her mother's stories kept
her awake at night, but she wouldn't have it any other
way. She didn't want to forget her, and she had so little
left. A five-year-old's memories are easily written over.

But she knew it had been stormy the night her mother
was killed. She was sure. In her mind she saw a hideous
face pressed to the dark glass. Her steps faltered. No,
that was just a childish fear brought on by stories of the
Goblin King.

Goblins didn't really exist.

Around her the silence was complete. She stopped
and turned. There was no one around. It was like she
was the only person in the whole of the park. Her nerve
weakened. Running through the park was usually safe,
as there were other people. Her stomach tightened as
her gaze darted to the shadows in the scrub. There was
nothing there, but she couldn't laugh at herself. She
should've stayed closer to the café and the car parks.

Nadine took a couple of steps backward, then turned
and ran back the way she'd come. She couldn't force
herself to run on through the deserted park as if everything was as it should be. Something was wrong; the
danger plucked a warning along her spine.

She was overreacting and letting a stupid childhood
fear get the better of her, but her feet didn't slow. And
the fear didn't vanish. It wrapped tighter, and every
rustle in the scrub made her run faster. As she ran, she
cursed her stupidity. It was fine to be afraid at night,

but to allow her fears to take control during the day was too much. But she couldn't make herself stop; she just wanted to get back to the bench and wait for Meryn.

A branch swept across the path and caught her in the shins. She let out a yelp as the pain shot up her legs and she fell. Her hands hit the asphalt and she was knocked to the side. A man loomed over her, a stick in his hand.

For a second she didn't move, then adrenaline flooded her system and took away the stinging on her palms. She scrambled back—if she could get to her feet, she could outrun him. Her legs were knocked from under her again by a second man. She glanced at their faces and remembered the sketches from the TV.

Two men. These were the violent bag snatchers the news had warned about.

She wasn't about to be a statistic. Anger made her move and she retaliated, kicking, determined to get one to the ground to give herself a chance to get up and flee. He swung his leg at her ribs. She rolled away, hindered by her backpack and the now loose earbuds from her MP3 player.

She had nothing of real value. Why her?

The men laughed as they continued to deliver strategic jabs. And she kept lashing out. Then one grabbed a fistful of her short hair and tried to drag her off the path.

"Game's over, you lose," he snarled.

The adrenaline became ice in her blood. *Like hell.* They were not getting her into the bushes. She screamed, hoping someone would hear but knowing the park was empty and most people wouldn't risk their lives to help another.

A hand clamped over her mouth. She bit and thrust her

fingers up and into his eyes, not caring about the potential damage. She wasn't going to die here. Why hadn't she just waited at the bench? Her attacker screamed and released her; before she could get up, the other man let out a strangled cry and went silent. With her heart beating hard Nadine turned her head and saw Meryn stand up…the other man remained lying on the ground.

He glanced at her, his lips curving for a second before his smile froze. The man who'd been holding her charged at Meryn. Meryn moved sideways and seemed to barely raise his hand, then her attacker was falling to the ground, with Meryn never letting go as if he were merely guiding the man down. She'd never seen a man move with such fluid grace. More like a dance than violence.

The man jerked as he hit the ground and immediately tried to rise.

Nadine watched as Meryn calmly shifted his grip on the man's arm. "If you ever touch her again, I will find you and I will kill you. Do you understand?"

The man spat at Meryn and Meryn tightened his hold. "If I ever see you thieving in the park again, or even stepping foot in the park, I will kill you. Do you understand?"

This time the man whimpered.

"Answer me."

Nadine held her breath, not wanting to move and draw attention to herself. She'd never seen Meryn so—it wasn't rage. It was far more controlled, colder, calculating, fierce. Gone was the heat and the smiles. His face was blank, his attention on the man—yet she was sure he knew exactly where she was, where the other man was, and who was moving—hell, who was breathing.

She knew she was seeing who Meryn had been before his wife's death. This was the soldier more than capable of killing. And he was doing it to protect her.

"Yes." The word was forced out as if even drawing breath hurt.

Yet she felt no compassion for the man. He'd had none for her.

Meryn lifted his knee but didn't release the man, and the man didn't move. "Be a man and get a job."

"Yes. Yes," the man hissed, as if he'd agree to anything if he was freed.

Meryn relaxed his grip but still didn't let the man up. "If you turn and attack, I will make sure you don't get up. Understood?"

Nadine had no doubt he was capable of following through on every threat, probably with his bare hands.

The man nodded. "I understand."

"Be smart." Meryn let go. The man lay on the path unmoving. His friend also lay on the path, still. He hadn't moved since Meryn had dropped him.

Meryn glanced at her and her eyes widened. His eyes were cold, steel murder. She had no doubt the next person to breathe wrong was dead and that he could do it without shedding a drop of blood.

He offered her his hand. She hesitated. That hand had just taken down two men without any effort. How many men had Meryn killed while in the army?

"They will live," he said as if he sensed her fear. The hardness in his eyes melted as his lips curved and the dimple formed.

That was the man she knew. She reached up and took his hand. His fingers closed over hers and he hauled her into his arms. He embraced her, his cheek against hers, his lips finding hers for a brief kiss.

"You're all right?" he whispered against her lips.

He'd saved her, defended her from the thugs. If he hadn't shown up…she suppressed a shiver as the adrenaline left and the chill of shock took over.

She swallowed and tried to find calm. "Yes. Thank you."

Moryn lowered his gaze as heat crept over his skin. He'd done nothing someone else wouldn't have. He'd just been closer. Her hands held his shoulders like she was scared of letting go, and he didn't want her to release him. In the corner of his vision, one of the men moved. He drew back, breaking the contact and missing her touch in the same heartbeat.

"We should go. Can you walk?"

"I think so."

He slid his arm around her waist as she limped next to him, in no rush to be free of his touch, but he'd seen the fear in her eyes for a heartbeat before she'd taken his hand. His fingers moved of their own accord, over the light fabric of her clothes, feeling the firmness of the muscles beneath. She was the first woman he'd held in his arms since Idella.

Cold cut his heart. If not for him, Nadine would never have been in danger. The thieves had targeted her because they'd seen him and Nadine together. He was sure they'd been watching his old campsite and waiting for his return. When he'd failed to show up and they'd seen Nadine, they'd gone for the next best thing.

"I'm sorry I was late." He should have been at the bench, waiting for her. Not checking his old campsite to see if the men had come back.

"I was worried you were having second thoughts when you weren't at the bench."

Second and third thoughts. Doubts about whether he could be the man she wanted and needed. Yet when he was with her none of it mattered. He just wanted to live and revel in the moment instead of always planning and plotting.

"Some. You?"

She gave a small shrug. They continued walking, the woods giving way to the rolling green lawn. Her steps became steadier but she didn't pull away. Meryn realized she wasn't leaning on him because she needed to; she was doing it because she wanted to. Her hand rested on his hip and her body was pressed along his side. Yet he could feel the tension in her muscles beneath his hand.

Eventually she spoke. "Are you taking me back to your place?"

He had been leading her to his house, subconsciously wanting to satisfy the desire coursing through him. He didn't break step but he knew the timing was wrong. What she needed was a place to clean up, have a drink and a rest.

"Is that okay?"

She nodded. "How long has it been, Meryn?"

What could he say that wasn't a lie? According to Dai's lie a year had passed, yet he couldn't keep lying to Nadine. He didn't want her to know only a man built of false truths and fake pieces of identification.

He stopped walking and turned to face her. "Too long."

She traced his jaw, then leaned in and touched his lips with the barest of kisses. It quickly deepened. He had been alone for too long, swords and gold and blood had been his life. Even in the Fixed Realm, before the curse was laid, life had been lived on the edge of a Roman sword. But in Nadine he saw a glimmer of a future and it glittered with an allure he knew he wouldn't be able to resist. Moving forward didn't mean losing his past—he would always have that; it was what had shaped him and it was a part of him— but he was no longer a part of it. Her teeth raked his lip in a promise of things to come. A hot shiver coursed down his spine and spread.

"Come on." He glanced over her shoulder, back the way they'd come. So far they weren't being followed, but he didn't want to risk another confrontation. He slipped his arm around her and began walking. "They won't be scared of me forever."

This time they walked faster. As they approached the white building, Nadine glanced up to take in its full size.

"Nice." She gave him a cheeky grin.

Would she find it nice inside? After seeing Roan's house he knew this was much more modest. Would it be enough to impress her?

"I like it." He opened the door without a key and then the one with the number two on the front. He knew that symbol now. Some of the letters and numbers were staying in his head, but his writing lacked the neatness and flow of Dai's. He could probably spend the next year learning and practicing and still not be caught up on the simple things people took for granted.

She unclipped her backpack and let it fall to the floor.

Her gaze darted around his house before landing on him. Her eyes were lit with a desire he'd liked seeing. For all his doubts she wanted him, and that had to be enough.

He took her hands. "Are you sure you're all right?"

"I am now. Thank you for being there." She touched his cheek.

She'd had him tamed the moment she'd first touched him with kindness and led him out of the screaming mess of his memories. With Nadine, life was worth fighting for. He would fight for her.

Meryn lifted her hands and kissed her scratched palms. "I will always be there."

She drew in a sharp breath but didn't pull away. "This isn't quite how I imagined the morning going." Her voice was shaky.

"I know." He lowered her hands. "And it doesn't have to be today."

He wanted it to be today. Thoughts of her had kept him up half the night as he'd wondered if he still knew what to do. It had been so long, but then he looked at her damaged hands and knew today wasn't the best day to be doing anything.

Nadine lifted her chin. "I'm not going to let them ruin the day. I'm here, you're here." She smiled and placed a light kiss on his lips. "Which way to the bathroom so I can clean up?" she asked as she pushed off her shoes without unlacing them, wincing as she did.

"This way." He stepped back to show her, knowing that each step also led them closer to his bedroom.

She followed without hesitation, as if her mind was made up. In the bathroom Meryn turned on the tap and wet a washcloth. "Show me your hands."

"They're okay." But she held out her palms anyway.

He dabbed at the dirt and scratches. As injuries went, the only thing wounded was her pride and their plans. It could've been so much worse.

She watched him work, her gaze tracking his every movement. "My knees," she whispered.

He lifted his gaze and saw the heat in her eyes. Without speaking she peeled down the pants, exposing her thighs. He drew them down the rest of the way so she could step out of them. He knelt on the floor, but didn't feel the cold of the tiles. He touched the washcloth to her knee, then placed his lips on the scratch. Her breath hitched, and he kissed a little higher up her leg. When he glanced up, she was watching, her lips parted. Slowly she lifted the edge of her skin-hugging top, revealing her stomach. Then in one move she pulled it off the rest of the way and let it fall on the floor, leaving her in her black underwear. His blood surged. She was beautiful. Like an exotic goddess made of flesh and seduction.

He stood and placed the washcloth in the sink. Then claimed her mouth, her lips opening to him, matching his hunger.

"Join me in the shower." Nadine beckoned him forward.

His shaft hardened further as a forgotten longing filled him, and he'd do whatever she asked of him.

"You start," he said as he unbuttoned his shirt. He needed a moment to rein in the desire that wanted to claim her even though his mind warned that this was a bad idea. She didn't know who he really was; she was attracted to the lie Dai had made up and he had told her. Yet when she looked at him, nothing else mattered.

He shrugged out of the dark striped shirt and her gaze

skimmed over his chest and down. Whatever it was she was looking for, she found it and was pleased, her mouth turning up at the corners.

"Okay, I'll get the water going." Nadine removed her last few pieces of clothing then stepped into the shower.

Meryn swallowed. She was waiting for him. She wanted him. He needed her more than any gold he'd ever craved as a goblin.

He stripped off his trousers, shoes, and socks, and went after her. Water spilled from the spout and onto the woman underneath. Lust drew tight in his belly like a bowstring ready to release. The glass door was open and she was smiling, so he stepped in. Hot water hit his skin, like heavy rain but without the chill. He caged her with his arms against the tiles unable to resist her any longer.

"You have woken a hungry beast." He leaned in and took advantage of her mouth.

She moaned and met his attack with her own. Her fingers feathered over his hip, along his shaft. Then gripped. Her hand was as sure as her kiss, sliding over his wet flesh and forcing a groan from his lips as she caressed his length. It had been so long he'd forgotten the simple joy of being with a woman.

"If you want more from me, you'd best stop."

She grinned against his lips, but her hand stilled and the movement of her fingers became more subtle—a tease, not a demand—circling and stroking and bringing life to sensations he'd forgotten could exist.

He cupped her breast and felt the weight in his palm, her dusky nipple already hard. His thumb swept over and pinched. She gasped as he played, learning her reactions. Meryn lowered his head to take the other in his mouth. She arched her back, small noises of pleasure catching at the back of her throat. He'd never heard anything quite as sweet. He kissed his way up her neck, tasting the water off her skin, then found her lips. She kissed with a hunger that matched his, as if she'd been waiting for him.

When his hand slid lower, over her belly and between her thighs she eased her legs apart to allow him access. He didn't want to rush, but every time he moved forward she was ready and waiting. His fingers slid over her slick sex and dipped into her core. She moved her hips as if seeking more. Then she angled his shaft, wanting to replace his fingers.

He resisted the temptation, distracting himself with her lips. But her hand around his shaft was insistent. Her nails pressed into his shoulder. Meryn lifted her against the tiles, and she wrapped her legs around his hips. Her gaze locked on him, dark with lust and wild with need. Her breathing came in heavy pants.

He paused even though he wanted to lower her onto him and possess her. She wiggled in his hold, using her heels to force him closer, the head of his shaft already nudging against the heat of her core.

But he wouldn't be rushed.

For the first time in two thousand years, he was human and in the arms of a woman he was falling for. He wanted to savor every moment. The little rush that accompanied every glance, and the swoop and fall of the first kiss. The rising of his heart as he looked into her eyes.

He eased into her slowly, enjoying the sensation and intending to hold on to it for as long as possible. Her hands traced over his skin, leaving heated trails in their wake. She cupped his cheek as she kissed him, stealing his breath as he thrust into her. He reveled in the sensation of having her arms and legs wrapped around him as he buried himself deeper. Slick and hot. It was almost too much after living with so little for so long. He slid his fingers between them and teased her clit, wanting her to find release first. Her head tipped back and her lips parted. She rolled her hips, wanting more. And he moved with her, giving her what she wanted. She gasped and tightened around his shaft, tempting him to let go.

Meryn held back, not wanting it to be over, not yet, but it had been too long. He withdrew from her heat and let his seed be washed down the drain with the water. He didn't want to get her pregnant. He wasn't ready for that. He wasn't sure he was ready for this. Being with Nadine, while amazing…was different. She was changing him, or maybe he was changing to fit the time.

The water drummed on his back and reality returned. The moment where desire replaced thought was over. If he let go of Nadine, would she leave now that she'd got ten what she wanted? They couldn't stay in the shower forever, yet moving was too hard.

She sighed and rested her forehead against his. "I think I made a mistake."

Chapter 17

BENEATH HER HANDS HIS MUSCLES TENSED AS IF bracing for a hit. She traced her fingers over his shoulders; even now she couldn't stop touching him. "We should've used a condom."

How had she let that happen? She was usually so careful, but her brain had stopped working once his fingers had started moving. She knew exactly what he meant when he said he thought only of the moment when he was with her, because she felt the same.

"I withdrew," he said, but his words were uncertain.

Nadine drew her head back to look him in the eye. "I'm not worried about babies. I'm on the pill. Who have you been with since your…" She left the sentence hanging, unable to finish it.

This was not a conversation they should be having while her legs were still around his waist and he was holding her against the wall. Still, they would have to have it sometime.

"No one." He lowered his gaze as if he were watching the water swirl down the plug. "I'd been with her since I was sixteen."

She hugged him tighter but the distance was already there. Her words had forced a wedge between them. "I'm sorry. Oh God, I've made a mess of this."

He'd been with his wife since he was a teenager. Venereal diseases weren't really going to be an issue. Plus he would've been tested in the army.

"No you haven't. There was always going to be someone after Idella eventually. I'm glad it was you." He kissed her and eased her legs to the ground.

She kept her arms around his neck, needing to hold on to him in case he changed his mind and walked away. In his arms she hadn't had to pretend; he'd given her exactly what she needed without her hinting or asking. Unlike other men she'd dated he wasn't trying to be something other than who he was. He was Meryn, recovering from the loss of his wife, unemployed, and none of the things she'd thought important and everything that was. He had true heart. One that had been broken.

He'd become a part of her life by accident, yet she struggled to imagine a life without him. "I'm glad it was me too."

She shivered as her skin cooled and the heat that had burned in her blood melted away. She would always be the woman who came after his first love. What did that even mean? Was that a good thing or a bad thing?

She had no history to compare with. Her own boyfriends had come and gone more out of convenience than any real feeling. Love brought pain and the man in her arms was living proof. She wasn't that brave or that strong, but it was already too late. The moment she'd kissed him it had been too late.

Like a princess in a fairy tale she'd fallen into his arms even though she knew happily-ever-afters weren't real.

Meryn reached out and turned off the tap. "Come and rest."

She nodded. "Will you stay with me?"

He smiled and the dimple appeared. "Where else would I go?"

Nadine glanced way. Of course, this was his house. She finally knew where he lived.

He drew away, leaving her wet and naked and cold without his body next to her, then handed her a towel.

She dried off with one eye on him as he toweled dry. He had scars on his fair skin, the pale-pink shiny lines of old wounds. Beneath the marks marring his flesh, muscles moved. Hard and lean. While she'd seen him fight with dangerous efficiency, she couldn't put him in uniform. He didn't seem the type. He was too…pretty. Gray eyes, the dimple, those lovely lips, and the casually unshaved look.

"Why did you join the army?"

He turned, completely at ease being naked. His gaze remained on her face, not sneaking a peek while she finished drying.

"To defend my home and protect my family."

"That's very noble."

Meryn shrugged and his gaze traveled to take in her half-covered body. No, he didn't sneak a look; he did it without hiding. And she didn't feel the need to hide.

"Being a nurse is no less noble."

"It's hardly frontline combat."

"Saving lives is always frontline combat." He hung up his towel and walked into the bedroom, leaving her to follow.

This time she took in the details she'd missed in her hurry to get to the shower and try and put the morning back on track. She hadn't intended on being in the shower for their first time. The bed seemed much more appropriate, and yet she wouldn't change it. It had happened in a rush of pent-up lust.

"How long have you lived here?" The bedroom was neat and practical but without a real personal touch. A house but not a home.

"Since my cousin arranged the purchase." He shook the sheets to straighten them, and she tried not to smile. He was making the bed just to get back in and make a mess.

"You came over to be with family?"

"They insisted." He sat on the edge and glanced over his shoulder at her. "I was lost for a long time."

Nadine slid into bed next to him. He put his arm over her and she turned to snuggle into him. In her mind she saw him as he'd first appeared in the emergency room— wild, disheveled, and weighed down with pain.

"You never did tell me why the police brought you into the hospital."

His sigh slid down her spine. "I wasn't coping. I was living rough for a while, hoping to numb the pain. I'd fallen when they picked me up. I guess I looked worse than I was."

"Will it happen again?" She twisted to look at him.

"If I block out my family, they cease to exist. If I remember and hold on to the good parts, they still live. It took me a while to realize that was what I had to do."

Nadine eased back onto the pillow. "Will you ever love again?"

"Yes. What is the point of living without loving?" He placed a kiss on the back of her neck, his touch sending shivers down her spine to her belly.

"I don't know." She didn't want to be alone. She wanted someone to share her life with, but she'd only seen love destroy and wound. Yet, despite the murder of his family, Meryn still thought love was worth the hurt.

Either his heart was stronger than hers or the love he'd had with his wife had been something great. Something bigger than she'd ever seen or experienced.

"You've never been in love." It wasn't a question. He knew that if she'd truly ever been in love then she would know its value.

Nadine worked her lips between her teeth. "Maybe I have."

"You would know if you had. You would carry the memory with you long after it ended."

"Love always ends. Why would I want to risk my heart on a fantasy?" Even as she spoke she knew she'd already crossed that line. She'd let Meryn get under her skin and lodge in her heart. An arrow so fine she'd never felt its sting.

Meryn was quiet; his breath tickled her skin. She closed her eyes as exhaustion crept through her body.

After a minute he whispered, "How do you judge the highest mountain if you've never stood at the bottom? An endless flat plain gets dull."

The dull plain followed her into sleep.

Beyond the wall of the castle, the world was flat and barren. The land and sky merged in the distance to form a solid gray that was mirrored in the man's eyes.

Meryn smiled at her. His hair was roughly cut and hanging in his eyes, but his beard was neat and full. She touched his arm to make sure he was real. He was, like the last time she'd dreamed he was here. She wasn't alone in her castle anymore.

Now she had company, a knight to protect her even

though the dream world was breaking apart. Like all fairy-tale knights, he wore a cloak and sword. And like all princesses, she wore a beautiful gown that swept the stone floor.

Once she'd been safe here, but like the last few times, her castle was slowly deconstructing. The gardens and fountain that had filled the gap between castle and wall were gone. Pieces of path showed through the dust where Meryn had followed it to the door. She'd hoped the castle would begin to fix itself, but every time she imagined it whole, nothing changed. The maze was gone, and the forest that should've been on the other side of the wall hadn't come back.

She pressed her hands to the glass and stared into the endless gray twilight, trying to bring back the sky and grass. "Where has it all gone?" Why had the Shadowlands invaded her dream after all this time?

"Come away. It's not safe." Meryn took her hand and drew her back.

"This is my dream. Why can't I fix it?" She pulled free to scan the desolate landscape again. Everything she'd built was gone. Tiny cracks formed around the window in the brickwork. Her castle was decaying as she watched. Soon there would be nothing left.

"I don't know, but the goblins are coming."

As she watched, a half dozen goblins climbed over the wall and dropped into what should've been garden. She stepped back as fear made her blood run cold. "They shouldn't be here."

"We need to hide, let them take the gold, and we'll be safe."

Then she noticed the gold coin on the windowsill.

Who had put it there? She hadn't. She would never do something so dangerous. The goblins were being drawn to her castle because of the gold. Meryn was right; they weren't safe here. "Hide where?"

Glass shattered. She spun as the shards fell to the floor like rain, breaking into ever smaller pieces on the stone. A hideous gray face with a hooked nose and long, pointed ears peered through. Long-fingered hands reached for her, yellowed nails scraping her skin.

Too late she reacted, reaching for Meryn, but he didn't move. He couldn't move. His arms remained locked by his sides even as he struggled.

"No!" she screamed as the goblin seized her around the waist to pull her through the window. Her dress tangled around her legs, preventing her from fighting back.

Meryn watched in horror, his eyes widening.

"Please, help me." She elbowed the goblin, trying to get free, but he yanked her onto the windowsill. She was going to fall and die. That would be better than being taken. She dug her nails into his arm, drawing black blood, but he didn't let go. "Meryn, please." Her voice was frantic and panicked.

"I can't." In his hand was her mother's cross. As he stared at his hands the skin grayed, his joints thickened. His fine clothes became rags and his hair matted and clumped. Meryn was becoming goblin. He couldn't help her; he couldn't help himself.

This was her dream, but it shouldn't happen like this. She couldn't will the goblins away. She looked at Meryn; his eyes were goblin yellow and locked on the gold in his hand. "No!"

Then the goblin dragged her out the window and they fell.

She woke with a gasp before she hit the ground in her dream. Strong arms held her still and for a heartbeat spurred her panic on. She struggled against the embrace, her legs tangling in the bed sheets.

"Shh. It's only a dream."

But her heart still raced, pounding hard from a fright she'd imagined. Her mother's stories were taking over her sleep, and each time they became more terrifying. Now she was involving Meryn.

Her hand covered Meryn's as she eased closer to his warmth. His hands were normal, not gray. It was just a dream, fueled by Meryn's tragedy and her mother's death. She closed her eyes hoping to find sleep again, but imprinted in her mind was the image of Meryn going from man to goblin, knight to monster, as she'd been pulled out of the window by cold greedy hands.

She shivered and tried to fake sleep, hoping the real thing would find her, and failed. She was wide awake and she wasn't the only one. Behind her, Meryn was awake. His fingers made small circles on her stomach. He didn't press her about her dream. Maybe she should just go home…to her empty bed. Lying next to someone was a luxury she'd never allowed herself. She never let her guard down in front of anyone—except Meryn. With him, she could share her secrets and he didn't laugh or recommend counseling. And in exchange, he'd exposed his dark past.

With a sigh she relaxed. It was nice having someone there when she woke up from a nightmare. She was safe in his arms. Daylight kept the room bright and free of shadows, but when darkness came, would she be able to sleep at night knowing Meryn was there?

Nadine rolled over to face him. "Were you asleep?"

He opened his eyes, gray and endless. "No."

"You stayed in bed with me."

"You asked me to."

He probably thought she was a bit of freak. "I don't usually have nightmares." Not a total lie, but not exactly the truth either. She couldn't remember a time when she hadn't had nightmares. Building the castle as she went to sleep each night had helped. But they still came, usually when she least expected them. Like now. She should be happy, but instead she was scared of her own dreams.

"You can't help what you dream."

Maybe not, but when did she get to sleep without fear? "Don't you want to know what the dream was about?"

"If you want to tell me."

Nadine's lips curved. The start of the dream had been fine. "Promise you won't think I'm crazy?"

He placed his hand over his heart. "On my honor."

"I was a princess in my castle, and you were there."

"I'm sorry to have been so terrifying."

"I wasn't scared of you…although I don't know why you were there." Why had he appeared in her dreams? Was it just because she was spending too much time thinking about him? No other boyfriend had ever invaded her castle.

"What happened?"

"There was nothing beyond the castle walls, just gray. Like I was in the Shadowlands."

"How did you get there?"

"I don't know. It never used to be there; there used to be all kinds of other things beyond the castle walls, but it's all gone." It was gone. She couldn't go back anymore. Would she be able to stop herself from returning to her castle when it had been a habit for so long? She sighed and got to the worst part of the dream. "Then goblins broke in and took me while you watched."

Meryn closed his eyes in a slow blink. "I wouldn't let that happen. I would fight."

"You couldn't move."

"It was your dream; therefore, you had the power to release me."

That wasn't the first time she'd heard those words. The best way to combat a nightmare was to take control, to alter what was happening. But she'd never been able to do that. The fear made it impossible for her to do anything. So she gave into it, and it fed and grew. Now she was dragging other people into her nightmare and forcing them to watch. She didn't tell him the rest of her dream. He didn't need to know she'd imagined him turning into a goblin.

"I'll try that next time." Hopefully there wouldn't be a next time. She placed her lips on his, wanting to forget what she'd seen.

His tongue flicked against hers and his hand slid lower. She shifted her leg and hooked it over his thigh. His touch warmed her skin and tightened the desire building in her belly. Her eyelids flickered closed as his fingers slid over her clit, moving as if he knew exactly what she liked. A moan slipped out and she couldn't stop herself from rocking in rhythm. She needed more, so she drew him to her.

He rolled over her, pressing her into the bed, sealing her mouth with a kiss. His strength and power and desire were hers. She wriggled her hips, wanting to feel him inside her. But he teased, drawing out the inevitable. Heat coiled low in her belly as her fingers kneaded his butt, wanting more, but like this, caught beneath him, she couldn't rush him, and didn't want to. She gave into his touch and he took his time stroking and caressing until she came.

"Say my name," he whispered against her lips.

"Meryn." Her voice was light and breathy.

He thrust into her and took her over the edge again. This time, she didn't care how far she fell, as she knew Meryn would be there to catch her. His name formed silently on her lips.

They moved together, pushing harder, taking what they needed. He groaned words she didn't understand as he came deep within her. Their bodies locked together.

She stole another kiss, not wanting to lose the moment—not wanting to wreck it like she had last time.

He gazed down at her, his eyes dark with unreadable emotion. Something stirred in her heart. Did he love her? Oh God. Was he going to say it? It was one thing to know it, another to acknowledge what was growing between them and name it. She held her breath, not sure what to do.

Meryn eased out of her and lay beside her. The words, while unspoken, lingered around them. She couldn't say them. She never had, not since her mother's death. And she knew Meryn hadn't said them since his wife's death. Yet they were there and it was only a matter of time until one of them spoke first and forced the other one to action.

Before the moment could become really awkward, she slipped out of bed and went into the bathroom.

Meryn was still lying in the bed when she came out, tempting her to slide back in, but she needed a moment to catch her breath. She didn't mind fast lust, but love… could that develop this fast?

"Would you like a drink?"

"I'm fine." He paused. "The glasses are in the kitchen above the sink. There's milk and orange juice in the fridge."

She walked out of the bedroom. Beneath her feet the carpet was soft and thick. No doubt real wool, not the synthetic, hard, nylon rental carpet she had. The living space was big and airy. It could easily feel like home if it were given a few personal touches. At the moment, it was furnished with simple but costly items. Leather sofa—real leather. Big screen TV with all the bits beneath and all the wires carefully hidden. No doubt the cabinet was real wood and not veneer.

He may not be working, but he hadn't been joking when he'd said his family had money. She opened a few cupboards in the kitchen just to see what was in them. Nothing out of the ordinary except it was all very neat. Stuck to the fridge was a calendar with scenery of Wales, beautiful but harsh and straight out of another time.

Nadine opened up the fridge. Fruit, some veg and steaks, no beer. With a shrug she closed the door and got a drink of water. As she sipped, she scanned the rest of the apartment. And she realized what was missing.

There were no pictures of his wife and children. She frowned. In fact, there were no photos at all. She poured the rest of the water down the sink. Why did he

not have any pictures? Was it still too painful? There'd
been no pictures in the news article either. She walked
back toward the bedroom, but her gaze was caught by a
pile of papers on the dining table under a gold bracelet
shaped like a Celtic torque. She'd walked past them
before and taken no notice. Now she looked.

The writing wasn't English. The lettering was
wrong. She nudged the paper and saw a second sheet
with more of the same lettering. It looked a bit like
English lettering—only different. She tilted her head,
but the words made no sense. Was it code? Then she
realized what she was seeing. Latin. Her blood ran cold
even as her skin burned. Something wasn't right. She
glanced toward the bedroom, but Meryn hadn't come
out. He trusted her...now she wasn't so sure the trust
went both ways.

He'd come into the hospital speaking Latin. What
kind of soldier spoke Latin? Hell, what kind of soldier
read Latin?

A glint of gold under the paper caught her eye. She
lifted the corner already knowing what it was, the shape
too familiar.

Her mother's crucifix.

Her stomach contorted as if she was going to be sick.
Blood rushed from her head, making the room spin. Her
hand went to her throat where the necklace had hung.
She hadn't lost it. It hadn't fallen off. Meryn had stolen
it. She couldn't breathe.

Why would he do that?

She snatched up the cross, taking back what was hers.
Her bag was by the front door. Without thinking, she
ran over to it and started pulling out the clothes inside,

the ones she'd worn to work. She didn't care about her running clothes. She had to get out of here.

"Don't go."

She spun at the sound of his voice. Meryn stood naked in the bedroom doorway. He must have realized she was taking too long.

"You stole my cross. You…" She couldn't speak. Anger clotted up her words in her throat. "Why?"

"I don't know."

"Bullshit. Were you ever going to give it back or was it some kind of sick trophy?" She gasped as fear fisted her heart. She didn't know this man at all. "Where are the pictures of your wife and children?" Everything he'd told her was some kind of lie to get close to her. "Why do you have letters written in Latin? What the hell is going on? How many women do you suck in with your sob story?"

Oh God, oh God. She'd had unprotected sex. Shit. Meryn hadn't moved, but she'd seen him fight. "Are you some kind of serial killer? Are you going to kill me?"

"I would never hurt you."

"Too bloody late."

"I took the cross because it was gold and I had no choice. I never expected to see you again. Then I didn't know how to give it back."

The gold in her palm pressed into her flesh. Gold. He's taken gold like a goblin. She glanced at him again. Her dream was still fresh in her memory, snagging on her thoughts and tangling them until they made no sense.

"What do you mean you had no choice?"

He jaw tensed. "I needed it. I thought it would block out the pain the way it had before."

His words didn't make sense. None of this was making sense. She shook her head. Her blood was sharp, like razors in her veins, cutting and shredding her heart.

"Before when?" But in her mind she was seeing him as she had the first night, covered in gray dust. It hadn't been concrete; it had been something much, much worse. Shadowlands dust. Except the Shadowlands only existed in her mother's story—it wasn't a real place.

She looked at the naked man in the doorway. In her dream, she'd watched him turn goblin. He'd been with her in her castle surrounded by the Shadowlands. He was going to kidnap her and take her back to the Shadowlands.

Meryn was a goblin.

No, goblins weren't real.

"Who are you?"

"Meryn Knight."

Was it his name? It was someone's name, but there'd been no photos.

"And the letters? Why are they in Latin?" She flung her hand out and pointed to the papers.

"My cousin wrote the letters in Latin because Decangli was never a written language."

"Nobody speaks Latin." She didn't even know what Decangli was.

"I speak it."

"What the hell kind of Special Forces are you? What did you do in the army?"

"I planned battles for the king."

"What king? I thought you grew up in Wales."

"The king of the Decangli."

"I've never heard of the Decangli."

Meryn rubbed his hand over his hair, then over his

jaw. "Do you want the truth or a fight? Do you want to run or to understand?"

Run. She should run. But her feet remained glued to the carpet.

"How do I know I'll get the truth?" she demanded.

"I am not a liar." Then he softened his voice. "But I left out pieces."

"Lying by omission."

His face hardened. "Just go. Run like you always do."

Nadine stared. How dare he? He knew nothing about her. And she knew nothing about him. If he'd been a casual date, it wouldn't have mattered, but her stupid heart had gotten involved in what could have been good sex and someone to talk to.

"I want to know whose bed I was in." She crossed her arms. She wasn't going to turn tail and run from Meryn. Her blood was pumping and she wanted a fight—a fight so they could break up whatever had started and she could walk away knowing she'd done the right thing in leaving.

Chapter 18

MERYN FLEXED HIS FINGERS AND FORCED OUT A breath. He didn't want Nadine to know who he was. He didn't want to see fear in her eyes every time she looked at him, but he was her nightmare. He was the goblin who'd stood by and watched her mother kill herself after being taken during the solstice. However he was also remembering what it meant to be a man, and that meant being honest with those he loved. Starting with Nadine—even if that cost him her love. What they had would never be real if she didn't know who he was.

"Fine. But let me speak."

"Fine. Don't trip over your lies."

"I speak Latin and Decangli because they are the languages that were spoken when I was born. My wife and children were killed by Roman Legionnaires. There are no pictures because there were no cameras. All I have left are my memories. The happy ones cut as deeply as the bad ones." He took a breath and studied Nadine's face. She didn't believe him. One eyebrow was raised and her arms were crossed. "I was cursed to the Shadowlands with my king."

Meryn let his words settle like the fine gray dust of the Shadowlands. They coated everything and sucked out the life and joy. Her eyes widened and her lips parted, but she didn't speak, so he took a step forward into the living room.

Maybe he should've told her sooner. Maybe he shouldn't have let her poke around his things, but he didn't want to hide his past. He didn't want to spend his second chance at life living Dai's cleverly created lie. He wanted to be himself and to be known for what he did, even though it had all happened so long ago.

"I know the story of *The Goblin King* because I lived it. I spent nearly two thousand years trapped in the Shadowlands."

"You're a goblin."

"I have lived as a goblin. After I was made to watch Idella's murder, I gave in to the curse. It was easier to want nothing but gold than to remember her screaming at the sight of me in a body that wasn't mine." He glanced at his hands. Even now they seemed strange, like they belonged to a man who had lived another life. In a way they did, because he would never be that man again. Too much had happened.

"You stole gold like a goblin."

"That was a mistake."

"The mistake was mine. I should've known better." She picked up her bag and slung it over her shoulder.

"Nadine, please."

"No. I don't want to hear it. There is nothing you can say that will change my mind. Were you ever going to tell me you're a goblin?"

"Would you have believed me if I'd told you? I told you what I could about my life and tried to protect you from the rest."

"You lied to me about everything."

"No. Do you really want to know about everything I've seen and done? Do you want to know how hard I fought to keep the Decangli free? How many people I saw die? Do want to know how brutal goblins are when they see a speck of gold? I live with these memories every day. You don't have to."

"I have a right to know who I'm sleeping with."

"And now you know. Does it make you happy?"

"You're a goblin."

"I was born a man and will die a man, becoming goblin was a twist of fate." And while not one he'd want to repeat, it had enabled him to meet Nadine and experience a life so far from anything he could've imagined. "If I hadn't become goblin, we wouldn't be standing here talking. I'd be long dead. I've gotten a second chance at living."

She shook her head. Her eyes were hard, like her tears had frozen and left only ice. She hated him, hated what he was, hated that he'd hidden the truth.

"Goblins don't get a second chance." She opened the door.

Meryn took a couple of steps toward her.

"Stay away from me."

"There's something else you should know."

"Oh yeah? What?" She spat out the words.

"While I was in the Shadowlands, I saw a woman who'd been taken by the goblins at solstice."

"Was I next on your list?"

"No." He frowned. For a moment he considered staying silent, but knew if he did, it would just be another lie he was keeping from her. She should know the truth. "Your mother disappeared on the winter solstice." He paused, letting the words settle.

Nadine didn't move. Her fingers whitened against the door handle.

"Your mother was taken by goblins. Your father is innocent," Meryn finished.

She stepped back. "You don't know that."

"I see the resemblance every time I look at you."

Nadine shook her head. "You bastard." Then she left and slammed the door after herself. The room echoed, but the tension remained.

Meryn sank to the floor and leaned his head against the wall. His fragile heart cracked again as the screaming filled his skull. This time there was no ice-cold curse to take away the pain. There was no way out. He was trapped in his own nightmare. His nails dug into his scalp. But nothing stopped the ragged edges from cutting through the hurt and dragging him down. He closed his eyes, and tears clogged his eyelashes.

Sunlight crept across the floor. He grew cold. But he was used to that. He was also used to the hunger that followed. He knew he had to move, but he didn't know how. What did he do now? The screaming continued. He tried to smother it, to silence it. He should never have gotten involved with Nadine. He should've remained faithful to his wife. But it wasn't his wife his heart ached for. She was long dead. The woman who'd just been in his bed and in his arms was the one he wanted. Nadine gave his second chance meaning when the world around him made no sense.

Meryn scrubbed his hand over his face. He'd told her love was worth the hurt and he couldn't live up to his own words. It was much easier to believe them when standing at the top, instead of stranded at the bottom. His hands fell to his side. The house was silent, waiting for him to do something.

If this were a battle, how would he win her back?

Nadine turned her face to the window of the nearly empty train, but she didn't see the city passing by. She sniffed and tried to swallow the ache in her throat.

Lying bastard. Everything she thought they had was a goblin lie.

The points of the cross dug into her palm. She wished she'd never found it. Then she could've ignored all the things that weren't quite right about Meryn. There were so many of them, and yet there'd been so many things that she'd liked about him. She'd liked him because he was different. He was different because he was a goblin and every word had been a lie.

Her eyes brimmed and tears crept down her cheeks. She swiped them away. She didn't cry. Not now, not ever. Certainly not for a man who claimed to have lived the fairy tale of *The Goblin King*.

He was either a goblin or insane…no matter how much she'd rather Meryn be crazy, she knew that wasn't true. Which meant he'd spent a couple of millennia as a goblin hoarding gold and fighting and stealing women.

Yet he'd never hurt her. He'd saved her from the thieves. And when she'd left, he hadn't tried to stop her—because he was goblin, so why would he care? But she'd seen the pain in his eyes. Old or new it didn't matter; he'd laid open his past for her to see and she hadn't believed him. Her heart clenched like it would never beat again.

The memory of Meryn wild and covered in gray dust rose like a rotting corpse in a stream. Only now it made sense. He'd come straight from the Shadowlands. When he said he'd lived rough for a while, he'd meant in the

Shadowlands. When he'd said he was numb, it was because he'd been goblin.

Her body shook as she tried to hold back the tide that threatened to drown her. His words echoed in her ears.

You father is innocent.

Nadine opened her fist. For days after her mother's disappearance she'd refused to open her hand. When they'd finally pried it open, the cross was coated in blood. If Meryn were telling the truth, he'd seen her mother die and done nothing to save her from the goblins.

She couldn't put the cross back in his apartment and forget finding it any more than she could un-hear the truth or un-know the monster hiding in the man. But all she wanted was his arms around her, making her feel safe again. She hated herself for that weakness. For falling for him and needing him. Until Meryn, she'd never needed any one and had never risked her heart on something as dangerous as love.

The train stopped at her station and she got off, knowing people were staring at the crying woman. They could all go to hell.

Her shins and back ached from the attack. But between her thighs ached for a very different reason— one she wouldn't forget in a hurry. She sucked in air like it would be her last breath. She'd broken up with men before and it had never felt like she was dying. Meryn wasn't a man. He was goblin and he'd stolen the cross and her heart.

Had he taken her mother?

He'd said he had seen a woman in the Shadowlands, not that he'd taken her—but he could be lying about that too. Is that what her father had been hiding?

She unlocked her front door, her memories and nightmares colliding with everything her father and Meryn had said. It had been midwinter when her mother disappeared.

No. It was a fairy tale, nothing more. Goblins weren't real. They were a myth to scare children into behaving and not being greedy. But Meryn had known the story—a different version of it. Had he really lived it? She opened her hand and looked at the cross. In the bathroom she looked at the torque he'd given her.

A gift from another life. A life where it had been more than jewelry and a sign of rank. His clothes, the claim that he'd been waving a sword, and his lack of language. The ill feeling in her stomach swelled and crashed against her lungs.

What he wanted her to believe was impossible. He couldn't be a Celtic warrior returned from the Shadowlands. It was easier to believe in goblins than that.

She changed clothes, the skin on her palms tender and raw. But she remembered the touch of his lips on her flesh, the way he'd stepped in and defended her from the thugs without hesitation. She wanted to believe him. She wanted to be able to trust him. She squeezed her eyes shut and tried to push down the hurt, but it wouldn't go.

There was only one person who could answer her questions about goblins, who knew almost as much about them as her mother. And who had always pleaded not guilty to her murder—her father.

Maybe he wasn't guilty. She had to know if the secrets he was hiding were about goblins too. Had goblins taken her mother on the winter solstice like Meryn claimed? But why serve time for a crime he never committed, why never tell her that he was innocent and goblins were to blame?

And if they had taken her mother to the Shadowlands, what did that mean? Did that mean Meryn really knew the Goblin King? Had the curse really been broken? Was he really a man with a second chance?

Her father was the only person who would be able to prove Meryn's story. She snatched up her car keys, not sure if the truth would make what Meryn had told her better or worse. Could she love a man who'd been goblin?

Chapter 19

MERYN HAD WALKED THE PATHS OF KINGS PARK without seeing. He half started down the road to the hospital where Nadine worked, then turned back and headed home. He needed a better plan than just turning up and asking for a second chance.

He was everything she hated. Goblins had ruined her life as a child and so far he wasn't doing a great job of proving that he was any better. Would there have ever been a good way to tell her?

To tell anyone? He sank onto a chair at the dining table and cradled his head in his hands. No matter what he did, he would always have the same problem. No one would ever know who he was and he'd be stuck. A man without a past was a man without a future.

There were only two people he could talk to who would understand—his cousins. But that would mean admitting he told Nadine about the curse and goblins. He sat without moving, staring at Dai's Latin lettering without being able to read a word of it. He picked up the bracelet and felt the weight of it in his hand before putting it on. The words unscrambled and became clear. If only the answer was as easy to see. Once, he'd have never sat alone, dwelling on a problem; he'd have discussed it with Roan. He wanted his tribe back; he wanted a family again. He wanted Nadine.

He rang Dai, and within moments, his cousin was standing in the living room.

Dai glanced around and seemed to sense this wasn't a social call. "What's wrong?"

Meryn drew in a breath. How did he explain that he'd screwed up everything? "I need some advice."

Dai raised his eyebrows as if waiting for the rest of the story.

"I think I should tell you and Roan at the same time." Because whatever he said wasn't going to go down well.

"Right. Everyone is at my place." Dai held out his hand.

"Everyone?"

"Eliza, Amanda, Brigit…now you. You can meet the family." Dai smiled.

Great, the last thing he wanted was to be admitting his failures in front of everyone. "Maybe I shouldn't have rung."

"Meryn, they want to meet you. Whatever the problem, it's not going to get any worse if you stop for dinner." Dai turned the things Meryn had once said back on him. He'd once been the one reminding Dai to take a breath. Maybe some of things he'd said had made a difference and had helped Dai…maybe Roan and Dai would now be able to help him.

"Very well, but I need to act tonight." Meryn gripped Dai's hand, and the lurch and jolt of translocation followed. This time when he opened his eyes he was back in the tower he'd escaped from. The tower was actually a very nice apartment, furnished very sparsely but filled with people who all turned. They weren't looking at Dai, who'd just appeared out of nothing; they were looking at him. Meryn forced a smile.

"Meryn, so glad you came." Roan clasped Meryn's forearm in greeting. "You met Eliza." Eliza nodded. "This is Amanda and her daughter Brigit."

Amanda ran her gaze over him and made a quick assessment before smiling. Brigit narrowed her eyes and took a step forward. "Were you a goblin?"

"Yes."

Her eyes lit up. "Did you steal lots of gold?"

"Brigit, help me set an extra place at the table." Amanda steered Brigit into the kitchen.

"I won't stay; you're obviously in the middle of something." Why had Dai brought him here? This was a bad idea.

"Don't be silly." Eliza glanced at Roan. Whatever the message she was trying to convey, Roan seemed to understand.

Roan opened up the balcony door, the glass now whole. Meryn remembered using a chair to break the glass and escape. The three men stood outside. Roan leaned against the railing. "What's going on?"

For a moment Meryn couldn't speak. He'd come so far since the first night he'd stood here, before climbing down and fleeing into the city...only to be arrested for carrying a sword a short time later. Yet in Nadine's eyes he was still a goblin.

"I told Nadine about my life as a goblin." As Meryn spoke, he realized how naïve he must sound, to think he could tell the truth and have someone love him anyway.

Dai muttered what could only be a filthy curse in some language Meryn didn't speak.

"Why did you do that?" Roan rubbed a hand over his very short hair.

"She already knew about goblins, as a child her mother told her your story." Meryn glanced inside and watched the women talking. Brigit laughed, the sound carrying outside and cutting open the wounds he'd thought healed. He could see love, hear the affection, and yet he was cold and hollow and had nothing. "Amanda and Eliza know the truth. Why should I expect less?"

"That is different." Roan crossed his arms. "We don't talk about the curse or goblins for our own safety."

"Meryn has a point. Plus, if Nadine already knew the tale, what difference does it make?" Dai ran his finger along the top of the metal railing.

Roan shook his head. "It's too late now anyway. The words can't be unspoken."

Meryn wished they could be—or at least spoken better.

Dai looked at Meryn, the glimmer of magic in his eyes. "What happened after you told her?"

What was Dai seeing? Was he looking for lies? "She ran. I thought that if I explained I'd lived her mother's story, that would make it right. But I am everything she hates."

"Not hates. She doesn't hate you." Dai blinked and his eyes returned to normal.

"I need to find a way to win her back. That is why I called you. I don't know what to do. You two have both been there and fought that battle." Meryn pointed to the door where the women were serving up the meal as if there was nothing odd going on. They knew about magic and goblins, they knew about the men's past. Roan and Dai didn't have to lie with every breath.

"Her mother told her *our* story?" Roan was frowning.

Dai glanced at Roan and then at Meryn. "Does she know how the curse broke and what happened to us?"

"Yes, I told her the curse was broken by love long before I told her I'd lived the curse." Meryn shook his head. He was always going to be an ex-goblin from her mother's tale.

"No, no. Tell her the real story," Dai said.

"I did and she didn't believe a word."

Eliza pulled open the door. "Dinner is ready if you are."

"Almost." Roan smiled at her, then turned back to face Meryn. "She won't be angry now, and you've had time to cool your heels too."

"She won't listen to me; she thinks I'm a goblin. I don't even know if she'll see me." His plan so far totaled going to the hospital and praying that she would see him. He knew it was the kind of plan that would fail. Maybe he shouldn't have bothered coming; his cousins weren't helping.

"Write it down. She may not read it straight away, but she won't be able to ignore it forever." Dai smiled like he'd solved everything.

The idea was good. He could rewrite her mother's story, filling in the gaps with truth. He was the only one who could give her mother's tale its proper ending. There was only one flaw. "I can't write."

"Leave that with me." Dai opened the door and went inside to have dinner.

Meryn bit back a sigh and followed. He felt like an intruder on their family dinner. But as he ate and spoke, he kept imagining Nadine there. She'd like to meet

Roan, the king her mother had been obsessed with, and no one would have to watch what they said around her, as she knew about goblins. Mostly Meryn wanted what they'd had for those few short hours when she'd been in his arms. He'd never been so human, or so easily wounded. This time he wasn't going to give up; he'd fight for her. For them.

After dinner, Dai took him aside. With a little magic, Dai got a pen to transcribe whatever Meryn said. After a few false starts, both men were happy with the way it was working and the language it was writing in.

Meryn picked up the pen. Not a large weapon, but certainly deadly if used to stab. He spun it in his fingers. Written words would have to work where talking had failed. And if he failed?

He wouldn't let himself think of that. If one dreamed of defeat, the battle was already lost. He drew out a clean sheet of paper and recalled everything Nadine had told him about her mother's Goblin King fairy tale. It wasn't hard when he imagined her lips speaking the words.

"Start." The pen stood ready for action, his only soldier in his fight to win back Nadine. In Latin, he began his retelling of *The Goblin King* tale.

Eliza and Roan had gone home, and Brigit was in bed before Meryn was happy with what he'd done. He carefully folded up the papers, then Dai took him home.

"Good luck. Let me know how it goes…or better still, bring her around to meet the rest of us." Dai put his hand on Meryn's shoulder briefly. Then Dai stepped back and was gone with little more than a sigh of air.

Luck had nothing to do with it. Battles were about planning and understanding your opponent—that, and having the best weapons. Would a few sheets of paper be enough to win back Nadine's heart?

—✦—

Outside the small apartment, in a nondescript brown building in a dodgy suburb, she hesitated. Nadine cast another glance at her car. It wasn't new, and it wasn't flashy either. A small, cheap coupe shouldn't be high on thieves' lists. But that didn't mean some kid wouldn't take it for a test drive and then set it alight.

It would be fine, and if it wasn't, at least she had insurance.

She knocked on the door and tried to ignore the peeling blue paint and the faint traces of graffiti that someone had attempted to scrub off, and waited, her gaze flickering over the parking lot and other apartments. Many of the curtains were closed as the residents didn't want anyone peering into their lives. Solomon was home. She'd rung on the way over, but she hadn't said why she was coming.

The door opened. Her father stood there in tracksuit pants and a T-shirt. He looked at her and nodded. Then he let her in, as if he knew why she was here without her breathing a word.

His apartment was sparsely furnished with odd pieces. Nothing matched. It wasn't like the home she'd grown up in; her mother's touch was missing. But it was still more of a home than Meryn's spacious apartment. This place was lived in.

"Tea, coffee?"

"No. No thanks." She glanced around, not sure what to do. On top of the TV was a picture of them as a family. Her mother was smiling at her father. She closed her eyes and turned away as the heartache threatened to crush her again.

Her father looked at her, resignation lined his face. He knew she wasn't here to chat. "Why are you here, Nadine?"

She took a breath—she could only do this once—and jumped. "Mum used to tell a story, *Le roi des gobelins*. Was it real?" Had the Goblin King been a cursed Celtic King as Meryn said?

"Michaline loved fairy tales. She believed there was truth in all of them."

Maybe there was more truth to some. "She used to say goblins ran the earth on winter solstice. Have you ever seen them?"

Solomon sighed and sat down on the sofa. "Yes. When we were dating, she made me sit up one night with her to watch the Wild Ride. At first I saw nothing but shadows and moonlight. Then it became clear—an army riding straight out of Hell made up of gray demons."

"Did you see the goblins take her?"

"I don't know for sure what happened. Maybe it was goblins, maybe it was humans. Only you know the truth."

Nadine wiped her eyes with the back of her hand. The tears wouldn't stop now they'd started. "I don't remember."

Flashes of her nightmare played in her mind like an old film. The face in the window. The monster that hid in the shadows and crawled around her sleep.

"You do. You just locked it away to protect yourself. Only you can set the memory free."

In her mind, the glass broke for the last time.

Only it wasn't her being dragged out the window

by goblins in her dream; it was her mother. The person left holding the cross and doing nothing wasn't Meryn. It was her. She'd watched her mother be stolen and done nothing.

Her legs buckled and she knelt on the floor. It was her fault her mother had died.

It was her fault her father had been imprisoned. If she'd remembered… If she'd done something, anything, she would've had a family.

Solomon was at her side, holding her the way he should have done twenty years ago, "I wish I'd been there. I'm sorry, Nadine."

"I should've stopped them."

"You were a child."

"I should've remembered and spoken at your trial." She lifted her head. "You're innocent. We have to clear your name."

"No. No one believes in goblins. I want to move forward. I don't want to look back."

"I'm sorry I never wrote you or came to see you."

"Prison is no place for a little girl. I don't blame you for anything." Solomon smiled even though his eyes were wet.

She hugged her father for the first time in two decades. She knew the truth and had her family back. "You don't hate the goblins for what they did?"

"How can I hate a creature so damned they gave up all emotion in exchange for greed? They suffer every day in a hell of their own making."

But Meryn hadn't given up everything for greed. He'd been cursed along with the king of her mother's story. "Is it possible for a goblin to get free of the Shadowlands?"

"At solstice?"

"To be a man again."

"I don't know. I guess his heart would have to out-weigh the goblin's greed. It would be a rare man to claw his way back."

Yet that was what Meryn had done. Could Meryn really be one of the men her mother had talked about? "What about the Goblin King and his men?"

"If the curse broke maybe, but how much of the man would be left after living so long in the Shadowlands?" Solomon studied her as if wondering at her sudden interest.

That first night Meryn had been more goblin than man. He'd admitted as much and proven that by steal-ing her mother's cross. But now? He'd shown her his heart and still ached for a two-thousand-year-old loss. No goblin would feel such a wound.

But had he really given up being goblin? Could she trust him?

"If the goblins took her, you can't bring her back."

"I know." But she didn't share her mother's fate with her father. Telling him would not do anything but open an old wound. "I guess I just want an end to her story. It was always incomplete."

"That's what she always said, and she spent a lot of time looking for variants, hoping to find out what hap-pened." He shook his head. "If those men survived, they have served many life sentences."

Nadine looked at the floor. Her father had done twenty years. Meryn had done twenty centuries for dar-ing to stand against the Romans and support his king, something that he should've been rewarded for, not punished for. The sheer amount of time made her head spin. Meryn had stepped out of ancient history. The army he'd served in had fought with swords against the Romans.

It was too much when all she wanted was a simple life. A boyfriend who hadn't crawled out of her worst fears, one who hadn't watched her mother die alone in the Shadowlands.

"Not every story has a happy ending. If your mother's tale is true, the chances are better that those men gave in or went mad. You're so like her, believing in the fairy tales."

"They were all I had when I was growing up. I used to wish she'd walk through the door and take me home."

"I used to wish she'd be found alive and well, even though I knew in my heart she was gone. I'd seen the goblins pass the cab. I knew she'd planned to watch. I never thought they'd take her."

Nadine closed her eyes as the fragments reformed. "She put a coin on the windowsill to bring them close enough for me to see. She was hoping to see the Goblin King."

Chapter 20

IT WAS MIDNIGHT WHEN MERYN WALKED DOWN THE hill and into the city. His eyes kept a careful watch on the dark shadows lining the street. While nothing moved, the tension in his gut didn't leave. He was completely unarmed. He'd left the knife he'd stolen at home, in an effort to prove he could fit in and that he was no longer a goblin or a soldier. Without a weapon, he was naked…and he had no armor. Nadine could cut out his heart with just a few words, and yet if she did, he knew he could survive the injury. He'd rather live and be happy, but he knew that he didn't deserve a second chance with her, not after stealing her mother's cross.

Tucked into his jacket pocket were a few sheets of paper. Even now he didn't know if it was right or if it would work. He crossed the empty roads and passed closed shops. In front of the hospital, he paused. Last time he'd been here the police had brought him, more goblin than man, confused and scared. He touched the healed wound on his head. This time he wasn't injured. Could he just walk in?

He had no backup plan. He didn't know where Nadine lived, only that she worked here at night and ran through the park in the morning. If she wasn't here, he would have to wait for her; although if it was him in her situation, he would find somewhere else to run.

What did he have to offer her?

Nothing. He was hardly a suitor of worth. He stared up at the hospital building. She hadn't cared before…No, she hated that he'd been goblin. So did he, but he couldn't change his past any more than she could change hers. All he had to offer was a future filled with love.

He drew in a breath of cold night air, rolled his shoulders, and walked through the glass doors marked emergency. A wave of heat, sharp white light, and bitter antiseptic rolled over him. He pushed through, even though he'd rather wait outside in the cool air. This time the waiting room was nearly empty.

Like the police had done when they brought him in, he walked to the counter. Nadine wasn't there; her friend Gina was.

"Can I help you?" Gina's gaze raked over him as if his presence offended her.

"I'd like to see Nadine."

Gina raised her eyebrows and looked away. "This is emergency not a dating service. Do you have an emergency?"

Meryn stood his ground even though he wanted to leave. He didn't have a medical emergency, but if he left now, he'd wonder the rest of his life about what might've been with the woman who knew half the story of the Goblin King and his men. "If I don't get to see her and make amends, I will have lost her forever."

The woman glanced up from her paperwork, but this time she really looked at him. Her eyes narrowed a fraction. "You hurt her."

The nurse drew the first blood in the battle with her pointed comment. He'd truly wounded Nadine and she'd told her friend. He deserved this woman's scorn, but he didn't turn away from the heartache. He embraced it. Living meant feeling. He would rather hurt than be numbed to everything but gold.

"I didn't mean to."

"Why would I let you see her?"

"Because...because I love her and need another chance to prove it." He wished he'd had a chance to tell Nadine how he felt before everything had fallen apart.

Gina considered him for a moment before shaking her head. "Then you'd better double up like you have appendicitis."

Appendicitis? Meryn frowned.

The nurse rolled her eyes. "Grip you stomach like you have sharp pains and I'll get you through the door."

He grimaced and folded his arm across his gut like he was stopping it from falling out. The nurse ticked a few boxes on a form. "What's your surname, Meryn?"

"Knight, as in shining armor."

The nurse's lips moved as she tried to hide a smile. "Let's get you through so you can be seen."

"Thank you," he said through his teeth as if raked with pain.

"Don't thank me yet."

She indicated the door at the side and Meryn walked over, still holding his stomach. Was it for the benefit of the people waiting or the other nurses who'd watched them speak? For a moment, a stab of guilt leant its weight to his faked illness. He was taking up nurses' time when there were people waiting. He glanced again at the few people in the waiting room. There were no children and no one was bleeding or unconscious. And while he was sure they wouldn't agree, he had to see Nadine.

Gina took him into a small room. "I'll let Nadine know you're in here. If she won't see you, you'll have to leave. And if you make a scene, I'll call security."

"I understand."

Gina hesitated. "I've never seen her so upset. You must have really gotten to her." Then she closed the door after herself.

Meryn sat on the edge of the high, narrow bed. His nose wrinkled at the strong smell that seemed to be part of the hospital. Beyond the door he could hear talking, someone crying. But in the room it was quiet, still, and bland. Different shadow of white and off-white blended together as if someone had created a sterilized version of the Shadowlands.

It was strangely calming. He let out a sigh and rolled his shoulders. The muscles in his back remained tight, as if he were bracing for a blow he couldn't yet sense.

What if Nadine refused to see him?

Should he wait for her outside the hospital and hope to see her? The building was huge. If he waited on the wrong side he might never see her. Did he try again tomorrow? Or did he walk away, knowing she could find him when she was ready?

He flexed his fingers and forced his mind to be still. Chasing himself in circles wouldn't make the waiting pass any faster. Better to be calm. Or at least try and be calm. He closed his eyes and breathed as if he had no worries. Those moments before a fight were always clearest. The plans were made; everything was ready. Nothing else to be done except fight. What was at risk and what was to gain hung in the balance.

For the man that he'd been, it was the promise of

a better life for his family. He'd seen how the Roman soldiers treated the young women of the Decangli. His daughters weren't going to be whores to the legion. He'd supported the rebellion in the hope of being free from the invaders.

For the goblin he'd become, it had always been about gold. Life wasn't worth living without more.

For the man he was now, it was about restoring honor and being someone worthy of loving, being human and all the hurt and joy that entailed. That meant accepting that Nadine may not be able to see past her fear of goblins and see him as a man.

She may not want to see him at all.

"There is a gorgeous guy faking appendicitis to see you in room two." Gina pulled Nadine aside.

"There's a man here to see me?" Nadine caught up with Gina's rapid whisper.

"Gray eyes, fashionable stubble, you know, the boyfriend you brought to my wedding, the one you refused to talk about today even though your eyes were red from crying."

Oh God. Meryn was here. "You admitted him?"

She wasn't ready to see him again. Maybe she'd never be ready to see him. He was wrong for her. He was an ex-Celtic goblin. What if he turned back?

"No. I snuck him in and put him in a private examination room. What happened?"

"Nothing happened." Nothing she was going to share anyway. She'd almost called in sick to avoid seeing Gina, but spending the night at home alone hadn't appealed, so she'd come in and plastered on her fake, I'm-fine smile, which apparently Gina now saw through.

"So you didn't fight with your boyfriend and he likes to come begging to see you because he enjoys apologizing for no reason?"

"Okay." She had to tell Gina something so then she could go and get rid of Meryn. "We argued and I learned something about him, and it's not going to work. Now you can tell him to leave."

Gina shook her head. "You can do that. He didn't look like the type who just lets people walk away without a reason. Damn, I can't believe you let him go after one argument. Everyone loved him at the wedding, even Bryce. What did he do, try to get to know you?"

Nadine crossed her arms. "Very funny. He knows too much. It's weird."

Having someone to talk to about her family and her fear of goblins had been nice, but it had gotten out of control too fast. Meryn made her realize that it was possible to fall in love, before stealing her heart and becoming her worst nightmare. She suppressed a shudder even though her skin craved his touch. She didn't know if she could get past the time he'd spent as a goblin. Did he deserve a second chance when he'd lied to her?

"That 'weird' is called a relationship. And if you don't get used to it and give people a chance, you'll end up like my canary-loving, single aunt."

"I don't even like pet birds." They should be free to fly, not caged. "Please get rid of him…tell him I'm busy."

Busy had been her excuse during school and university. Now it was that she worked unsociable hours. While she liked men, she didn't trust them. But Meryn had been there when the thieves had attacked. He'd told her everything when she'd demanded and she'd repaid him by yelling and running.

"If you don't want to see him, you go and tell him it's over." Gina pointed down the corridor to room two. "And I promise not to let him in again."

"No. I'm working." She could be just as stubborn as Gina.

"Take a break. Seriously, Nadine, men like him don't come around that often. So unless he's an ax-wielding maniac, give him a chance."

What could she say? He was a sword-wielding ex-goblin?

She wasn't sorry the truth had come out but she was scared of who he was, of the life he'd lived over the past two thousand years. He had life experiences she couldn't relate to…and he was trying to adapt to the modern world. Nadine frowned. He was actually doing a really good job. Better than she'd be doing if she'd been thrown back into Roman-occupied Britain.

But she still didn't know what to say to him and she wasn't ready to talk to him about anything that had been said. "Okay. I'll get rid of him."

Gina shook her head. "You're throwing away a man willing to grovel to get you back."

Nadine gave Gina a half smile. "Meryn doesn't grovel."

While he'd stood naked and argued with her, she couldn't picture him on his knees for anyone.

"Oh yeah, what does he do?"

"I don't know." Why had he come back? Hadn't it been clear she didn't want to see him again when she stormed out? In another day, maybe two, she might be ready to think through their fight. And in a day or three she might have convinced herself that it wasn't worth the hassle being with someone. The tiniest part of her wanted to know why he was here. He'd clawed his way back from goblin, become a modern man, and ensnared her heart in the process.

"Find out," Gina said.

Nadine stared at her supposed friend who was refusing to get rid of the man she shouldn't have snuck in. "Fine."

She strode down the corridor determined not to give Meryn a chance to explain. He was wrong—wrong for her, wrong in this time. She pushed open the door. The anger and hurt she'd been holding on to like a shield fractured when she saw him. For a heartbeat she paused, unable to move. When she was near him she couldn't think of anything but him and everything he'd been through to get to where he was. A man, not a goblin.

It was much easier to be upset when she wasn't confronted with the reality. She didn't hate him, but she didn't want to love him either.

She took the final step into the room and closed the door, but she remained near the exit, so she could escape at any moment.

Meryn stood but didn't approach, as if he knew they were doing a strange kind of dance, each being careful not to startle the other and provoke a response.

"Why did you come here?"

"To see you."

"I don't want to see you." How could he have stood by while her mother died?

The muscle in his cheek twitched. If he smiled, a

dimple would form, but he wasn't smiling now. He was as wounded as she was.

"I did many things I'm not proud of as a goblin. I should have acted to help your mother. But I didn't know what to do. Goblins don't think the same as men. They crave gold and battle and a human queen if they can steal one. Even if I'd saved her, she would've still been trapped in the Shadowlands. No human deserves to live there."

How long had Meryn spent as a human in the Shadowlands, a place so barren nothing grew? She knew her mother's stories, that goblins could only ride the Fixed Realm during solstice. But humans? How did they escape the Shadowlands once taken…? She didn't know. How had Meryn gotten free? Had he slipped through at solstice? She squashed the rising sympathy for everything he'd suffered.

"You acted goblin. You stole from me. You could've returned the cross. Hell, you could have dropped it on the ground and let me find it while out running."

"I was scared. The world has changed so much since I last walked the Fixed Realm. Gold was familiar. Then I couldn't give it back because it reminded me of you. As I got to know you more, I wanted to return it, but I couldn't find the words. I could never just drop it and act like I never took it. That would be dishonest."

"You lied to me about who you were."

"No I didn't. I let you draw your own assumptions and didn't correct you. I will make it up to you if you give me a chance." He took off a heavy gold cuff and placed it on the bed. "Without this I can't read."

"Why not?"

"I never learned. Very few people could read when I grew up." He pulled some papers from his jacket. "I can't write very well either, and it's in Latin. English is hard to read and write even with magic."

"I can't read Latin." But that didn't stop her from being curious about what he'd written.

"Use the bracelet."

She eyed the bracelet; it was beautiful, delicately engraved with knots. She wanted to pick it up and try it on. But she knew her fairy tales. If something looked too good to be true, it was probably going to knock the princess unconscious to be dragged back to the Shadowlands.

"How does it work?"

He shrugged. "Magic."

"You want me to believe in magic?"

"You believe in goblins."

"What kind of magic? Fairy godmother or evil witch?"

Meryn frowned. "Neither. My cousin, Dai, learned magic while in the Shadowlands. He is more powerful than a druid."

Ah. The cousin who'd arranged the house. "You weren't alone in the Shadowlands."

"The king in your mother's stories is Dai's brother, Roan. We were cursed with him. I succumbed. They didn't. It was Dai who brought me back to the Fixed Realm." He tapped the papers. "It's all here, including the ending. You told me once the story was incomplete. It's not. Not anymore."

Nadine shook her head. Fairy tales didn't come true. They weren't real. They were stories designed to scare children into not speaking to strangers and to not be

greedy lest the goblins take them away. But her mother
had believed there was a grain of truth in every tale.
She'd stayed up and seen the Wild Ride with her mother
when she was five and had blocked it from her mind, yet
the fear of the storms and howls had stayed with her. A
shadowed memory she didn't want to recall.

"Her story is real?" All of it. Not just the bit about
goblins and the Shadowlands.

"Yes." He was watching her as if he expected her
to run.

She should be running. None of this made any sense.
Magic and goblins and curses. And yet it did. This was
the only way Meryn made sense. And she needed to
know how the curse broke. To find out what happened
to the king and his men.

She took a couple of steps. Her fingers touched the
gold bracelet. Curiosity bubbled in her veins like soda.
If her mother were here, she wouldn't be hesitating.
She'd be grilling Meryn and asking to meet the King
of the Goblins.

Nadine picked up the golden bracelet and put it on.
She would finish what her mother had started. The
Latin lettering on the paper jumped into focus and
became words.

*Once upon a time there was a king called Roan. He
ruled the Decangli. When he was young, his lands were
invaded by the Romans. His brother, Dai, was taken as
a slave to ensure Roan's good behavior.*

*For a time, the Decangli wore the shackles while in
secret they plotted rebellion. When the time came to fight,
they learned they had been betrayed. Knowing they only
had one chance, Roan urged caution and a delay. The*

druid argued for the fight; he hated Roan and used the disagreement to his benefit. The druid, convinced Roan had betrayed his tribe and taken Roman gold, cursed Roan and all the men who had taken his side.

They were banished to the Shadowlands. But so was the druid, because his hatred of Roan was so great.

The traitor Drem, cousin to Roan, told the Roman General of the curse. The general killed Drem and then used the curse to force Roan to destroy all that was left of the Decangli. Men, women, and children were killed so there would be no more rebellion. There were no more Decungli.

The king's second, Meryn, gave in to the curse after watching his wife and children murdered. The others, after watching this, vowed to die before fading to goblin.

Brac, a fierce fighter, attacked the druid, believing the druid's death would free them, and was killed.

The youngest warrior, Fane, killed himself, unable to cope with the harshness of the life they were forced to live.

Slowly the curse began to take hold. They hoarded gold like goblins. No magic Dai found could break the spell. Eventually Anfri, the eldest, faded. Roan shot him, keeping the promise that none of them would become goblin like Meryn.

One day Roan was summoned to the Fixed Realm by a woman. They fell in love; she was able to look past the goblin he was cursed to be and see the man he once was. The curse broke, freeing Roan and his brother Dai.

Dai was able to put his past behind him and find love. But then he realized that Meryn had also been freed from the curse and was trapped in the Shadowlands. He

risked his life and future to go back and rescue him. But
the creature he brought back was more goblin than man.

Remembering caused Meryn pain and for a while he
just wanted to forget and be goblin again. But a woman
reminded him of the thing he'd been missing as a goblin,
something that couldn't be bought with gold. Love.

Tears welled in her eyes, but she blinked them back
as she took off the bracelet. She gave it back to Meryn
with a trembling hand. She'd lost her family, but Roan
and his men had lost everything. Family, tribe, way of
life, humanity, and some of them, their lives. Yet Meryn
had fought his way back from a wasteland that devoured
hope and soul to stand before her, wanting nothing but
another chance.

She never gave people second chances. She'd always
had to protect herself. But then no one had ever bothered
asking for one. She wasn't worth the time. Not foster
parents, friends, or boyfriends—she ended it before they
got a chance to hurt her first.

It was already too late for that with Meryn.

They'd had their first fight and he'd come back for
more. Her lips turned up at the corners. "How does your
story end?"

"I'm hoping the knight wins back his lady." He
moved closer, close enough to touch, almost close
enough to kiss.

She scrunched her toes in her shoes, wanting to say
yes but terrified of what that would mean.

"What if it doesn't work?"

"We can make it work." His fingers grazed her cheek
and she leaned a little closer. "Believe in your own fairy
tale. You deserve a happy ending."

"So do you." Nadine placed her lips against his in what was supposed to be a gentle kiss that deepened as his hands swept over her hips and pulled her to him.

For a few moments nothing else existed in the world except them and the kiss that sealed her fate. She would always be safe in his arms. Her fingers slipped under his shirt, needing to feel he was real and not something she'd imagined. If this was a dream, she didn't want to wake up. She'd found a man who would hold her heart safe. A warrior from another age. A knight in gray, dusty armor.

Chapter 21

NADINE WALKED THROUGH THE HOUSE ONE LAST TIME, her heart fluttering with excitement and nerves. It had been her home for years. It was familiar and comfy, and while she had only rented it with Gina, it had been theirs. Although in truth, over the last two months, she hadn't spent much time here. It was too easy to stay at Meryn's place.

"Is that everything?" Meryn stood in the hallway, his thumbs hooked into his jeans pockets looking every bit the modern man, right down to the fashionable stubble.

Nadine bit her lip and nodded. There hadn't been much to take. The furniture had been secondhand to start with and was staying in the house for the moment for Bryce and Gina to use. So far they hadn't found a house they liked within their price range.

Price wasn't a problem for Meryn. After spending her life keeping careful track of her savings, it was an odd concept for Nadine, and one Meryn grappled with too. All he'd done so far was buy a car, not even a fancy one—and he'd only done that after she'd convinced him that he drove well enough to get one. Having experienced his cousin's translocation magic once for herself, she knew why Meryn had been so keen to learn to drive.

"I think so." If there was anything left, she could always come back. She glanced at Meryn again. She loved him. She knew she did because she couldn't bear to be away from him, but a small part of her still thought she was rushing. Jumping too soon into his bed and house. When he'd first suggested that she move in permanently, she'd laughed and said not without a ring.

He'd taken her seriously.

Two days later as they'd lain in his bed, he'd given her a ring—simple, elegant, and detailed with tiny knot work around a diamond. Her fingers traced the square cut stone as she walked toward her fiancé. The word was still strange on her tongue. The little things Meryn did that gave away that he had been born two thousand years ago made her smile. The way he picked up modern life amazed her.

What was his family going to say? That it was too fast? Would they think she was only after his money? They'd been friendly and welcoming, but now? Meryn wasn't concerned.

Meryn didn't seem to fear anything.

Even her nightmares. With him, they had lost their intensity; she could go nights without a dream, or maybe now that she knew the truth, her mind could rest. She took his hand, and his fingers curled around hers.

"If we don't leave soon, Gina will be back and I can't do good-byes." She forced a smile but tears were stinging her eyes. She'd never imagined she'd be the one leaving first, and she'd tried not to think about Gina leaving.

"You'll see her again."

"I know, but it won't be the same." Nothing would ever be the way it was.

"If everything stayed the same, you wouldn't be living; you'd be existing."

"True, but…"

Meryn raised one eyebrow.

What could she say? Her feet weren't exactly cold, but it was a big change and she was still getting used to the idea of having someone she could count on. Someone who knew her and understood her and didn't run a mile. But there was no one else like Meryn and she wasn't going to let him go, even if holding on scared her.

Nadine shrugged. "I've never lived with a boyfriend before." Whereas he'd done all of this before—true, in another time and place, but it was more than she'd ever done.

He stopped walking and they stood in the doorway, the white van parked in the street beyond loaded and ready to go. "I'm not comparing. I can't." He touched her cheek, then leaned in and placed a soft kiss on her lips. "So this is as new for me as it is to you. I wouldn't have asked if I didn't want you there. I love you."

A smile tugged at her lips and she looped her arms around his neck and kissed him properly for the last time in her old house. Her tongue traced his lower lip, then his mouth opened to her. She closed her eyes, and for a moment, nothing else mattered except his hands on her hips pulling her close as their tongues met. It was in those moments she could lose herself and forget everything else. They were just two people getting on with their lives. Only a few knew the truth about how unlikely that life was.

"Okay, let's do this." She pushed down the remaining butterflies that were dancing in her stomach.

Meryn released her and stepped outside while she took a breath and closed and locked the front door. She took a moment before she turned. She'd been in many foster homes, but none had been her *home*. This place had come close; she'd belonged here, but in her heart she'd always known it was temporary.

What she'd wanted was family. That was what made a house a home.

With Meryn she'd found that. He started walking toward the van and pulled the keys from his pocket.

"You're not driving." She called after him. A car was one thing, a moving van, even if it was only small, was another.

He turned and offered her the keys. "I'm driving tonight."

She'd known he would if only to rub it in to Roan that he'd learned to drive faster—and without damaging a car. Every couple of weeks they all got together—Roan and Eliza, Dai and Amanda and Brigit, Meryn and her. At first she'd felt like an interloper eavesdropping on history, but now she looked forward to the evenings and the conversations that to anyone else would sound impossible. Tonight was also the first time her father was invited.

It had been Meryn's idea and everyone else had agreed; after all, he knew about goblins. She'd half expected her father to refuse, but instead he'd accepted, wanting to meet the legendary Goblin King.

Her stomach gave a flutter as the van lurched forward and she hoped everything would go smoothly.

———∾∾———

Meryn watched as Roan turned the pig on the spit. Its flesh sizzled and popped as embers floated past. Not quite suckling but close enough. If he closed his eyes, he could almost imagine he was back in Wales in the heart of Decangli country, surrounded by his tribe.

Two thousand years ago this wouldn't have been possible because of the shadow of Rome. Celebration had been curtailed and meetings were held in secret. His lips curved. He was glad to be surrounded by family. Here everyone knew of the curse and there was no need to hide.

Female laughter glided across the night accompanied by the lower murmur of the men as Dai spoke to Solomon. It hadn't taken much convincing for Solomon to be invited to the gathering. Solomon knew all too well the damage goblins could do, and what was a tribe without elders? Or children?

He glanced at Nadine but knew they were both a few years away from going down that path. The women were admiring Nadine's ring, but he couldn't hear their words. He was just glad Nadine had liked it and had decided to move in on a permanent basis instead of living between the two houses.

"That didn't take long." Roan nodded in the direction of the women.

"I didn't see the need to wait." He knew what he wanted…Nadine knew what she wanted, but sometimes it seemed like she expected it to be snatched away if she reached for it. Hopefully now she'd realize he'd meant it when he said he'd always be there. He took a sip of his beer, enjoying the warm evening.

"How's the writing going?" Roan asked.

"Good." Better now he'd realized that by typing on a computer he didn't need to write anything by hand except his name. He was never going to have the same neat script as Dai or Roan, but it was passable. "I've enrolled in a few college classes for next year."

"What are you going to study?"

"History, I want to catch up on what I've missed."

There was another round of hugs between the women, but this time Eliza was the center of attention. Meryn looked at Roan, knowing he'd been keeping a secret, then slapped him on the shoulder. It looked like there was going to be another child in the little tribe, the first Decangli born in nearly two thousand years. "Congratulations."

"She said I wasn't allowed to say anything for another two weeks." Roan looked a little shocked.

"*You* weren't allowed to say anything. She can tell other women." Meryn made an effort to keep a straight face.

"Hey, are you going to show me the ring?" Roan called out.

Nadine walked over and held out her hand for Roan to see, but she grinned at Meryn. Gold Celtic knots surrounded a diamond.

"Congratulations." Roan kissed her cheek.

"And you too. Eliza said we can't marry until she's had the baby." Nadine slipped her hand into Meryn's. "A wedding and a baby, it's exciting."

"If we were to wait for Dai, we'd die of old age." Roan grumbled with a smile.

"At least that is a problem again," Meryn said. His gaze drifting from Eliza, Amanda, and Brigit to Dai and Solomon.

"Dad seems to enjoy chatting with Dai." Nadine

stared across the yard. She and Solomon were still mending their relationship; including Solomon in their gathering was important.

"That would be because Dai is speaking Nuer." Whether Dai had just learned it or already spoke it, it didn't matter. He was enjoying himself and Solomon looked thrilled to be able to use a language he hadn't used in years.

"Oh. I haven't spoken to him in his language since I was a child."

For a moment Meryn was sure he saw a shimmer of regret. "Go. Join them." His arm fell away.

"I couldn't. It's been two decades."

"Give it a go. Your father will appreciate the effort. Besides you could always switch to French." Meryn gave her a kiss and after a couple of uncertain steps Nadine left. He watched her walk away, her skirt swishing around her calves.

"Any joy getting your sword back?" Roan gave the pig another turn. The scent of cooking meat filled the air.

Meryn nodded. Dai had helped with the paperwork. "I have to identify it next week."

Roan raised an eyebrow. "The police have more than one?"

"Apparently. And then I have to ensure it is locked up and kept safe." Meryn laughed. "The police are worried about the sword and not the person wielding it."

"Whatever makes them feel safe." Roan shook his head in disbelief.

Beyond the patches of light, darkness clung to the corners of the yard. They all knew too well what hid in those shadows. Safety wasn't automatic; it had to be guarded and defended. Locking up one sword would do nothing.

Behind Roan was the memorial for the people they'd lost. Before them was a future they couldn't have dreamed while under Roman rule and couldn't have hoped for while trapped in the Shadowlands.

Despite everything, the Decangli lived on, changed but not defeated. Rome had failed. They had won. They were free.

Acknowledgments

It's said it takes a village to raise a child and a book is no different. So many people have input—it wasn't until I went to the Sourcebooks office that I realized just how many people there are working behind the scenes. The first thing people see is the cover and this series has been blessed with great covers by Don Sipley. My editor, Leah, made sure the book was as tight as it can be. The Winkgirls read my early drafts despite the typos, and my family spent a day traipsing around Kings Park with me as I made notes. Without all of these people, there would be no book. Finally, to my readers who love my goblins as much as I do: without you, there'd be no one to share the story with. Thank you!

About the Author

A civil designer by day and an author by night, Shona Husk lives in Western Australia at the edge of the Indian Ocean. Blessed with a lively imagination, she spent most of her childhood making up stories. As an adult, she discovered romance novels and hasn't looked back. Drawing on history and myth, she writes about heroes who are armed and dangerous but have a heart of gold—sometimes literally.

The Goblin King

by Shona Husk

Once upon a time…

A man was cursed to the Shadowlands, his heart replaced with a cold lump of gold. In legends, he became known as

The Goblin King.

For a favored few he will grant a wish. Yet, desperately clinging to his waning human soul, his one own desire remains unfulfilled:

a willing queen.

But who would consent to move from the modern-day world into the realm of nightmares? No matter how intoxicating his touch, no matter how deep his valor, loving him is dangerous. And the one woman who might dare to try could also

destroy him forever.

—⁂—

"Shona Husk put together an amazing story
about loss, love, redemption, and discovery…"
—*Night Owl Reviews* Reviewer Top Pick

For more Shona Husk, visit:

www.sourcebooks.com

Kiss of the Goblin Prince

by Shona Husk

The Man of Her Dreams

He is like a prince in a fairy tale: tall, outrageously handsome, and way too dark for her own good. Amanda has been hurt before, though. And with her daughter's illness, the last thing she needs right now is a man. But the power of Dai King is hard to resist. And when he threads his hands through her hair and pulls her in for a kiss, there is no denying it feels achingly right.

In a Land of Nightmare

After being trapped in the Shadowlands for centuries with the goblin horde a constant threat, Dai revels in his newfound freedom back in the human realm. But even with the centuries of magic he's accumulated, he still doesn't know how to heal Amanda's daughter—and it breaks his heart. Yet for the woman he loves, he'd risk anything... including a return to the dreaded Shadowlands.

Praise for The Goblin King:

"A wonderfully dark and sensual fairy tale."
—Jessa Slade, author of *Seduced by Shadows*

For more of the Shadowlands series, visit:

www.sourcebooks.com

Enslaved

by Elisabeth Naughton

GRYPHON—Honorable, loyal, dependable…tainted. He was the ultimate warrior before imprisonment in the Underworld changed him in ways he can't ignore.

She calls to him. *Come to me. You can't resist.* But Gryphon will not allow himself to be ruled by the insidious whispers in his head. And there's only one way to stop them: kill Atalanta, the goddess who enslaved him. But with so much darkness inside, he can't be sure what's real anymore. Even the Eternal Guardians, those who protect the human realm and the gods, want to exile him.

Finding Malea is like a miracle. Somehow he doesn't feel the pull of the dark when she's near. And he's determined to keep her as near as possible, whether she wants him close or not. But she's a temptation that will test every bit of control he has left. One that may ultimately have the power to send him back to the Underworld…or free him from his chains for good.

Praise for Enraptured:

"A spellbinding and wickedly sexy thrill ride that turns the heat up. Ms. Naughton continues to rock the Greek Mythology world with another entry in her brilliant Eternal Guardian series." —*Bitten By Paranormal Romance*

For more of the Eternal Guardians series, visit:

www.sourcebooks.com

The Lord of Illusion

by Kathryne Kennedy

He'll do anything to save her...

Rebel Lord Drystan Hawkes dreams of fighting for England's freedom. He gets his chance when he finds a clue to opening the magical portal to Elfhame, and he must race to find the slave girl who holds the key to the mystery. But even as Drystan rescues Camille Ashton from the palace of Lord Roden, it becomes unclear exactly who is saving whom...

For the fate of humankind lies with Camille...

Enslaved for years in a realm where illusion and glamour reign, Camille has learned to trust nothing and no one. But she's truly spellbound when she meets Drystan, a man different from any she's ever known, and the force of their passion may yet be strong enough to banish the elven lords from this world forever...

Praise for Kathryne Kennedy:

"Enthralling...a passionate love story."
—*RT Book Reviews*, 4½ stars

For more Kathryne Kennedy, visit:

www.sourcebooks.com

Untamed

by Sara Humphreys

Layla Nickelsen has spent years hiding from her Amoveo mate and guarding a devastating secret. But Layla's worst fear is realized when the man who haunts her dreams shows up in person…

William Fleury is as stoic as they come, until he finds Layla and his feelings overwhelm him. She won't let him get close, but then an unknown enemy erupts in violence and threatens everything Layla holds dear…

———

Praise for the Amoveo Legend series:

"I loved this book. I'm looking forward
to many more in this series."
—*Night Owl Reviews* Reviewer Top Pick

"Fast-paced paranormal romance with
fantastic world-building."
—*The Book Girl*

"Outstanding…red hot."
—*Publishers Weekly Starred Review*

For more Sara Humphreys, visit:

www.sourcebooks.com

Prince of Power

by Elisabeth Staab

Wizards and vampires have been mortal enemies since the beginning. Now Anton, son of the Wizard Master, has one last chance to steal the unique powers of the vampire king's beautiful sister, Tyra...and then kill her. But when he meets Tyra face-to-face, everything changes...

Tyra will stop at nothing to defeat the wizards, until Anton saves her life and she suddenly sees an opportunity she never could have imagined...

As the sparks ignite between them, together they could bring an end to the war that's decimating their people, but only if they can find a way to trust each other...

—⁓—

Praise for King of Darkness:

"Hot, sexy, and on-your-toes action."
—*Seriously Reviewed*

"One tough heroine, an absolutely sexy hero, and an interesting host of supporting characters you're going to love."
— *Night Owl Reviews* Reviewer Top Pick

"Action-packed and sexually charged."
—*RT Book Reviews,* starred review

For more Elisabeth Staab, visit:

www.sourcebooks.com

Deliver Me from Temptation

by Tes Hilaire

When things go bump in the night, Logan bumps back. Vampires, demons, succubi—you name it, he's fought it. His job as a Paladin angel warrior is to protect humans. Not fall for one.

Detective Jessica Waters protects humans too—with her Glock and a good set of handcuffs. She doesn't believe in fate. But if anyone looks like a gift from the gods, it's Logan. And he clearly knows more about her case than he's letting on…

—∾∿—

Praise for Tes Hilaire:

"A stellar paranormal romance."
—*Romance Reviews*

"Dark, sexy, and intense! Hilaire blazes a
new path in paranormal romance."
Sophie Jordan, New York Times
bestselling author on Deliver Me from Darkness

For more Tes Hilaire, visit:

www.sourcebooks.com